10/17

# Water in May

ISMÉE WILLIAMS

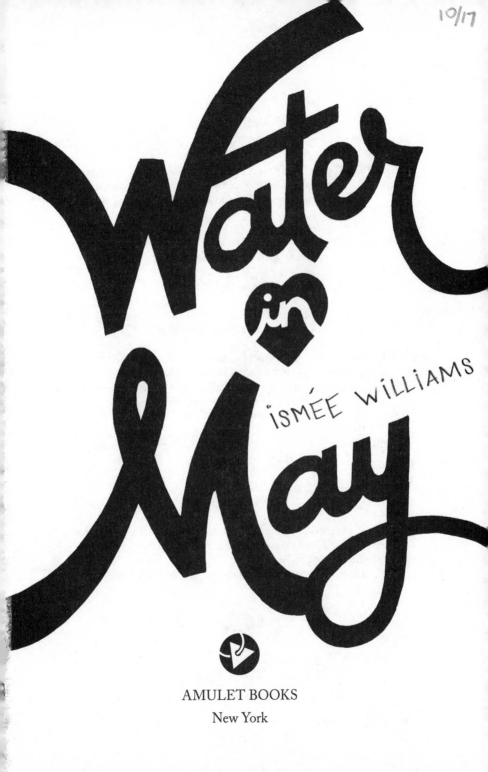

AMULET BOOKS
New York

Cataloging-in-Publication Data has been applied for and may be obtained from the Library of Congress.

ISBN 978-1-4197-2539-5

Text copyright © 2017 Ismée Williams
Book design by Siobhán Gallagher

Printed and bound in U.S.A.
10 9 8 7 6 5 4 3 2 1

Amulet Books are available at special discounts when purchased in quantity for premiums and promotions as well as fundraising or educational use. Special editions can also be created to specification. For details, contact specialsales@abramsbooks.com or the address below.

ABRAMS The Art of Books
195 Broadway, New York, NY 10007
abramsbooks.com

*For all the Angelos*
*And . . .*
*For Charlie, whose heart and mind touched so many*

# GLOSSARY OF DOMINICAN SLANG

**agitada** - Excited; in a state

**anda el diablo** - Damn

**anjá** - Wow

**alelao** - Someone who is stupid

**arrecho** - Erect

**asopado de pescado** - Soupy rice fish stew

**avión** - Easy woman, sexually

**baboso** - Idiot; a liar

**boca agua** - Impetuous person who speaks without thinking

**boca de suape** - Big mouth; someone who gossips

**brava** - Angry

**bugarrón** - Slur for a gay man

**cacata** - Tarantula; slang for an evil woman

**caché caché** - Cool; looking good

**canillas** - Skinny legs

**can** - Party

**carajo** - Hell

**chan** - Friend, bro

**cherchando** - Chatting it up

**chévere** - Awesome

**chata** - Flat-butted person

**chichí** - Baby boy

**chin** - Little bit

**chopo** - Low-class person; very rude

**concho** - Oh my gosh!

**¿cómo?** - What?

**¿cómo te sientes?** - How do you feel?

**coño** - Damn

**cuero** - Slut

**culero** - Asshole (Mexican)

**¿dímelo?** - What's happening?

**¿dímelo-chan?** - What up, man?

**¡diache!** - Damn

**echate pa'ca** - Come here

**embarazada** - Pregnant

**enchulao** - In love

**fajar** - To fight; to beat up

**fo** - Bad smell

**freco** - Fresh; rude

**frío** - Cool

**furufa** - Ugly woman

**gallera** - Female expert on cock/rooster fights

**grajo** - Body odor

**¡güay!** - Wow!

**güebo** – Slang for penis

**la hada** - The cops (general Spanish)

**hijo de la porra** - Son of a bitch

**hijo de machepa** - Someone who has nothing; son of rotten luck

**hombre** - Man

**loco** - Crazy

**maldito** - Damn

**mande** - Excuse me/what? (Mexican)

**manin** - Brother; "bro"

**mano** - Brother; "bro"

**manso** - Cool; chilling; easy

**mayores** - Old people

**mala pata** - Bad luck

**medio pollo** - Coffee with milk

**mentiras** - Lies

**mira** - Look

**mofongo de ajo** - Smashed plantains with garlic

**moreno/a** – Dark skin

**morenito/a** - A person with a dark complexion

**nalgas** - Butt cheeks

**ñame** - Idiot

**nieto** - Grandson

**novio** - Boyfriend

**ofrézcome** - Damn

**orale** - Hey there (Mexican)

**oyé** - Listen up

**óyeme** - Listen to me

**pájara** - Lesbian

**papi chulo** - Good-looking guy

**parejero** - Someone who is vain

**pariguayo** - Dumbass

**patuche** - Slang for a marijuana-filled cigar; a blunt

**peliar** - To fight, slang

**pelmaso** - Stupid

**pendejo** - Idiot

**perros y gatos** - Dogs and cats

**pinta** – Short for *pintalabios*; lipstick

**el pipo** - Damn

**porquería** - Silly crap

**porra** - Hell; bitch

**puta** - Whore


**¿qué lo que?** - What's up?

**¡qué cheposo!** - How lucky!

**qué bolsu** - A person who doesn't know how to do anything; also a person with big testicles

**qué mono** - So cute

**quillao** - Mad


**rata** - Low person; scum

**ratreria** - Dirtball


**tato** - Slang for "esta todo"; everything is good; bye

**tecato** - Someone strung out on drugs

**te lo juro** - I swear it

**to' ta frío** - Everything is cool

**todo 'ta bien** - Everything is okay

**tu ta'** - You are

**tu ta' pasao** - You're crazy

**tu ta' cloro** - You're cool

**vaina** - Thing

**¿veldá?**- Is it true?

**ven acá** - Come here

**vete pa'l carajo** - Go to hell

**yunque** - In a mood to fight

# TWENTY WEEKS

H is name ain't Dr. Love. *Coño.* You're messing with me, right?"

Yaz smacks me in the shoulder. She's doubled over, fingers clamping her mouth shut. Her purple silver-studded nails press dimples into her cheek. She's trying not to laugh.

"What?" I ask her. My cell slips as I shrug my shoulders. "They expect me to believe this guy's name is Dr. Love? A heart doctor? How stupid do they think I am?" I squat and snatch the phone. I wedge it back in the crook of my neck. "Like if Toto called for a penis doctor and was told the guy's name was Dr. Weiner he would believe them?"

Toto is Abuela's boyfriend. That's not his real name. It's just what my girls call him. Because his hairline's low. And he's bulky. Like one of them fighting dogs. And he's got these small hands and feet.

Yaz is gasping, cherry lollipop-colored lips pressed almost outta sight. Teri is giggling, fingers smoothing down long strands of inky hair. Heavenly's screen is three inches from her nose. She's probably browsing posts from her favorite designers.

She doesn't respond to my joke. But she thinks it's funny. I can tell.

"Your appointment with Dr. Love is scheduled for nine thirty on Thursday, September eleventh." The lady on the phone can't wait to get rid of me.

"Nine eleven? No way, José. Give me another date."

Yaz kicks me in the thigh.

"Hey!" I circle an arm around my belly, my finger pointed, already wagging. "Watch the baby!" I catch my phone as it tries to fall again.

"Like she was anywhere near your uterus." Heavenly rolls her eyes. Thick clumps of mascaraed lashes make everyone else look like a clown doll. On Heavenly, it looks good.

Phone Lady gives me a different appointment.

I hold the phone away from my face and turn to my girls. "Does Monday, September fifteenth, at ten work for *youz* guys?" I fix each of them with my you-better-be-there glare.

"Whatever you think, Mari." Teri's smiling like I just told her I won some money off those scratch cards at the bodega and I'm takin' them all on vacay. "I'll come," she says, as if her expression ain't enough. We was all excited when I found out about the baby. But Teri was the one who went out and got a book. And read it. Teri was the one who told me when it was time for my first doctor's appointment. Found the clinic I should go to.

"*Weez* guys will be ready." Yaz strikes the air above her with her fist, like Dazzler from the X-Men. She been doing that same dumbass pose since we chased Ricky Lopez down 173rd Street all the way to Broadway for her backpack. That was in the third grade. We been besties ever since.

Heavenly's acrylics tap-tap-tap on the face of her phone. It's the second one Jo-jo's bought her. As long as it texts and fits in the pocket of jeans that show off the curves of her *nalgas*, Heavenly don't care what logo it has or when it came out. But Jo-jo does. Only the best for his girl. I don't mind, seeing as I got to keep her old one. She's promised Yaz this one once it goes outta style. Heavenly's bottom lip slides out like she's gonna apply more *pinta*. But her eyes, they be smiling. "Ten on Monday? Perfect. I hate Mr. Sansone's English class."

Phone Lady's still talking. I can hear her squawks even with the phone a foot off my ear. I press it back into the space between my shoulder and cheek and catch the end of what she's sayin'. "And please arrive twenty minutes early to fill out all the necessary paperwork."

Twenty minutes? For paperwork? You gotta be kidding me. "*Coño*. Listen," I say, trying to be nice seein' as Yaz knows what I'm thinking and is giving me those lizard eyes. Like my swearin' is some bug she's fixin' to eat with that long tongue of hers. "I was just there yesterday seeing my baby doctor. She told me I had to make this appointment. Don't you have all my info in some system?" I know they do, 'cause every time I go I have to stand there and wait for them to pull it up.

Silence. Then, "You have our number if you need to reschedule. Is there anything else I can help you with, Miss Pujols?"

*Miss* Pujols. I've gotten over the way white folks say my last name—*Poo-joe-ells*. It's actually better than how it sounds in Spanish—*Poo-holes*. Yeah, I won the instant scratch-off lottery with that one. But what I hate most is that they always call me "miss." I know I look young. But we're on the phone. She can't see me. And I'm making a pregnant-lady appointment. Shouldn't that make me a Ms. or a Mrs.?

"No." I wanna say something else. But Yaz, with that sharp lizard tongue of hers, is staring at me hard. My upper lip itches. I scrub at it. I need a nap.

Yaz mouths something at me, pointing to her dimples.

"Oh . . . And, uh, thanks."

I hang up.

I hear the music when we're still under the overpass. Fort Washington Park, squeezed between the river and the highway, is more parking lot than park. But summer nights, as long as rain hasn't flooded the river, all of Washington Heights squeezes into it. Families come. *Los mayores* in folding chairs play dominoes. Cans of Quisqueya sweat in their cupholders. Kids climb the playground like monkeys, stopping to shout for food. Next to the cars, grills smoke and a *mamá* or *tío* or *abuela* seasons and flips and shouts back to the playground, "*¡Un minuto más!*" One more minute!

Even if you have no family, this is the place to be. There's music and dancing, and you're surrounded by people who love the same music and dancing you do. You don't need no money to get in. Don't need no ID. All you need is your tribe. Your friends. When we started coming here, before even Heavenly needed a bra, I used to take Yaz's hand and close my eyes and let her lead me across broken-glass sidewalks and grass that was mostly dirt. I used to imagine that the *ba ba-da ba ba-da* was a real tambora drum. That the peal of horns came from real trumpets and saxophones. I even pictured an old man bent over the rounded metal sleeve of a *güira*, brushing it with his pick. I never been to Santo Domingo. But my girls told me enough so I didn't mind opening my eyes and finding car stereos instead of bands. I know how real merengue is made, even if I never seen it done. When you dance, it don't matter how the music comes. If you can feel it, like a thrum inside you, it don't matter how it got there.

The first time I noticed Bertie, it was at this park. He was dancing with some *morenita*. A girl older than us. She didn't care that Bertie wasn't in high school yet. 'Cause he could spin her around. Lift his hand and ease her into a dip. Snap his wrist and bring her right back to him.

We were sitting on one of the rundown picnic tables facing the setting sun. The bench was broken. Splinters of wood separated Yaz's and my feet. And I watched that *morenito* dance the legs off a full-grown woman. We'd convinced Teri to come that night, even though she was afraid of partying, afraid of meeting boys and men. She was shaking like the A train hurtling from 125th to 59th. Living with two older brothers and a mama always at work taught Teri what made men get up in the morning. And she'd seen what Heavenly's mama's boyfriend had done to Heavenly's mama. It wasn't that the rest of us hadn't. We knew it was like some sorta power, getting men to look at us. Even if they was probably just looking at Heavenly and her *nalgas*.

Besides, we told Teri, not every man be like Heavenly's mama's boyfriend. Just gotta find one who'll treat you right.

Heavenly had three men circling that night. One on either side trying to keep her attention, another across the way at a different table, a girl already on his lap. Yaz and Teri and I were placing bets on who Hev would choose. My quarters were on the *chan* who was already taken. I remember the Mister Softee I bought myself with my winnings. I shared it with Bertie. Turns out, besides music and dancing, we also both love ice cream.

The smell of charred barbecue mixed with the warm dirt and the wet plant scent of the river reminds me of that night two years ago. Except that was the beginning of the summer and this is the end. School starts tomorrow. Other than a few weeks in the DR for Hev and Ter, I've had the whole summer with my tribe. But when school starts, all those folks I don't care about, half-friends, quarter-friends, and flat-out enemies, are gonna hear about my baby. Bertie's and mine. Can't wait.

We find ourselves one of the picnic benches by the water, one of the new ones made of that fake wood that'll never break. Just as we settle in, Hev raises her hand and calls out. Jo-jo's here, his too-cool leather jacket hanging off his too-broad shoulders—no matter it's warm enough for a tank top. Though the sun's nearly set, he keeps on his gold-rimmed shades 'til he's right in front of Hev. When he pushes them onto his hair, his dark eyes see only her.

Heavenly stares back at him, the curl of her mouth sly. He turns, and kisses all our cheeks.

"*Tato, chicas.*"

As she and Jo-jo head to the playground, we catcall them. Yaz hollers something about not corrupting the innocents. One of the nuns in Yaz's after-school used to yell it at her all the time. Jo-jo snakes his arm around Hev's waist, pulls her against him, and gives us a show. We whoop some more. Heavenly gives us the finger. Jo-jo grins.

Juan Luis Guerra croons from a car window. "*Ojalá que llueva café en el campo.*" It's one of Bertie's favorite songs. Even though he don't like rain and he don't like coffee. But he's not in the throng of bodies making more dirt of the grass. He's not tearing up the asphalt either. The lot's full, the entrance blocked by an NYPD barricade. A royal-blue Mazda RX-7 zooms off the highway. Someone pushes the barrier to the side and the Mazda skates through.

Yaz has broken away and is *cherchando* with a guy whose open collar shows a larimar-stone necklace tangled in the chain of a thick gold cross. He doesn't seem to mind that Yaz is snapping her peppermint gum at him or that you can see the wet glob of it between her teeth when she grins. He's got those light gray-blue eyes that look good against golden Dominican skin. He's gonna ask her to dance. Or at least get her a drink. Teri's watching, half-fascinated, half-afraid.

I touch Teri's hand to get her attention. I jerk my head toward where the Mazda parked. She nods and follows.

I slow as we get closer. Sergio Vargas has taken over where Juan Luis Guerra left off. I try to keep my hips steady. But the baby inside me loves merengue as much as I do. My papi loves merengue. That's what Abuela says. So I guess it runs in the family.

My Bertie is leaning through the open window of the Mazda's passenger door. I don't know if he got out of it or if he's been waiting, hanging with his *manin* by the trees or against the parked cars. His arm slips across to the driver. I imagine hands bumping, fingers snapping. Bertie stands. Did he slide something into his back pocket? *Coño.* The Mazda backs out. Teri tracks the car—now mostly afraid and only a little fascinated—as it zips from the lot. The engine revs as the Mazda skids onto the highway.

I think about going over there. Checking Bertie's pockets. I think of finding the Mazda's driver—I don't want to say his name—and doin' to him what I been doin' to all the Ricky Lopezes in my life. You threaten my tribe, you threaten me.

I think of the baby inside me.

I grab Teri's wrist, pull her toward the river. "Wanna dance?" I don't want to be in a mood. I feel great. I'm not tired. Got no morning sickness, never did. No heartburn. Don't even feel pregnant. I touch the small mound of my belly.

Yaz waves us over. The sparkly pink-orange of her nails is the current color of the sky. The guy with the larimar necklace is dancing with her. Yaz introduces us to Yefri and pushes him over to Ter. We help Ter out that way. She's so quiet, she'd get no action otherwise. Yaz tugs me a few steps away from them, and then we're both moving, arms and elbows up, hips sliding. "Suavémente" is blasting from a speaker someone's placed on the roof of a car. Yaz is kissing her fingers, circling her hands, mouthing the words at me as if I'm her long-lost lover. She's trying to turn my smile into a laugh. She knows that's what I need.

Hands take my hips. My back warms as someone presses against me. "Kiss me," Bertie sings to Yaz's lip sync. "Kiss me, slowly." My Bertie moves with me. We're so close, it's like we're one person. His arms encircle my waist. Gently, he turns me.

His eyelids are heavy. Maybe he's thinking about kissing me. Maybe he's trying to hide his bloodshot eyes. I can smell the *patuche* on him. I told him he can't smoke near me anymore 'cause of the baby. But he's not smoking. Not right now.

He takes my hand in one of his. His other holds my back. He nudges me away, then pulls me in. *"Echate pa'ca,"* he breathes.

No one bumps me. We're surrounded by a wall of elbows and thighs, butts and backs. Bertie's careful. His arms are a cage around me. He gives me his lazy smile. His fingers graze my stomach. He winks. He *is* a good dancer. I wonder if he's better than my papi.

Yaz is dancing with Teri. Guess Yefri wasn't all that. Too bad, 'cause his eyes were *manso*. Teri's watching me and Bertie. She's all fascinated. Not one bit afraid.

I tug Bertie close. I tell him, "Dance with her." Bertie holds my gaze, kisses my fingers. He takes Teri's hand. He twirls her, and she shrieks. She doesn't have his baby in her, so he don't have to be careful.

Yaz and I are back together. Her arms paddle the air, beating an invisible drum. She's left off lip-synching. She's crowing out the lyrics. Don't matter that she's outta tune. Sweat drips between my shoulder blades. The sun is five seconds from disappearing. A Jet Ski whizzes by—the music is so loud I can't even hear it. I get a whiff of roasted meat and my stomach snarls. The baby inside me's got an appetite. I feel warm, inside and out. I'm alive, alive, alive.

Teri shrieks again. Pure laughter. Soon, Heavenly and Jo-jo will find us. We'll go to the twenty-four-hour diner on Broadway and Jo-jo will buy us dinner. We'll have to drag Yaz, dancing and singing, the whole five blocks. Bertie will order me ice cream. Maybe I'll let him sneak me into his room after. I'll wake in the careful cage of his arms.

# TWENTY-ONE WEEKS

I'm on a cold table, practically naked. I'm under a cold sheet. My butt's asleep. The paper crinkles when I wiggle. It rips. Now my naked butt is right up against cold, hard plastic. Where other naked butts have been. *Chévere.*

"I'm so excited to see her!" Teri's feet salsa the floor though she's sittin' down. She wrangles her cell out of her olive-green Old Navy schoolbag. The one that was her brother's before her. "You think they'll let me take a picture of the picture?" She positions the phone in front of me. She's been documenting everything. Fine by me. Means I don't got to do it. But Ter can get a little *agitada*. Last week, I said hell no to some *carajo* idea to make a cast of my belly. Like, who would ever want that?

"Baby Angela!" I poke my stomach and make a face for the video. "This is yo mama talkin'." I lower my voice and hum Darth Vader's theme.

Heavenly snorts. She does that sometimes when she laughs. Once, we was all at McD's during that Monopoly game they have, the one where, if you win, you get tickets to the World Series or somethin'. Teri peeled her sticker off real fast—she can never wait—and leaned over, tellin' Yaz to hurry up and peel hers. She was even more excited 'cause the Yankees was in the playoffs. Yaz turns, all calm, like she the queen of Santo Domingo, and says, "What? You wanna know if we gonna be sittin' next to each other?" Heavenly snorted so big, *leche* came out her nose. We all got sprayed. We was so loud, hooting and slapping the table, they kicked us out. I had McFlurry in my hair for three days. It was on my coat all winter. All 'cause my fancy fashionista friend snorts.

Yaz goes to the machine next to me. It's part brown, part white. Like *medio pollo*—coffee with milk. It looks like some fancy vacuum cleaner, those ones with all the parts hanging off the sides so rich people can clean their curtains without getting the dog hair from the floor on them. Only this one's made for a giant. Bigger than those Smart cars we always make fun of. Yaz's palms are up, fingers counting one another like she's deciding which nail polish to choose. "*¡Anjá!*" she says. "This thing is huge! Was it this big at your other appointment?"

"I don't think you're supposed to touch that." Teri glances at the door. She's gumming her lips. Like she's tryin' to spread gobs of old lipstick smooth again. She does that when she gets nervous. Which is probably half the day. But not usually when she's with me.

"Doctors always run late. We waited for like half an hour for the last one. Won't hurt for me to take *un chinchin* of a peekypeek." Yaz picks up something that looks like a wand and jabs the air with it like it's a sword. She steps over the cord so it's between her legs and holds the wand up in front of her crotch. She thrusts like she's onstage with Beyoncé. "*¡Qué arrecho!*"

"Yaz!" Teri's face goes all red. She and Yaz be opposites when it comes to the deed. Not that Yaz is an *avión* or anything. She just talks like that. Fact is, she only been with one guy more than I have. But that's three more than Ter, who's still making up her mind about the whole thing. Like I said, she be the nervous one.

"Why won't this TV work?" Heavenly, the only one of us tall enough to reach, presses buttons on a monitor hung from the ceiling. Her black skirt is some fake snakeskin. It matches her heeled ankle boots and lace knee-highs. Up top, she's got an off-the-shoulder cable-knit sweater the color of custard caramel. Jo-jo supports Hev's fashion habit. It's nice having an older man with a job to pay for stuff. Especially when Hev shares so much. Hev jabs the TV again. "What's the point in having it here if we can't watch our shows?" Heavenly's got more experience in the man department than all us combined. Not surprising given the Nicki Minaj butt that sits atop those long legs. But while Heavenly shares her stuff, she don't share much of what goes on in her boys' beds. "I'm a doer, not a talker," she says. It ticks Yaz off. Yaz and me, we made a promise when we was twelve to tell each other everything. She was the one crammed in the

stall with me when I found out baby Angela existed. We jumped
.up and down, hugging and screaming 'til the coffee-shop guy
banged on the bathroom door. I was gonna trash the place. Stuff
the two toilets with paper and squirt soap all over the floor. To
get him back for ruining my moment. But Yaz pulled me out by
the hand saying we didn't have time 'cause we had to celebrate.
It was one of those crazy May days where the sun got confused
into thinking it was August. We skipped school and sat on a
rock by the Hudson, sucking on *pipas*, chucking the shells at
pigeons and making lists of what we was gonna do different
from our parents.

"Now show me the belly!" Yaz is pointing the *vaina* at me.
She does a hip circle like she's JLo this time. At least the plastic
stick's not near her crotch no more.

"Here." Teri, not looking at Yaz, folds the sheet down from
my stomach. She sits back on the chair, wedges her hands under
her legs.

Yaz puts the tip of the *vaina* on my belly button.

We all hear the knock at the same time the door opens.

Teri lets out a yip. Her phone slips off her lap, clatters to the
floor.

"It helps if you turn it on first." A Prince Royce face under
blond hair and above a white coat smiles at us like we're little-
kid cute.

"*Qué papi chulo,*" Heavenly mutters as Doc Hottie pulls the curtain in front of the doorway. *Coño,* she's got that right. He's even hotter than Heavenly's Jo-jo.

Doc Hottie steps around my feet. "Here, let me help you with that." He takes the wand from Yaz, puts it back on the machine. He extends his hand to me. "It's nice to meet you, Ms. Pujols. I'm Dr. Love. I'm one of the doctors who'll be performing your fetal echocardiogram today." He covers my belly with the sheet again. "We're not quite ready yet. I don't want you to get cold."

Huh. Too late for that. I want to complain about the too-cold table and the too-cold sheets, but I like him. And it's not just that he's hot. *Bonus!* Teddy-bear blond hair, eyes gold like a caffeine-free Coke can with a little bit of Pepsi blue, stubble so I know he doesn't take himself too seriously, glasses so I know he takes *this* seriously. It's that he called me "Ms." and introduced himself. A lot of peeps think I'm difficult. I'm not. Not really. You want me to show respect? You got to do me one first.

Teri and Yaz stare at Doc like he's a fudge sundae on Friday night. They're following some crazy diet where they only eat sugar on the weekend. Just makes them eat more of it, but they don't listen to me. Heavenly has let off with the TV. Her eyes track Doc as she takes a seat and crosses her legs, straightening her back to show off what she's got that I don't. Comes from having a black mama. My dumbass mama was white. Wasn't 'til I got pregs that anything real showed up on top. *Coño*, was Abuela relieved. Bertie was crackin' juiced, even though he'd told me before he didn't care they was so small. Teri and Yaz, their mamas are *morenitas*, so they filled out just fine.

"Hi there, I'm Dr. Love." He's offering his hand to Yaz. She reaches for it like it's her mama's necklace. The one her papi gave her before he split.

"I'm Yazmeen." She gulps but her grin's still there. "I'm Mari's cousin."

We ain't no cousins. If we was related, we'd be sisters. Yaz is just scared he's gonna throw her out. Teri read something about how only family members should be coming to these appointments.

"My name's Teri." Teri's voice is like a three-year-old scared the doctor's gonna give her a shot. Her fingers barely touch Doc's before she pulls them back. "I'm her cousin, too." Don't know why she's sounding like that. She knows I'd never let those hospital guards lay a hand on her. Or Yaz. Or Heavenly. You want me, you gotta take my girls, too. Don't matter that I'm pregs. My fist still knows how to swing. When Bertie and me first met, he called me *la galla*, after those fighting cocks back in the DR. Said if he could bet on me, he would, 'cause I always win. I didn't mind the nickname. I always thought it was stupid they only ever let the boy birds fight. That's Dominicans for you.

Bertie don't call me that no more. But sometimes, when we in bed, I give him a few *cluck-clucks*. It always sets him off laughing.

Heavenly's standing again, hands smoothing down her skirt. "Cousin Heavenly." She says her name like it's something you're not supposed to think about in church. Her grip on Doc's hand is solid. Like she's not planning on letting go.

"Pleased to meet you all." Doc doesn't look surprised I have so many cousins. Or that none of them look like me. He flips a switch on the machine. It's like he reached right into me and flipped my squirming stomach over. I grip the small mound of my belly. I squeal and kick my toes. Yaz squeals back. She grabs a piece of Doublemint from her bag and scurries to the other side of the bed so she can see better. She grabs one of my hands and one of Teri's. Pretty soon, we're all giggling. Even Heavenly. It's like we all kids again, squeezed into one of them cages on the Wonder Wheel in Coney Island, waitin' for it to lift off and show us the beach, the ocean, the sky.

Doc Hottie is working the keyboard. He hasn't let off smiling. "You're all excited, I see." *Coño.* He even has Prince Royce's dimples.

There's another knock and Doc looks up. "Is it all right if another fellow—another doctor—joins me?"

I shrug. "Sure." The more docs want to look at my baby, the better, far as I'm concerned.

Yaz whispers behind my hair, "Maybe this *médico es para mi*." She's grinning.

Heavenly aims a glare dead at her. "Then I call him." She points toward Doc Hottie, *my* doctor, with her chin.

I slap her wrist off my table, bring my thumb to my chest. *No way, he's mine*, I say with my stare.

"Fine." She sits back, flicks her hands up. Her silver rings catch the light. "You're right. Guess I need to get knocked up first." She scrolls her phone, looking bored again.

A woman doc enters. She's blond, too, but not a real blond like Doc Hottie. She goes to stand behind him. She doesn't even look at us.

"Hey, she's a woman." Teri's chewing her lip again, looking all confused. "You said it was a fellow."

"By 'fellow,' I mean a doctor-in-training, a pediatrician studying to be a cardiologist." Dr. Love finishes typing. He turns to the TV hanging behind him. He finds some hidden button and powers it up. My name and today's date show along the top of the screen. "Ladies, this is Dr. Goldstein. Dr. Goldstein, Ms. Pujols and her cousins."

Goldie head-bobs us then goes back to reading the sheet in her hands. "This is the HLHS rule out?" she asks.

I jut out my jaw. I don't know what she said. I know it was about me. About the baby. Weren't many rules in my house growing up, but not speaking Spanish in front of English speakers was one of them. It just be rude. Even my abuela, who never went to high school, knows that.

Doc Hottie doesn't answer the other doc. It almost looks like he's making a point of *not* answering her. He takes a seat in front of the machine. He adjusts his chair and the height of the table I'm on. He asks permission to lower the sheet and apologizes for the temperature of the jelly he squirts onto my skin.

Goldie frowns at my belly. "Are we sure she's twenty-one weeks? She doesn't look that far along." I look at Doc Hottie's face. Bertie's mama said the same thing. That I'm too skinny. She calls me *canillas*—"chicken legs"—or "chata"—flat butt. I hate that woman. She's such a *cacata*. She didn't even believe us that I was pregnant 'til I peed on a stick in her own bathroom.

Teri pats my leg. Heavenly's nose is still in her phone, but her hand is warming the top of my foot. Yaz squeezes my hand even harder. My girls, they got my back.

"The OB scan confirmed it. She's just thin, Miriam," Doc Hottie says.

I pluck at the edge of the sheet. "Yeah, Abuela—my grandma—she keeps trying to feed me more. I eat a lot, I swear." Abuela cooks me breakfasts of *huevos fritos* and *tocino, salchicha,* fruit, and always *pan* with *mantequilla.* I don't know what it is with Abuela and bread, but ever since I told her about the baby, she pushes it on me like a dealer. No matter that she hadn't made a meal for me since I started to use deodorant. "I just don't gain." I shrug again.

"You lucky," Yaz says, squeezing my bony hip. "It's 'cause you got that *flaquita*, *blanquita* mama."

Yeah, I'm lucky all right. I won the parent lottery. My mama ditched me with Abuela when I was eight. Said it was because of a new job. More like a new boyfriend. Weekly visits turned to monthly. Monthly turned to Christmas. Christmas came, I got a card. Haven't seen her white ass for like five years. At least there's *mi papi*. I know where he's at. Sing Sing. I write him. Every month. Sometimes he writes me back. I know *he* loves me. He wouldn't have done what my mama did if he had a choice about it.

I look at my belly. It is little. But it's round. Inside it a baby is growing. *Mi bebé*. And I can't wait for her to come out.

I pinch Yaz back. She pretends what I did hurt, but then she's all smiles and taking my hand again. She's just trying to make me feel better. It's not like I don't know what men in the Heights are attracted to. It's sure not my skinny booty. Bertie's the exception.

"Tch-tch!!" Heavenly swats at Yaz. "Sit back, mami. I can't see."

The wand sinks into the jelly on my skin. It's different than the one Yaz was playing with. Wider. And not as long. I hold my breath. Yaz and Teri do, too. On the TV, black-and-white speckles grow big and then small. It's quiet. Too quiet.

"I can't hear nothing. How come I can't hear it?" Yaz says real loud.

Doc Hottie adjusts a button. A sound fills the room.

*Ba-dump, ba-dump, ba-dump.*

It's the most beautiful sound I ever heard.

Yaz claps and shrieks. Teri laughs and holds up the phone. Heavenly smiles real big. So big, I see her gold cap, the one she got in DR and is always trying to hide.

"Sorry, we usually keep the volume turned down," Doc Hottie says.

"Why? Why would you do that?" I ask. "Us mamas want to hear our babies."

"Us aunties, too!" crows Yaz.

Doc Hottie nods. He's focused on the screen. Goldie is, too.

"I bet she'll have your eyes, Mar. Big and brown." Yaz grins at me.

"Nuh uh. I want her to have Bertie's eyes. Gray-green." My baby is going to be U-NIQUE. Green eyes are the rarest. So she's going to have those.

"As long as she don't get Bertie's ears." Heavenly smirks. Girl's got a point. Bertie's got big ears.

"Do you know the sex yet?" Doc Hottie's looking back at me.

My face goes warm. Is he stupid or something? The man is looking at a baby inside of me. How does he think it got in there?

He tilts his head since I'm not answering. His gold-blond hair brushes his cheek. Most guys I know have their hair real short. Only way to tame the kink. If Doc lost the glasses, it'd be like he's going for some *manso* rock-star look. It works for him. Even with the glasses.

"Do you want to know if it is a boy or a girl?" he asks. And suddenly he's not a rock star. He's something more. It's like a hot, kindly lion is staring at me.

Oh. My face goes even warmer. I'm not usually such an idiot. "It's a girl," I say.

"Did Dr. Millar tell you that?" That's my real baby doctor. She's this super nice lady with frizzy hair who's always late. I pegged her around Abuela's age, though the nurses were sayin' she just came back from having her third baby. Reminded me of the Duane Reade bags Toto lugs into the apartment, his contribution to their living arrangement. Even doubled-bagged, I can always see the tampon boxes, pressed up against the toilet paper and Clorox. Those tampons ain't for me no more. The thought of the two of them getting pregs makes me feel like when Teri told us about her brother going to emergency for an ear pain. The doctors found a *cucaracha* in his ear. Alive. *Gross.*

The doc's still looking at me. I almost forgot he asked a question.

"Nah," I say. "Doc Millar didn't tell me either way. I just know she's a she."

Something takes shape on the TV. It kicks up bubbles of water, but I don't feel nothing. Is that . . . a leg?! Two legs? But there's something else.

"Doc, is that what I think it is?"

"What do you think it is?" He smiles at me. All rock-star hair and nerd glasses.

Heavenly sits forward, frowning at the image. "Does that baby have three legs?"

"Two legs," Doc Hottie says. "And a boy part."

*What?!*

"A boy part?" I repeat. "You mean that huge thing in between the two long things is a PENIS?!"

Doc Hottie blushes. Doctors aren't supposed to blush. My face goes all warm. Again.

"Oooh, Mari's em-BAR-rassed!" Yaz's silvered fingernails are tripping up my arm. *Coño,* this fuckin' white skin of mine. I can barely ever hide what I'm thinking. "And she's *embarazada*!"

Yaz sweeps her hands from below her boobs out and around to her thighs, ballooning an invisible stomach. She roars a laugh.

I elbow Yaz hard. In the boob.

"Ow!" But she's grinning.

"Sorry to disappoint you, Ms. Pujols. But you are having a boy."

*A*y, *chichí! A boy! ¡Un señorito!*" Yaz shouts. She's pounding the bed. Heavenly lifts her swan-neck arms and gives a whoop-whoop. She takes a pic with her cell and starts texting. Teri's blinking, smiling her cheek-hurting smile.

I stare at the screen. At the penis on the screen. This kid is smart. It's like he knows we're watching. He's showing it off.

My chest swells. *A boy.* A little man. My arms encircle my belly, sticky gel sliding all over them. Teri takes my fingers, grips them 'til they're numb. There's gel all over her now, too. We're both laughing. I thought I wanted a girl. I wanted someone just like me. Girls love their mamas more than boys do. But boys love their mamas *and* take care of them. This is better. This is so much better.

A knock and the door opens. A short lady who looks like she loves flan a little too much introduces herself as Dr. Stevenson. She's got floppy gray hair, like one of those dogs whose eyes you can't see. A pair of half glasses pinch her nose. They're I'm-trying-to-be-cool purple even though she's so not. She says she's the attending, whatever that means. Another doc attending to me, I guess. Pudgy Purple goes and stands behind Doc Hottie. She's giving him directions. Goldie moves back. She's looking at the same screen we are. The one hanging from the ceiling. Her face is tilted up, catching the little bit of light in the dark room. That's how I know something is wrong.

Yaz leans over my stomach, gives a peace sign as Teri snaps a pic. Heavenly is reading out boy names from some celebrity baby name list on her phone. Yaz says something about Bertie's ears being cute on a boy. But I'm looking at Goldie.

There is no penis on the screen. It's the heart. I know because it's moving. It's beating. Colors, blue and red, rush through it. Goldie is frowning. She shakes her head, like the screen's disappointed her. What's wrong? Is it the colors? Are they off? I knew we were coming to see heart doctors. But Dr. Millar said this was only a precaution because she couldn't see everything she wanted to. She said the baby was in a difficult position. Everything's going to be fine. Everything has to be fine.

Yaz, Heavenly, and Teri are quiet. They're looking at me. Watching me watch Goldie. Waiting.

Pudgy Purple is murmuring. Telling Doc Hottie to show her this, show her that. Isn't Doc Hottie my doctor? Why is Pudgy Purple even here? Everything was fine 'til she arrived.

Doc takes the wand off me. He smiles, but it's not a real smile. It's a smile Prince Royce would give a fan who's asked for an autograph. He wants to sign it. But he doesn't have a pen. Or he's rushing to another show. Either way, it's not the fan's fault. Either way, it's a pity smile. I should know. I get them all the time.

"Why don't you get dressed, Miss Pujols? You and your friends can join us in the other room." Pudgy Purple is talking. I can't get anything from her face. It's like we're those men Toto watches on TV late at night, the ones who play poker for days without stopping to shower or sleep.

Three white coats file out. The curtain shrieks as Goldie pulls it behind her. The door thuds shut.

"¿Qué fue eso?" Yaz exclaims, hands on hips. She looks as if one of the men at the bodega insulted her culo. She rips off a piece of paper from under me and pushes her gum into it with her tongue. She crushes it in her fist and flings it to the trash. Her sass is her shield. Heavenly's cell is up by her face again. Her nails click, click, click on the screen. Teri's fingers worm together. She's looking at the machine, like she's just now seeing it resembles a giant vacuum.

"You didn't get a picture," Teri says. "They didn't ask if you wanted a picture."

I slide off the table. I walk into the bathroom, leaving the sheet behind. I could care less if they see my skinny, white, naked ass.

"Wait." Teri scratches in her bag. A tissue, a tampon, and three pennies fall out. "Here." She thrusts a wrinkled photo at me. It's black. But a tiny, bright shape, like a bean, is in the center. Baby Angela, June 30, ten weeks.

She kept it. From all those months ago. Of course she did.

My heart is the drum of feet on our rickety fire escape. I tell myself I could be wrong. About Goldie's face. About Doc's smile. Sometimes it's hard to believe the things you say to keep yourself together.

I shake my head at Teri. My neck feels hot. It's the one place the sun always tries to burn me. "You think I want a picture of my son with a girl's name on it?" I flick it away, giving her my fierce, don't-mess-with-me grin. My lip itches like crazy, but I won't touch it. I show them my bare ass and shut myself in the bathroom.

"The fetus has a birth defect called hypoplastic left heart syndrome. Half of the heart is missing."

Those are the last words I hear. I pretend to listen. I'm good at that. But what more do they need to say? How can a baby live like that? With half a heart?

We're at a huge table. The three white coats and the four of us. They asked if the baby's father could come, but I shook my head at them. I'm not calling Bertie for this. He'd understand even less than me.

Pudgy Purple is doing most of the talking. Teri is sniffling in the corner, that tissue that fell on the exam-room floor now wadded in her hand. Heavenly keeps tapping at her phone. Like she's texting. Goldie keeps giving her ice-pick looks. But Heavenly's taking notes. That's what she does when it gets all *coco-loco*. She gets all cool and businesslike. Like she's one of the girls working in Jo-jo's office. Yaz is holding my hand under the table. She has her listening face on, too. When she squeezes my fingers, sound gushes through the pretend cotton over my ears. Words I know like *risk* and *death*. Words I don't know like *catheterization* and *transplant* and *neurodevelopmental deficits*. I put more pretend cotton over my ears.

Pudgy Purple says something that makes Teri bawl. Yaz is breathing fast, sideways looking at me. Her grip is so tight I can't feel my fingers.

"We'll give you a few moments to think about everything." Pudgy Purple stands, comes to my side of the table. Her hand touches my shoulder. It must weigh no more than a feather, 'cause I can't feel it.

"Are you sure there isn't anyone else you would like to call? Someone else you want to be with you?" she says.

My gaze is a knife. I would stab her with it if I could.

It's my age. She thinks a fifteen-year-old can't handle this without a proper grown-up. But she don't know the grown-ups in my life. She thinks I'm stupid and got pregnant by mistake. But she don't know me.

I wanted this baby. He's no mistake. I love him. And he loves me.

"Maybe her grandma?" Yaz's voice has never been so quiet.

"She's at work, but I got her number." Yaz takes out her phone.

Pudgy Purple looks at me. Her card-playing face doesn't react to the boiling water spitting from my eyes. "Would you like me to contact your grandmother, Miss Pujols? Ask her to come in so we can all talk together?"

"No." Vipers, bullets, poison. I'm throwing everything in my head at her. But she don't see it. She don't feel it. "Like Yaz said, Abuela be at work. She don't like interruptions."

Pudgy Purple leaves. Goldie follows her, shaking her head at us. I glare at her, too. My hands coil like whips in my lap.

*You want a piece of me? Come on, let's go.*

I wait for that *chopa* doctor to say something. Anything. But the door closes.

"Mari?" Teri has stopped sniveling. She reaches over and pats my arm. "*Todo 'ta bien.*" She starts crying again. "*Todo 'ta bien.*" She doesn't even believe her own lies. Like I didn't believe mine.

Doc Hottie is still here. He hasn't said nothing for a while. I don't look at him. I don't want those blue lion eyes to disappoint me, too.

He rolls his chair around to my side of the table. He slides white paper in front of me. He takes a box of crayons out of his pocket.

From Goldie and Pudgy Purple, I expected it. Lady docs judge. Because they're women and that's what us women do. But him? He's leaving me with paper and crayons? So I can scribble? Like a little kid?

"How about I draw you a picture of your baby's heart?" he says. His massive hand pins the paper, rotates it toward him. "Dr. Stevenson did an amazing job explaining everything. But you know what they say about a picture."

He draws a heart. Like a Valentine heart. Who's he kidding? I laugh. I cackle at him like I'm a mad *bruja*. Yaz puts her arm around my shoulder. Heavenly comes closer. She switches her phone to video to record what Doc does and says.

Doc draws one heart first. A normal heart. He fills it with blue and red blood. Blue for the right side, red for the left. Below it, he draws something else. Half a heart. There's no red in it. Only blue. And purple. His voice is deep and steady. His words are slow and simple. He keeps going. Even when tears sting my eyes. He's not making fun of me. He's showing me he thinks I can understand this.

When he's done, five different hearts are on two sheets of paper. Normal and HLHS—that's what my baby's problem is called. On the other sheet is the way my baby's heart will look after the three different surgeries he will need to survive. His heart will never look normal. I get that. But the doctors will try to make it so the blood goes where it needs to. After the last surgery, both blue and red blood are there. But his heart will still be only half of what it should be.

I'm nodding, showing Doc I understand. But all I'm thinking is: How's my baby going to love me with only half a heart?

Doc stands. He moves his arm and his fingers cover mine. I'm clutching the first sheet of paper.

"Mari, I'm sorry. Truly, I am."

He leaves me alone with my girls, a broken baby inside me and paper hearts in my hands.

The apartment door opens, jingling with all twelve of Abuela's keys. It's minutes to ten. Her usual time. Toto's boots and construction hat have been at the door since eight, when I got home after crashing at Heavenly's. I didn't want to see Bertie. Not yet. Toto's in Abuela's room, doing whatever he does back there. He knows enough not to come near me. It took near three years, but Toto and me, we know how to get along. We keep our distance.

Abuela's making a sandwich when I come into the kitchen.

"You hungry?" She pushes a plate at me. Cheese, ham, salami, and pickles on buttered toast. I'm still not used to this. She's paid more attention to me in the past few months than she has in the past six years. I know it's all about the baby. But I don't care. It's nice to feel wanted.

"No. No standing while eating." She clicks her tongue. "You sit. Come, *la sala*." She waits for me to put the sandwich back down and picks up the plate. I take the five steps to the couch, slump down on it. Abuela goes back to the kitchen, returns with a glass of milk and her sandwich.

"*Leche* is good for the baby. Drink." She sits next to me. Starts to eat. The TV is on. One of her *telenovelas*. Do not mess with Abuela and her soap operas. Once, Toto recorded a soccer game over one by accident. She almost threw him out. The time I caught him in my room—going through my stuff—she didn't even make him apologize. Yaz said they were probably in on it together, looking to see if I was doin' drugs. I said they oughta know drugs wasn't why I act the way I do. They got nobody other than themselves to blame for that.

I stare at the TV. I wait for the man and woman who are pointing guns at each other to start making out before I speak.

"Had an appointment today. For the baby."

"¿*Veldá?* Good. The baby, she needs to see the doctors."

"It's a he. A boy."

Abuela puts her sandwich down and looks at me. "¿*Un varon-cito?*"

Is she mad or happy? I hold my breath, waiting.

"¡*Ay, mi amor!*" Her hug knocks me into Gato, who yowls and jumps off the sofa. "¡*Un principe! Ay, que bueno.* Teo! Teo!" she shouts to the back. "You tell him?"

I shake my head. Since when do I speak to Toto?

Toto's hairy head sticks out her door. "¿*Qué pasó?*" Abuela tells him it's a boy. He gives me a thumbs-up and goes back to his *fútbol*. Gato is slinking by, but Abuela scoops him up and asks him how he's going to like a little nephew. She moves his front legs as she pretend-answers for him. Despite his turned-back ears, the cat is looking forward to it. Abuela takes another bite of her sandwich, feeds the cat a piece of salami, and looks for the phone.

"Ay, I need to call Yael and Cila. And Rosa. I will be the first great-grandmother with *un nenito!* You know Cila, her daughter's son, he has the two kids—different mothers. But they both girls. And only one in Nueva York. The other in DR. But this . . . *¡Ay, Mari!* Is so wonderful to have a baby. Especially now. *Es como agua de mayo.*" It's one of those old-people sayings that doesn't make sense. "Water in May." No matter that I tell her it's April showers here. She says it like her mother and her abuela—who, she always points out, came from Spain—used to. She said it when I told her I was pregnant. She's thinking about how bad things used to be. Between us. Never talking. Only yelling. Slamming doors. The occasional broken plate or glass. And then one Sunday, after church when the priest had talked about some woman named Ruth and gone on about how children should stay with their mothers, I demanded to know where my mama was. Abuela had to know. She was keeping it from me. Abuela laughed. Said she wished she knew. Said she wouldn't have to put up with my ugly mouth no more if she did. I got so mad, I smashed all the photos in Abuela's living room. The ones of *her* family. Of people I never met. Thought she was gonna hit me. But she just dragged me, kicking and hollering, to my room. Locked me in. And then nothing. A year when Abuela and Toto pretended I didn't exist. A year when, at least once a week, I looked down at my nail-bitten hands to make sure I wasn't actually invisible. Hitting would've been better.

Angelo is like rainwater in May. He's what we needed when we needed it most.

"Think of all the beautiful blue he will wear." Abuela puts down her sandwich. She spreads her hands, as if I'm not going to believe what she's going to say next. "Your papi, he had this one outfit, so cute. I think I have in Santo Domingo. This weekend, I call Marco and ask him to look."

Marco. Her brother. My great-uncle. I've never even spoken to him, though they talk on the phone at least every other week. Abuela's always made it clear I belong more to the mama who dumped me, than to Papi, who's her son. That changed, too, when I told her I was pregnant. Abuela said she'd save up, and when the baby was born, she'd take us both to Santo Domingo to meet Marco's family.

Abuela finishes her sandwich, humming, laughing at her soap. I don't know how to tell her the rest. I've never seen Abuela this happy. Ever. And she's happy at something that's 'cause of me. I call Gato over with my fingers. He stares at me from the kitchen, wraps his tail around his feet. He doesn't move. He's a smart cat. He doesn't want any part of this.

I don't want to do it. But she needs to know. He's her family, too, right?

"Um, there's more," I say. "The doctor said there's a problem."

"*¿Cómo?* Problem? What kind of problem?"

"With his heart."

Her face goes real still. "But they can fix it, *¿sí?*"

I nod. "With surgery." I swallow hard.

Abuela's eyes are pointed at me, but she's not seeing me. She's watching something in her head. She puckers her lips, bringing out the wrinkles that always fill with lipstick and make her mouth look like it's sprouted tiny red feathers. They smooth out as she runs her tongue over her teeth. She lets out her breath and blinks. She swats the air with her hand, her smile coming back. "The doctors these days, they amazing. I saw on *Dr. Oz*, baby with whole new liver. Yellow as *mantequilla* before, but now white and perfect." She reaches over, puts her hand to my belly. "They will fix his little heart. And we will pray. I tell Padre Andrés, and he will pray. Maybe even *una misa especial.*" She gives my belly one final rub and pats it. "*Todo 'ta bien. En Dios lo creo.* Have faith in God, Mari. Have faith."

She marches to the kitchen before I can say anything else. I don't usually go along with what Abuela says. But tonight, I do. Because I want to believe it, too.

The TV's still going, but she turns the kitchen radio on. Abuela sings that *bilirrubina* merengue song as she washes the dishes. Hers and mine. I'm not allowed to clean anymore. On account of my condition.

S o what are you going to do?" Yaz holds the door to the bodega for me.

"About what?" We haven't talked about it since yesterday. No texts, no calls, no nothing. I'm pissed. That she left me hanging like that. She didn't even bring it up at school.

Yaz looks at Heavenly. Heavenly rolls her eyes. Pitbull chants *"I know you want me . . ."* from her back pocket. Hev whips out her cell and squints at the screen. Don't know when that girl's gonna get her eyes checked like I told her. She slides the phone into her jeans and glances out the window. She turns back to Yaz, pouts those big lips of hers and lifts a fur-vest-clad shoulder at me. So now they both gonna sass me?

I grab a bag of Doritos and a Coke. It's hot out. Summer's not giving up without a fight. The cold can feels good in my sweaty hand. I imagine the baby inside me, jumping, rolling, twirling. My little man wants a Coke, too. But then I remember I'm not supposed to have soda. Teri read that in a book. I open the freezer door and put the can back. I take an apple juice instead.

"It's not good for you," I say to my belly.

The chips are open before I pay. *"Coño* am I hungry," I tell

Bodega Man. I show off the inside of my mouth as I chew. These Doritos be mine now.

Yaz slaps a pack of gum on the counter. She snaps a bubble at Bodega Man and turns to me. "Have you told him yet?"

"Who?"

Yaz blows another bubble. She pops it with her pinkie nail. Yellow with blue stripes today. She's watching me like she's trying to figure me out. "Who?" she repeats. "*¿Qué carajo es ésto?* Your man, that's who." She nods toward the door. "Here he comes by the way."

"Three twenty-five." Bodega Man wants his money.

I dig in my pockets. I toss two rumpled singles at him. "Sorry. All I got." I open the juice and glug it down before he can snatch it away. I wipe my mouth with the back of my sleeve and put my hand on my stomach. "*Anda el diablo,* this baby be thirsty. And hungry." I grab another handful of chips.

Bertie ambles toward me, hands hanging from his back pockets. "Ey, mami. *¿Qué lo qué?*" He nods at me, his lips pursing in an air-kiss. He nods at Bodega Man and leans in front of me to fist-bump him once, twice, three times. They touch elbows as he pulls back. "*Oyé, chan. ¿En qué vaina tu 'ta?*" Bertie takes off his cap, punches it out, and puts it on backward.

Didn't know Bertie and Bodega Man were close. Doesn't surprise me. Bertie knows everybody.

*"Aquí, manito, todo manso. Pero . . .* Bert. This your girl?"

Bertie slides next to me. He's taller than I am, but he's just as skinny. He wraps his arm around my neck. He tweaks my nose and kisses my hair. I love it when he does that. Shows the other guys I belong to him.

*"Manin,* this my baby. And my baby's mama. Ain't that right?" He makes a kissing sound. I turn and kiss him, pushing chip bits into his mouth. He pulls back. "Yo, babe. That's gross." But he's smiling. He comes back, legs wide. His hands grab my butt as he leans me back, kisses me deep. "Oooh," he sighs, straightening. "I love that." He squeezes my *nalgas* again. "And I love this." His hand comes round to the front of my shirt. He bends his knees, looks into my eyes. "I hear you have some news for me?"

*What?!* What did he hear? I look around for Heavenly, glad I don't got scissors or anything else sharp, else I'd chop off her lemon-bleached rocker locks. I bet she's the *boca agua.* Yaz would never betray me. Teri hardly ever talks to boys, let alone cute ones. She only ever looks at her feet, her tongue and lips sticking together whenever Bertie comes round.

Yaz points to the door with her thumb. She knows what I'm thinking without me having to say nothing. "Jo-jo picked her up already. Date time. Did you know he has a new ride?"

I could care less about what car that *parejero* has. Jo-jo is so full of himself. I can't believe I let Bertie introduce his cousin's friend to Heavenly. Bet Jo-jo's the one who told Bertie.

"Beto, Beto." Bodega Man snaps his fingers at us. "She needs to pay up, *manin*. She don't got enough, *manin*."

Bertie takes his time looking away from me. He gives Bodega Man his lazy smile. He fishes in his pockets and comes up with only two dimes. "*Óyeme, chan*," he says, shrugging. "What can I do? You heard her. The baby's hungry. Hey, you going to that *can* tomorrow night? How 'bout I hook you up? Skinner's gonna be there." He waits while Bodega Man considers it. When Bodega Man smiles, Bertie smiles back. "*¿Tu 'ta cloro?*"

Guess what kinda car Skinner drives? I hate that *maldito hijo de la porra*. I hate that Bertie hangs with him. Told him that after the baby's born, he can't no more. Bertie's dumb enough to fall for Skinner's lines. He's always defending him. But he's smart enough to make sure Skinner and I never be in the same room. 'Cause if that happened, my fist would find Skinner's face real fast. Don't care if Skinner's name gets Bodega Man off my back.

Bertie's arm is round my neck again. He leads me to the door.

"Mar, you forgot this." Yaz takes my hand, slides the gum into it. She stares at me. *Tell him.*

I stare back and waggle my chin at her. *Looks like someone already told him.* She knows me like I know her. So she knows that's what I want to say.

Yaz frowns, shakes her head. *He doesn't know. Not everything.*

We're halfway out the door and Bertie's already shouting "Yo! ¡*Chan!* ¡*Tu 'ta cache-cache!*" at some blue-capped bro. His fist is up in salute. My mayor of the Heights. He ruffles my hair, kisses my cheek. Elvis Crespo pumps through the sunroof of a passing car. Bertie spins to face me, slides a finger through my belt loop. He does a few steps of merengue right there on the concrete. His other hand is out, palm open, beating the air. He's grinning.

Yaz is right. He doesn't know. He can't. He wouldn't be acting so normal if he did.

I shove open the door to my place. We kick our shoes onto the shaggy brown carpet that smells of breakfast eggs and bacon. No one's home. Bertie pulls me to my room, lifts off my shirt, undoes his pants. He drops to his knees, kisses my belly all over like he always does. I love this about Bertie. That he's sweet. That he treats me right.

I stop him when he gets to my underwear.

"We need to talk."

He looks up at me. His gray-green eyes are dazed. "You breaking up with me?"

"*No.*" He can be such an idiot. My hand moves to my stomach and his gaze drops. "It's the baby," I say.

Bertie stands. He sits on the bed. His mouth hangs open in that way that makes him look like he's twelve.

I sit next to him. I don't know what to say. I don't do candy-coated *porquería* so I just say what's true. "The baby has a heart problem."

Bertie says nothing at first. He takes my hand, weighs it in his. "I thought you was gonna tell me it was a boy. I didn't hear nothing about a heart problem."

I nod. I hold on to his hand real tight. "It is a boy. A boy with a heart problem."

Bertie looks away. He brings his fist to his mouth. He lets go of me and covers his face with his hands. There's a terrific crash above, like a casserole falling off a counter. The glass that sits on my nightstand rattles. The sip or two of dusty water in it shivers. Muffled shouts and the pound of feet rain above us. Mr. and Mrs. Rodriguez, our upstairs neighbors, are the oldest people I know. But they fight like *telenovela* stars.

Bertie still has his head in his hands.

"You okay?" I nudge him with my elbow.

He looks at me. His eyes are red. I don't think it's because he's been smoking. "¿*Veldá*? It's a boy, huh? *Diache*. That's great." He tries to smile. He takes a breath but starts to cough. He stands, moves away from me, coughing so hard he's choking. He does up his pants, shifts them back down so his boxers show. His hands hang on his hips. His head hangs on his neck. "What are you going to do, Mari?" He doesn't look at me.

What am *I* going to do? "What do you mean?" My voice is a knife sharpening. How is this all on me?

Bertie turns. "Is he going to live? Did the doctors say he's going to be normal?"

I grab my shirt. I yank it on. I go to my closet and get out a sweater. One that goes all the way to my knees.

I cross my arms and stare at my nightstand, past the dirty water glass. My kitten-a-day calendar, the one Bertie got me for my birthday, stares back at me. I wish I could tape the kittens from the last three days back up. White fluffy furball tangled in yarn. Orange-and-black paws sticking out from under sheets. Tabby clinging to tree bark. I wish I could go back. To before. When all I knew was the cackle of Yaz's laugh and the minty smell of her gum. Teri's shy smile when a cute boy comes near or her pretend stern one when she passes me a note reminding me of homework I'll probably never do. Heavenly rolling her eyes as I come out of her bathroom for dinner with her and her mama, wearing Heavenly's too-big bra on my head like a pair of horns. Bertie's warm hands sliding over my hips as he whispers for me to kiss him *suavemente*. My warm belly growing round with a baby whose heart is whole. But I can't go back. I threw those pages of kittens away.

"Mari, *¿qué dijeron?*" Bertie asks. "What did they say?"

Why is he making me talk about it? Why can't he be like Abuela and tell me everything's going to be fine? That God or the doctors or whoever will take care of it? Why can't he just hold me?

*Coño.* "They say they don't know, okay! They say it's really serious and he could die. Is that what you want to hear? That you put a baby inside me that's so junked he might not even make it? Thank you, Bertie. Thank you for that. *¡Qué bolsu!*" I make a rude gesture. "What a man you are!"

He looks at me. His mouth is open again. "Mari, *por favor, no te pongas brava conmigo.* Don't be like that."

"Maybe Skinner or Linner or whatever his name is can get you out of this. Maybe you have some friend who knows someone who knows someone else who can buy or sell something that will get me my healthy baby back! Remember the one we talked about? A baby that would love me—love us—forever?"

"*Chula*, baby, don't do this." Bertie still looks so confused.

I slap the calendar off the table. It smacks the wall and lands on top of my bag. My hands are fists. "Don't you call me '*chula*'." I want to hit him. I want to hit him so bad. It's not his fault, but he can't fix it. And I hate him for it.

I open the door, hold it for him. "Get out, Bertie. Go!"

He does what I say. *Gracias a Dios*, he leaves. I grab hold of the picture of a black kitten lapping milk. I rip it to teeny, tiny pieces. I go after the next one. And the next. Until my room is covered with torn-up kitten paws, kitten tails, kitten bellies. Until the entire kitten year is gone. I pace, crushing paper bits, until my feet hurt. I sit on the bed and pick lint and cat hairs off my sweater until I hear Toto dropping his boots by the door. I don't know what else to do and I can't stand it no more. I pick up my phone and text Yaz.

Yaz is lying on her bed, hands under her chin. Her nails throw purple shadows onto her cheeks, though they're painted a royal, shimmering blue. The color reminds me of an ad I saw on the side of a bus once. For some show called *Supergirl. Coño.* As if I'd ever watch some skinny, blond *puta* running around pretending to be Superman. Abuela's *telenovelas* be more realistic than that.

Yaz's room smells of paint remover. Little bottles of nail polish line the top of her dresser. On one side, cotton squares stained yellow and blue clump together like they're cold. Yaz rolls over. She stretches out a hand and examines her nails. She knows I been staring at them. There are tiny red hearts painted on each one. Don't know how Yaz does that. I seen her do it, with a brush as thin as an eyelash. How she keeps her hand so steady is what I don't get. If it were me, my nails would have red splotches all over them. Like they'd gotten into a fight and got all bloody.

"I'll do them for you if you promise to stop biting them."

I loosen my thumbnail from my teeth, slide my hand under my butt. Yaz has offered before. When we both started eighth grade, she and her abuela got me some polish that tasted like *fo*. Just taught me to peel it off before I put it near my mouth.

I rest my head against the wall and look up at the stickers covering the ceiling. Chewed nails seems like a really good problem right about now.

Yaz scooches forward on the bed 'til her head is hanging off it. She makes a pout, turning her face into a puppy dog's. "You told your papi yet?" she asks.

She's talking about the letters. The ones I write to him in prison. Abuela says my papi don't like visitors. A prison's not a place for a girl anyway. But every month, we send him something. Sometimes, I slip in extras. A ripped ad from a magazine showing a sunset over a beach. Ticket stubs from Yankee Stadium—not mine, just ones I found on the ground. A strip of blue flannel from the bottom of a Salvation Army bin that I got for free and that I imagine him wearing around his wrist or woven through his fingers. Abuela says blue is Papi's favorite color. But always, ever since I been stayin' with Abuela, even if we fighting, I write that letter, put it in the envelope Abuela leaves on the kitchen counter. I don't say much. Just enough so Papi knows I don't forget him.

I shake my head to Yaz's question. "Don't want to bother him," I say. He don't need to know about my problems. He got enough to be depressed about without me bringing him down.

I'm staring up at the words *You're a star!* written in bubbly letters. It was one of the last stickers we put up so it's not covered by any others. Underneath, *dous!* peaks from one side, while *ific!* peeks from the other. The feet of either Pluto or Goofy come out the top. They look like ears, or antennae, rising from the star. When we was younger, Yaz and I collected what we got from school, the doctor, dentist, social worker, case worker—anyone who gave a kid a sticker to keep them quiet—and put it up on Yaz's ceiling. We'd move her bed around the room, jump up and down on the mattress, peeled stickers balancing on our fingers, thumbs out to press them in. Her abuela never cared. She thought it was cute. Yaz loved the idea we were decorating. How she sleeps with all those My Little Ponies looking down at her is beyond me. I used to try to stick Shrek or Snow White over those freaky horse faces. But Yaz said she liked the ponies. When we switched to inspirational quotes, she made me promise to leave the ponies above her bed alone. We used to tape up a piece of construction paper to hide the ponies on nights I slept over. 'Til the summer Yaz swiped one of those eye patches from first class on her return flight from DR. Now when I'm at Yaz's, I put on the eye patch like a *manso* pirate, stretch out on her bed, and pretend I'm in first class. Compared to Yaz's, sleeping at Abuela's is like the last row of economy. You feel every bump of turbulence. And you're right up against the bathrooms, so you smell you-know-what the whole ride.

Yaz is watching me look at all the stickers. I wonder if she knows which one I'm searching for. Jasmine, from *Aladdin*. Yaz wore that costume three years in a row. When was the last time we played that guessing game? Beginning of the summer, maybe.

"So Carmen's cool, huh?"

Carmen's my abuela. I told Yaz what she said. After I told her what went down with me and Bertie.

"As long as she gets herself a *nieto*, she be good," I answer.

"But you told her everything, right? About the heart?"

I give Yaz a rotten-lemon look. "I told her there's a problem with his heart. She didn't want to know more. You know her, she makes her decision and that's it. No going back. She's got her faith."

Yaz snorts. "Faith in her rightness."

"More like faith in Dr. Oz. I was half expecting her to demand Dr. Oz do the surgery."

"He *is* a heart surgeon." Yaz blows on a nail, touches it, then runs her hand through her hair. "Wonder if Carmen knows that."

"If it's written in *People* magazine, she's gotta." Besides her telenovelas, ain't nothing Abuela loves more than her celebrity magazines. "Poor Padre Andrés." I tsk. He's the priest at *Encarnación*. "Don't think he knows Carmen's got more faith in Dr. Oz than him." Yup. She's got faith in everyone except me.

Yaz's laughter dies away. She rubs the back of her hand across her mouth. She's not wearing lip gloss today. Guess she forgot. She's watching me again.

"Carmen knows about the surgery then."

Why would Yaz think I would keep that to myself? "'Course she knows," I snap.

Yaz lifts her hands, as if I'm holding a gun and she don't want me to shoot. I slide my eyes away from her and scowl out the window. It's seven and it's already dark. Every fall, that's what I hate most. Not the cold. Not the bare trees. I hate that the sun pulls away. As if I've done something wrong.

My stomach growls. Yaz hears it. Wonder if she's going to suggest going to the park. I don't feel like dancing tonight. Don't feel like seeing Bertie. But I don't smell nothing cooking. Don't know if Yaz's abuela's even here.

Something hits me on the side of my head. I think it's a sock, but it's the black eye patch. It's Yaz's way of asking if I'll stay the night.

"We've got leftovers. *Arroz con pollo,*" she says, lifting one eyebrow. Used to drive me crazy that she could do that and I couldn't. We spent hours in front of the mirror with her coaching me. But my eyebrows are a pair. Stuck together.

My stomach grumbles again.

I stretch out my arms and hiss in a breath. "Didn't bring no clean underwear." There's school tomorrow.

Yaz reaches into one of the drawers. The room's so small, she doesn't need to get off the bed. A pair of panties smacks me in the face. They're cotton. With *coño* ponies on them.

"You know you always welcome to my undies. Long as you still fit in them!" Yaz rolls back on the bed cackling. Her feet scissor the air. She blows a bubble with her mint gum. Another something only she can do.

I ball the underwear in my fist. I think of hurling them back at her. But I don't want to get up from my spot on the rug. I'm glad Yaz knows me so well. I'm glad she hasn't asked me more about Bertie. More than what I told her. Which is that we had a fight. And I threw him out. I'm glad she knows I want to spend the night so I don't have to ask.

There's a pop as Yaz's bubble bursts. She clears her throat. She's looking down at her nails again, wiping them off one by one as if lint's got on them.

"Ever think of finding YKW?" she says.

YKW. You Know Who. It's our code. For my mama. I don't like to say her name.

"If you told her what's going on, maybe she'd come back? Maybe she could help?"

I take my time bringing my eyes down from the ceiling. I wait until I find Jasmine. She's in the corner near the old water leak, next to half of a yellow bird I think is called Tweety.

My mama's not like Yaz's. Yaz's mami is in the DR, working in one of those all-inclusive resorts. She's the concierge or something fancy like that. Yaz sees her every year. Sometimes more than once. Her mami actually comes to New York to visit. And she buys her things. And sends them money. How do you think they can afford the after-school with the nuns? If Yaz were ever in trouble, her mami'd be on the first plane back.

But my mama? She ain't coming back. I don't want her to. Not for this. She can rot in whatever little piece of hell she's hidden herself in. And she's hid herself good. 'Cause not even Abuela could find her. And Abuela wanted to. Real bad. She told me so. Remember?

I don't have to say nothing. Yaz nods. Turns onto her back. She spits out her gum. Reaches for a new piece. She lifts her chin 'til she sees me upside down.

"I know you gotta eat. But first," she points to the ceiling, "guess who I'm looking for?"

# TWENTY-THREE WEEKS

How have you been feeling?"

"Fine," I answer. Doc is in a good mood. He seems like someone who's always in a good mood. I try not to hold it against him.

"No significant bloating, increased urination?"

"No."

He doesn't say anything about my Sour Patch face or nasty tone. Teri and Heavenly look at the machine. They know not to try to break me. We didn't even talk while we waited.

I haven't spoken to Bertie since I kicked him out. Sure, I seen him—at school, during lunch, after school, outside the bodega. But I pretend he's not there. I'm waiting for him to get the balls to come to me. To apologize to me. For making it seem like this only be my problem. I been with my girls. Mostly Yaz. It's like old times, Yaz and me hanging out in her kitchen while her abuela makes us *asopado de pescado* and *mofongo de ajo*. My abuela never makes stuff like that, food that takes more than five, ten minutes to prepare. But Yaz's abuela, she's the best. I wolf down everything she gives me. Maybe one of these days, I'll actually look like a pregnant person.

The bottle makes a farting noise as jelly squirts onto me. "Sorry about that." Doc smiles his rock-star smile. Like he just hurt our ears with a scratchy tune-up sound. "Now, this will be a short scan. Just checking for any changes."

I stare at the screen hanging from the ceiling above my feet. It's still black. "Hey, aren't you going to turn it on?"

Doc glances at me. "Did you want to watch?"

"Uh, yeah." I rap my knuckles on my head and roll my eyes for my girls. Heavenly is typing on her phone. She's holding it too close as always. Teri stares at her shoes.

Doc turns on the TV. My baby boy, Angelo, swims into view. I stare at the moving picture. The wand presses into my belly and the baby kicks at it, like he's trying to push it away. I chuckle. My strong, feisty boy. I wish I could feel those kicks.

Doc lifts the wand off me.

"That's it?" I bark it at him. "It was so short!"

"I got what we needed. The main reason we wanted you back is so we can go over the fetus's heart problems and discuss any questions you might have. The nurse will bring you into the conference room after you change. All right?"

"Sure, I guess." *Coño.* Another opportunity to discuss doom and gloom. At least Pudgy Purple isn't around. Every other word out of her makes me feel stupid.

I come out of the bathroom, pulling my shirt away from my

sticky skin. "What time is it?" What I really want to ask is, *Where's Yaz?*

Heavenly shows me the screen of her phone.

"Yaz will be here, don't worry," Teri says. I give her a look. Yaz is usually the one who knows what I'm thinking.

The nurse takes us down the hall and opens the door to the conference room. Yaz is there, swinging side to side in her swivel chair. Her nails—pink with green polka dots—rap the table as if she's meaning to chip it.

I walk in and freeze.

Bertie stands. I couldn't see him from the hallway. He was sitting in the corner. He's clutching his baseball cap in his hand. He hardly ever takes it off. When he sees me looking at it, he puts the cap back on. He comes to pull out a chair for me.

Doc walks in, a packet of paper under his arm. He looks from Bertie to me and back to Bertie again. I hold my breath waiting for Doc's reaction. Bertie looks young. Younger than me even. He's not. I mean, he is, but only by months. He's old enough—we're old enough—to have a kid. *Coño.* Why did Bertie come?

Doc offers his hand. "Hello, I'm Dr. Love." They look ridiculous next to each other. Tall, blond hottie of a doctor with white coat, glasses, and tie. Not so tall, skinny Bertie, backward baseball cap hiding his frizzy hair, thick hoop of gold through the middle of one ear, jeans hanging off him, under-wear poking out.

Bertie's looking up at Doc. And then he's looking at Doc's hand. I'm scared he's gonna fist-bump it. But he gives Doc a regular shake.

"My name's José Humberto Valdez." Bertie glances at me. He's trying to figure out how angry I am. "I'm the baby's father."

"Welcome, glad you could join us. Please." Doc gestures to a chair. Bertie's still holding one out for me. I snatch it away and sink into it.

I narrow my eyes at Yaz. Since I'm not talking to Bertie, I didn't tell him about this appointment. And there's no way Bertie could find his way here by himself. Even with the address. This place is a maze.

"We'll wait a few more minutes. I understand others are join-ing us?" Doc looks at me. I don't know what he's talking about. Yaz's finger is going around and around, coiling up her hair then pulling it straight. The glittery nails of her other hand tap the wood. *Ba ba ba da ba. Dum. Dum.*

She's not the girl whose hand I held when her mama moved back to DR. She's not the girl who taught me what to do with a Tampax when I turned twelve. She's not the girl who got scared 'cause that skeevy guy—Manuel from MS 319—wanted more than she was willing to give. The girl who hugged me, tears coming down, when I confronted his sorry ass and told him what I'd do if he ever touched her again. She's not the girl I ate *asopado* and *mofongo* with last night.

I don't know where that girl went.

"Yaz?!" I pound my fist on the table.

She flies out of her seat, her eyes wide. "¿*Qué?* What?"

Out in the hallway, someone curses. In Dominican.

*Oh no.* No. No. No. No.

The door opens. In walks Abuela. Behind her is Josefina Payano, Bertie's mama. She's teetering on five-inch heels, her face painted like a whore's.

Really, Yaz? Bertie's mother?! I go to launch myself at Yaz, never mind there's a huge table between us. Bertie's hand takes my shoulder. Keeps me in my seat.

I whip around, glare at him. Señora Payano stoops to kiss him. She lowers herself into the seat next to Bertie, folding her freaky, long-nailed hands in her lap. I mean, I'm all for acrylics and mani-pedis, but why would someone want nails as long as their fingers? Yaz said it was so she could pick her own butthole without dirtying her hands. I almost laugh remembering that. But I'm mad at Yaz. Beyond mad.

Bertie's mama tosses her head, bringing her fake blond curls to the front of her shoulder. She doesn't look at me or say hi. This is our usual. That woman, she never respected me. Once I heard her in the kitchen talking to a friend about my *el hijo de machepa papi*. Yeah, my papi's in jail. But at least I know who he is.

Abuela takes a chair. Her face is paste-colored. Like she's been experimenting with bleaching cream again. She don't like doctors. She don't like hospitals. Unless they're on TV.

Abuela nods at Bertie. They're not besties either. Abuela's told me—and Bertie—that I'm ruining my chances by being with him. It's got nothing to do with our age or what Bertie does after school with Skinner. It's because Bertie is *morenito*. Because of my mama, I pass for a white girl. But Bertie, he's darker even than mi papi.

I take some breaths and unclench my hands as Doc picks up some markers from the table. Heavenly raises an eyebrow and gives Teri a look that says, *What's with this guy and the art supplies?* She and Teri sit next to Yaz, far from Bertie's mama. Señora Payano's perfume is worse than a *peo*.

Doc turns to draw on the whiteboard behind him. Teri copies Heavenly and takes out her phone to record. But I know this by now. I been studying the drawings Doc gave me.

Abuela wrinkles her forehead as Doc starts to speak. That's how I know she's paying attention. Bertie's mama picks at her nails. I don't want to think of what she's finding in there. Her lips pooch like she's got something sour in her mouth. Maybe she sucks her cheeks to hide that she eats guava pastries for breakfast, lunch, and dinner. *Dominicanos* like meat on their women, but Bertie's mama's moved way beyond that. She's so big, she might be able to take Jabba the Hutt in a sumo contest. After two or three sentences, the woman starts. "*Ofrézcome, que cosa tan horrible es eso.*"

I swivel my chair. The back and forth gives me something to do. Other than slap Bertie's mama's mouth.

She's still talking, but it's all breathy. Doc continues.

She butts in again. "*¡Ay, Dios mío!* Why me? Why my son?" She sounds funny. She always does. Because she sounds like a man. Her voice is deeper than Bertie's even.

I swing harder.

Doc stops. Señora Payano is peeling polish off one of the freaky nail-claws. She doesn't look up. Bertie and Abuela, Yaz, Heavenly, Teri—they're all watching Doc, waiting for him to go on.

Doc finishes drawing the messed-up heart.

Bertie's mama slaps her thighs with both hands. "This is not possible. How is this possible? This baby, he going to *die*."

Doc hasn't even gotten to the part about the first surgery. I'm rocking my chair so hard, it's making squeaky noises.

I grab Bertie's arm and jerk him toward me.

"If you don't get her to shut her big fuckin' mouth, we're going to have big fuckin' problems here." I'm whispering, but I'm pretty sure everyone in the room heard me.

Doc is watching me. A crease peeks out under the bridge of his glasses. I glare-dare him. Wait to see if he gonna tell me something. I don't want his pity.

Bertie puts a hand on his mama's shoulder. "*Mami, por favor. Quédate tranquila.* Just listen. We need to listen." She nods and leans on him. She's so fat it doesn't look possible, but Bertie's strong. Thin but strong. She rests her head on his shoulder. *Yick.* She looks up at him through bushy, fake eyelashes, all dramatic and sad. Her man voice asks for a tissue. If I didn't know Bertie came out of that woman, if I hadn't seen men coming out of her bedroom, I would have sworn she was a *pájaro.*

Doc pushes over a box of Kleenex.

I snort. This is bullshit. This drama and pretend sadness. As if she ever wanted me to have this baby in the first place. The *cacata* is probably psyched. The woman loves attention. She's trying to turn this into something about her. But this is about me and this baby. I'm about to say so, but the door opens.

"Good afternoon, everyone. Thank you for joining us." Oh good. The medical encyclopedia has arrived. Pudgy Purple looks at each of us. She adjusts the specs on her nose. Her poker-playing face is on. She doesn't even react when Bertie's mama heaves into a tissue.

Pudgy Purple takes a seat opposite Bertie and me. Her elbows are on the table, hands crossed one over the other. "Right, so where are we?"

Doc Hottie says he was just getting to the Norwood surgery.

"So you understand the baby is very sick." She's looking at me. I lean back in my chair, put my hands behind my head. I wait for the impossible-to-understand words that are about to come out of her mouth. Bertie, his mama, and Abuela aren't going to get much. It'll be perfect.

"He's going to need three surgeries, two within the first six months of his life. Even if he does survive, there is a high chance his heart will give out at some point and he could require a heart transplant."

Bertie's mama interrupts. "That's because he has only half a heart?"

Pudgy Purple swivels toward her. "Yes. Exactly." She goes on talking for a few more minutes. She doesn't use enough medical words. *Coño. Coño, coño, coño.*

Everyone is silent when Pudgy Purple finishes. Not because they don't understand. They're silent because they do.

"So how would you like to proceed, Miss Pujols?" Pudgy Purple is facing me again. I expect her to drum her nails. *Ba, da, bum, bum. Ba, da, bum, bum, da* . . . She doesn't.

I stare at the table. At the tiny patterns in the wood. At the lines that go left to right and the squiggles that go up and down like waves. They remind me of what I saw on the sonogram machine. Sound waves of my baby's heartbeat.

"Is there no hope then?" Bertie's voice doesn't sound like his. There's none of the bluff and bragging I'm used to. It cracks over the word *hope*. It almost makes me want to take his hand. Almost.

"There's always hope," Doc—*my* doc—answers. He's standing next to the board. He drew the surgeries while Pudgy Purple was talking.

Pudgy Purple still looks only at me. "The baby's life will be very difficult. If he survives."

Bertie's mama lets out another curse. "*¡Concho, hijo de la porra!* What kind of life is this? No life. That's what. And all these operations. They cost money. Who gonna pay for that?"

"We have social workers. To help make sure your medical insurance is in order. Miss Pujols should have already met with one."

Cacata Mama whistles out her exhale like she don't believe it. She's right about that. I skipped that appointment. Social workers and me, we don't get along.

Abuela's looking at me. It's like the bleaching cream on her face has spread. "*No sabía.*" She shakes her head. "I didn't know how bad." Her brown eyes are milky and faded. Like the color's bleached from there, too. "You no can do this, Maribel. I said I would help with the baby. A healthy baby. But this . . . ?" She opens her purse, fishes out a yellowed handkerchief. No one but fresh-off-the-plane Dominican drivers use those anymore. Them and my abuela.

She's looking at me with those color-bled eyes. "I no help you with this. To lose a child, after is born? *Horrible.* You have to take the abortion."

Teri starts to cry. Abuela covers her own face with the cloth.

Bertie's mama's mumblings have turned to "*Sí, sí. El aborto. Tiene que ser.*"

Heavenly jabs at her phone. Her mouth is all scrunched up. Yaz's nails press into the table so hard, they're going to snap. Neither of them look at me.

But Bertie, he's watching me. Waiting for me to look at him. I'm afraid to. I'm afraid of what I'll feel if I look at him. 'Cause right now I don't feel nothing.

Bertie leaves off waiting and leans over to me. I swing away from him, giving him my chair back. He asks me anyway. "Mari, what do you want to do?"

There it is again. Like it's my decision. Like I'm the only one a part of this. As if he had nothing whatsoever to do with this sicko situation.

I spin back around. I almost clip his face with the chair. "What do *you* want to do?" I yell it at him like I caught him in another girl's bed.

His mouth goes slack. "Me?"

"Yes. You. You want me to have the abortion, don't you?"

"*Sí*, tell her. *Sí, mi hijo,*" his mama chimes in.

I stand real fast. I'm going to smack her. But Bertie's faster. He's between us.

"You never wanted the baby, did you?" I mean to shout it at her. But I'm shouting at him.

"That's not true!" He looks as if I've slapped him.

His mama tuts me with her tongue. Stupid, fat *cacata*. I drive my arm past Bertie.

"*¡Ay!*" She grabs on to her hair as I almost knock it off. Who does she think she's fooling with that Barbie-doll wig anyway? I snatch again, throw it off her. Cacata Mama shrieks. It's like a battle cry.

*Bring it.*

Wide, warm hands take my shoulders.

"That's enough. Settle down." Pudgy Purple is pissed.

A voice, low and calm, speaks into my ear. "Take a breath. Get control. You don't want to get thrown out." Doc steers me into my seat. He doesn't let me go.

Bertie's mother is cursing. In Spanish *and* English. She's glaring at me like I'm a monster. Doc's grip is solid. If it weren't for him, I'd scratch that look off her face.

Abuela stands to leave. The handkerchief covers her eyes. It's not so the others can't see her; it's so she can't see me. She's shaking her head. "*Rata*," she says. "Worthless." She means me. This is the Abuela I remember. The Abuela who raised me the last seven years but hates me, who spends every minute she can at work. My mama told me her boyfriend's mother tried to get her to have an abortion. I was too little to understand what that word meant the first time she said it. But by the time my mama dropped me and drove off, the lights of her run-down Pontiac shrinking to tiny red pinpoints, Abuela's hands tight on both my arms so I wouldn't run after her, I knew what that word meant. I knew real good.

A uniformed guard comes from the hallway. He heads straight for Cacata Mama. Hate is still foaming out of her. Bertie is trying to settle her wig back in place without knocking her over. But she's like a cantaloupe on toothpick heels.

She stops hollering when she sees the guard. She plucks up her knock-off Louis V, humphs, and waddles out.

The guard makes a gesture at Bertie, looking to Pudgy Purple for instruction.

"Leave him," Doc Hottie says.

"Yes, but take the others. It's too crowded in here." Pudgy Purple has fingers pressed to her forehead. We probably ruined her week. Maybe her month.

Yaz squeezes my arm on the way out. I don't look at her. I feel like biting her. Traitor.

Doc releases me when it's just the four of us left. Bertie's still standing, his mouth open like he's a fish that's lost something.

"You two need to talk." Pudgy Purple stands. "Alone." She gives Doc Hottie a hard look. He follows her out. He hesitates at the door, glancing at Bertie. Someone else might think Doc was worried for me, that Bertie might do something to me. But Doc's nervous I might do something to Bertie. If my insides weren't crumbling, I would grin.

Doc leaves. Bertie and I, neither of us speaks. My pulse is a jackhammer crushing concrete. I close my eyes. I prefer this feeling. It's better than the alternative.

Bertie sits down. He leans on the table, hands holding his too-heavy head.

My heartbeat dies away. Until I can't feel it no more. I don't feel nothing. How is it I already feel empty?

"Mari." Bertie lays an open hand on the table for me.

I stare at it, not moving. "You never wanted the baby," I repeat.

"Yes, I did. I did want him." But he says it like he's trying to convince himself, not convince me. Bertie didn't like that I'd told him he'd have to cut it off with Skinner. He didn't like that his life—the part of it that didn't include me—was going to have to change. And from the beginning, his reasons for the baby were different from mine.

"You don't need him. You have her." I thrust my chin at the door. I don't want to think about Cacata Mama. She's an evil *puta*. But she's a good mother to him. Because she's *here*. Because she cares.

I bite my lips together thinking about how Abuela's gonna go back to yelling at me once the baby's gone. "You have her," I say it again. "I don't have nobody. I want this baby. I *need* him." My hands cradle my belly.

Angelo was going to be the one. The special person in my family—my real family—who would love me.

"You have me," Bertie says.

"Not the same." I give my head a furious shake. As if I'm stupid enough to think we're gonna live happily ever after like in a Disney movie. As if I'm blind and don't see that it's only ever the mamas holding chubby toddler fists at the park, keeping them close, making sure they don't fall. The fathers swoop in for *un besito* and a donkey ride. Then they disappear under the docks with new, prettier *morenitas*. I'm not that much of a sucker to believe Bertie and I would be different, that there was something special about us. I was just the sucker who thought I might be able to change my *carajo* life. That maybe I could make it better. I bite the inside of my cheek. The skin under my nose is on fire. I dig at my upper lip like I mean to scratch it all away.

"Shhh," Bertie murmurs. "It'll be okay." Bertie tries to take my hand. I shove him away and stand. He's standing now, too, arms reaching for me. But he can't fix this. I won't let him. I raise my fists.

"Mari?" The hurt in his voice almost breaks me.

I slam his shoulder, hissing as pain cuts into the back of my hand. It feels good to hit something. To let the hate inside come out.

Bertie stumbles back. My other arm is up, swinging for his jaw. He ducks out of the way.

Bertie's massaging his arm. His mouth hangs open. "*Tu 'ta pasao*," he mumbles. "You crazy. You know that?" He takes his jacket and leaves.

I'm on my bed, hugging my knees to my chest. My eyes are swollen, like that time I drank a whole cup of soy sauce at Empire on Jo-jo's dare. Only this time, I haven't been to no Chinese restaurant. I haven't eaten anything since yesterday. I don't want to leave my room. I don't want to see anybody.

There's thumping and smashing above me. Mr. and Mrs. Rodriguez are going at it again. Distraction's good. I had Gato in here with me before. Was hugging him instead of my knees. But he couldn't tolerate me for more than a few minutes. He only wants affection on his terms. He's like Abuela that way.

There's a knock on my door. It's probably Toto coming to tempt me with a peanut butter sandwich again. I never seen him in the kitchen, so I didn't know he could put food together. Peanut butter's not something Abuela would make. And I don't smell bacon or eggs. I bet she won't feed me or talk to me 'til I agree to what she wants. That Toto would ignore that and go through the trouble of finding bread, reaching the plastic container of peanut butter down from the high shelf, spreading it with a knife, cutting the sandwich diagonally—the way I like it—and offering it to me says something. I always thought he was afraid of her. She pays the rent. But maybe she's not here? Abuela was supposed to have the day off. We was going to go to El Mundo to shop for clothes for me. But that was before the hospital. Abuela probably called in to work. She's always preferred overtime to spending time with me.

My stomach churns. I have to eat something. I try to say, "Come in." All that comes out is a croak.

The door squeaks. Gato, the cat, yowls as he's smushed through the narrow opening. He glares at whoever's pushed him in, narrows his eyes at me, and slinks under the bed.

The door widens. Bertie steps in. He's holding the plate with the peanut butter sandwich out in front of him. There's a low murmur of a man's voice. Bertie turns and takes a tall glass of milk in his other hand. He holds that in front of him, too. The door shuts.

I cross my arms over my chest. I stare at my bedcover. It used to be *Star Wars*. Luke, Princess Leia, Chewbacca. Han Solo was my favorite, and I was pissed he wasn't featured. But at the store, it was either that or My Little Pony. After I told Abuela I was pregnant, she took me for a new one. Said I deserved something more grown-up. It's a tropical beach scene. There's even a palm tree with three coconuts in it. It was so I could sleep and dream under white sand and turquoise waters until after Angelo was born and Abuela took us to meet her family. I follow the curve of one of the palm fronds with my hand. Guess this is all of the DR I'm going to see for a while.

Bertie's been staring at me. When I look up, he quick-stares at the glass in his hand. There are tiny milk bubbles along the top of it. My stomach announces itself. I drop my arms, try to cover it.

Bertie licks his lips. "*Por favor*," he says. "*Tómatelo*. Please. You have to eat. It's not good for you not to eat."

I reach for the glass. He gives it to me. I drink it down, not stopping. When I finish, I let out an enormous burp. Bertie winces. I hold out my hand for the sandwich. He gives me that, too.

"You didn't say anything about the baby."

He tilts his head at me. I'm talking with my mouth half-stuck with peanut butter, so maybe he didn't hear right. I shove the rest of the sandwich triangle in my mouth. The empty glass of milk is teasing me. Making me regret drinking it all so quick.

"You didn't say it's not good for the baby. Not eating." I wipe the crumbs off my face with my sleeve. I push back in the bed, lean on the headboard. I leave the other half of the sandwich on the plate. It looks lonely.

Bertie winces again. He steps forward. He puts his hands on the sand of my coverlet. His fingers trace the edge of the ocean. I'm sitting at the other end of it.

"Mari," he says, looking only at the water. "We need to talk."

My eyes are so swollen, I didn't think anything else would fit in them. They're so dry, I didn't think any more tears would come out.

I grab up that lonely piece of sandwich. I hold it with both hands against my chest. I press it to my mouth, but I don't eat it. I use it to keep my lips still.

I hate being wrong.

I hear Bertie swallow. It's so quiet I'm not sure I'm breathing. Mr. and Mrs. Rodriguez must have made up. Or maybe they fell asleep. Old people do that sometimes.

"I . . ." He swallows again. "I don't want you to suffer. You suffer so much already. You don't deserve this."

The tears coming out of me dry up. A hot burning wave rises inside. I drop the sandwich onto the plate. I miss. It falls to the floor. Black-and-white paws shoot out from under the bed as Gato attacks it.

"What about you?" My voice is a solid metal bar, a railing leading down to the subway that you grab when you slip. I show him nothing.

Bertie nods. "We don't deserve this," he says. He looks for my hand, like he's going to take it. I push them both behind me. He reaches across the ocean and puts his hand on my socked foot instead. His palm covers the bumpy, pilled fabric. "We can try again." He whispers this. He's not sure how I'll feel about it. At least he knows that much.

He tugs at my ankle. Slowly, he pulls my leg across the sea that separates us. He starts to massage my foot. I don't know if I should let him. I don't want to be alone. But I feel so far away from him. Maybe this baby is God talking to me. Telling me I'm meant to be alone. I'm not meant to belong to a family.

The waves of anger inside me smooth and flatten. I feel empty.

And then I remember what he looked like. Little Angelo. Kicking away Doc's wand.

I scratch at my lip. "You didn't say anything about the baby," I repeat.

Bertie's rubbing my foot. His fingers take hold of my toes. He gives each one a little squeeze. His eyes are shut. When did he close them? "The baby's not here," he says. "You are. You are here."

"And you, too," I say.

He nods. He reaches for my other foot. I shift it away. I pull the one he massaged up against me, put a pillow on top of it.

Bertie lets out a sigh. "The doctor, she said this was the best way. She said this was the right thing to do."

I don't remember Pudgy Purple saying that. Maybe she did and I wasn't paying attention. My Doc never would have said that. He said there was no right decision. There was only the decision that was right for me. He said whatever I decided, he would be there to support me.

Bertie looks like he's going to say something else. If he says anything about us being too young, I'm gonna have to hit him. Because we talked about that. We talked about how three years is too young to lose your papi. Eight years is too young to be abandoned by your mama. Fifteen years is too young to get arrested for dealing. But it's not too young to become a father. Or a mother. It's not too young to make something that's gonna love you forever.

Bertie makes a sound. I think maybe he's trying to clear his throat. He's leaning with one arm against my bed, staring at the ocean between us. As if he doesn't know what he's looking at. As if he used to, but doesn't remember the words anymore. He looks so lost. So sad. I wish I hadn't drank all the milk. If I hadn't, I would give him some.

What Doc said wasn't right. It's not my decision. Not mine alone. Not really.

"Okay."

I'm not sure if I've said it or if I only thought it in my head. But then Bertie says my name. And he's crying.

I grab my other pillow, curl around it.

He holds his arm against his face. When he drops it, his skin is so pale it's almost white. I almost say it's too bad Abuela's not here to see him like this. She might like him better this way. I start to cry instead.

Bertie moves to my side of the bed. I'm terrified he's going to hug me. I push him away. I manage to utter the word, "Go." He stands there for a few minutes. He makes me say it again. And again.

When Bertie opens the door, Gato tears out from under the bed. Bertie yelps as Gato makes a break for it over his foot. It's nice to think that someone—even if it's just a cat—gets what he wants. It's nice to think someone is free.

I'm naked, underneath a gown, on a cold table. I should be used to this by now. But today is different. My hair is in a net. Everyone around me is in blue. Blue pants, blue shirts, blue gowns. They wear masks so I can't see their faces. So I won't know who's taking my baby away.

My stomach grumbles. Last food I ate was a day ago. There was some emergency at the hospital this morning. So I got to wait a few extra hours. A few extra hours of starving. A few extra hours of pretending not to be scared.

Teri and Heavenly didn't come. I wouldn't let them. It's harder not to cry when everyone around you is. Bertie doesn't even know it's today. He didn't want to know when it was going to happen. Wish I didn't have to know either. Wish they had some medicine that could erase time. And memories. Something safer than the *ratreria* Skinner deals. He offered some to Bertie and me for free. I said no. Nothing is for free.

I reach for my phone in my back pocket, forgetting I'm naked and that my stuff's in a locker. I was going to scroll back through my texts and emails, find any from Yaz I forgot to delete. I still can't believe she did that to me. Went behind my back like that and brought them all to my appointment. I wouldn't be here if I hadn't seen their faces as they heard about all the bad stuff. I wouldn't be here if Abuela hadn't threatened to throw me out if I didn't do the right thing. Maybe I wouldn't be here if Bertie had been brave enough to tell me what he really thinks instead of just parroting back what the doctor said. What his mama said. Maybe I wouldn't be here if I hadn't gotten so mad. Or so sad. If maybe I'd found the words to convince him. To convince me.

The door next to me opens. Another blue-masked person comes in. She introduces herself as the doc who will be putting me to sleep. Maybe she knows about forgetting medicines?

Someone puts stickers on my arms and legs. None of them say *You did it!* or *Great job!* They're doctor stickers, squares of gray and blue so sticky I'll have glue on my skin for a week. What I wouldn't give to look into a My Little Pony face right now. But that just reminds me of Yaz. Which makes the air inside my lungs burn.

I look around at all the unrecognizable eyes. I wish my Doc were here. He wouldn't make me feel stupid or weak. Maybe he'd make me feel less scared, too.

My hands go to my belly button. I press down, trying not to think too much. I take slow breaths. In. Out. I think about my mama, my dumbass white mama, and how she left me. How horrible of a kid I must have been for her to do that. How I must have scared her off like I did Bertie. I think about my papi, who I only recognize as a picture in a frame. Who I only know through letters that tell me he loves me. But he don't know me. Not for real. Maybe if he did, he wouldn't love me either.

Who was I kidding? Me? Be a mother? The kid would grow up and hate me. And leave me. Just like everyone else.

The machine next to me beeps. It's not a sonogram machine. It's bigger and swarmed with tubes and dials. I don't know why it's beeping. My stomach flutters. Like tiny bubbles tickling me from my insides. I feel it again. Against my hands. Flutters. Then a kick. I swallow the metallic taste in my mouth. I slide my fingers to the side of my belly. Again, a kick. Right beneath my hand. What a great time to start feeling him, huh? *Coño.* What is this? God's way of torturing me?

Kick, kick, kick. No matter where I put my hands. I feel it. I feel him. He's strong. And feisty. And suddenly, I know he's trying to tell me something. He doesn't hate me. Even knowing what I'm about to do to him, he doesn't hate me. He loves me.

I sit up. My gown slips off my shoulders.

"Miss Pujols? I'm going to have to ask you to lie back down now."

My feet hit the floor. It's harder and colder than the table. A wire snaps off me. The machine beeps again. It's beeping non-stop.

Hands take my arms. "Are you okay, Miss Pujols?"

Yes. No. I don't know.

I don't want this.

I want my baby. Even if no one else does.

"I'm sorry," I say. And I think I must be talking to God, because no one else in this room matters.

I clutch my gown to my too-small belly and run.

# TWENTY-SIX WEEKS

Teri takes my arm as we walk out of school after last
period. She squeezes through the puff of my coat.

I haven't told anyone. They all think the baby's
gone. But he's inside me, growing. Having a little secret is *manso*.
It's like just the two of us against the world. Well, three of us.
Doc's in on it, too. Only he don't know it's a secret.

Two black chicks by the water fountain see us and look away.
They whisper. Look back with those frown-smiles that are sup-
posed to tell me they know what I'm feeling and they be sorry.
As if they know anything.

At least it's getting better. Fewer glances and tongues
wagging. In class. During lunch. Outside the bodega. It's
like everyone in school and out is talking about me. Only this
time it's not about bruises and cut-up knuckles. A girl getting
preggo is not news. A girl getting an abortion, not news. But
a girl getting *un aborto* because her baby is messed up . . . That
be news. All a sudden, all these people—folks I never knew
or didn't like—be coming up to me. Telling me about how
their grandma or cousin lost a baby, too. Even Manuel, that
*pariguayo* who wanted in Yaz's pants, the one I beat the crap

out of, texted me a sad face with a tear. Like a *coño maldito bugarrón*.

Bet it was Yaz who told them all. She's the *boca de suape*. Big fuckin' mouth.

I grind my teeth together and remind myself to look depressed. But what I want is to hug my belly. Hug Angelo. He's keeping me together. Making me stay cool instead of yelling at those *putas* to drop the pity acts.

There's a shout. The bodies filling the hall split as a short, skinny *chan* shoots through. It's Saulo Reyes. His fists pump. He's clutching something. A crushed baseball cap. Not navy blue like Bertie's. This one's a pinstripe. Belongs to Alex De La Cruz, who isn't far behind, and who bellows like a bull. But he's teeth-clenched grinning as he charges after his friend. They're both part of Skinner's pack.

I pull Teri toward the door. I don't want to run into Bertie.

"You seen Yaz today?" Teri tucks her flat-ironed straight hair behind her ear. It's as if she knows I'm thinking about people I don't want to run into.

I did see Yaz. At her locker. Using that tiny mirror to reapply makeup to red-crusted eyes. Don't know why she been crying. Like she's got any right to be sad. What'd she think was gonna happen when she brought those folks to *my* doctor?

Teri and Heavenly are trying to patch things up between Yaz and me. Trying to make it better. Make me not hate her so much. Make me give her another chance. But that's not coming anytime soon.

"Who's Yaz?" I say. I fish an apple out of my pocket and chomp it real loud.

Teri squeezes my arm again. Makes me want to yank her hand off me. But right then, little Angelo kicks. I smile and take another apple bite.

Up ahead, Heavenly's leaning against a Camaro, her long skinny-jeaned legs out in front of her. Jo-jo's new ride. That's what you get when you have a real-life sugar daddy—Jo-jo's papi's known as El Rey de la Caña in the DR. 'Course Jo-jo works for his papi. That car is so red it's like one of those raspberry Ring Pop candies. Jo-jo and Hev have been giving me lifts, which I don't mind. All this pity be good for something.

Heavenly don't see us yet. She looks up from her phone, turns her head to someone calling. Yaz. They hug. Jo-jo sticks his arm out the driver's window, pulls Yaz down for cheek kisses.

I stop before we get any closer. Shrug myself out of Teri's arm.

I could care less if they want to stay friends with Yaz. Can't say I won't judge them for it, but I won't say nothing.

"See ya." I head for the 1 train. The subway's faster anyway.

I don't even get to the end of the block before someone's peeling off the side of a building, walking toward me. My fingers tighten around the pen I keep in my pocket for just this reason. I don't look at him head-on. But I recognize the side-to-side amble, the chest and shoulders that hang back as if still interested in what's behind, the feet and knees angled so they reach you first.

I let go of the pen in my pocket. I don't want to see Bertie. But I'm not going to hurt him.

He falls into stride next to me. He's done this a few times over the past weeks. Found me between school and home. Walked with me, not saying nothing. 'Cause really, what's there to say? As far as he knows, I ain't pregnant no more. As far as he knows, I got rid of the baby inside me. Because he wanted me to.

We're at the subway station. I start down the stairs. His footsteps follow me.

I stop. Turn around. I grip the cold metal railing with my bare hand. I'm not going to slip. "What do you want?"

He stops. Too close. I put some heat into my glare. He lifts his foot, rises up one step. Then another. His eyes are red. Even with the sky lit up behind him I see that. But it's not from crying. It's not from not sleeping either. My fingers clench the bar. I try to make them touch. To make a circle. But the handrail's too fat. *What are you doing, Bertie?*

He shrugs. For a moment, I think I've asked him that out loud. But he's answering my first question.

He licks his lips. He looks down. His hand is in his pocket, moving.

"You need anything?" That hand comes out of his pocket. It's holding a huge wad of cash.

I hiss at him, take a step closer while looking over my shoulder. What's he doing with all of that? What's he doing with all of that here?

But I already know.

Some lady with one of those portable shopping baskets is coming down behind us. Since we don't move, she has to go around. The wheels of her cart slam onto each step, rattling the metal cage of the basket. It's empty. Don't know why she don't collapse it and carry it down. She's not that old. She's muttering to herself, shaking her head. I can't hear if it's about us. I'm staring at her, waiting for her to look at me so I can give her one of my don't-mess-with-me scowls. But she don't look. She just goes right on past.

Bertie's still got the money out, offering it to me. When I look at him, I expect to find his eyes begging me to take it. But they're just red. And gray. The green in them is gone. His face looks like the blood's gone out of it. He looks like he might start muttering to himself. Like that crazy shopping-cart lady.

I go to put my hand on my belly. I put my hand on my hip instead. He's got to be pretty smoked if he thinks I be taking that money. I know where that money's from. Even if it wasn't Skinner's money, I wouldn't take it. Who does Bertie think he is to try to buy me off like that? Trying to pay off his guilt?

I turn and head down the stairs. Bertie doesn't follow. I almost yell back at him to stay away from those pushing *tecatos*. Like I told him before, they're not good for him.

On the platform, where there's no one who knows me, I press my fingers to my baby mound. Maybe I should tell Bertie. He *is* Angelo's father. But I'm still too burning mad. The mad part of me's glad Bertie feels guilty. 'Cause he should. 'Cause he deserves it.

I'm back on the exam table. Only I'm not naked like before. Doc said it wasn't necessary. All he needs is my growing stomach. It looks like a little moon, my belly. Whiter than it's ever been. At the beginning of the summer, when I told Abuela about the baby, she made me promise not to go in the sun. Said when she was pregnant, she got horrible brown spots on her face. She even got some funny line down the middle of her belly. So I stayed in the shade. All freakin' summer. Usually, I look forward to my tan. It lets me look the part. Lets me go to the diner, slide into the booth with Yaz, Heavenly, and Teri and not get raised-eyebrow looks when we all start rapping in Spanish. Abuela said my mama never could tan. She'd burn. I only saw that happen once. My mama never took me to the beach. Or to the park. Summers back then were a lumpy, orange couch with potato-chip crumbs on it and a TV with a whole lot of commercials. But one time, my mama took me to a place called Boca. I didn't speak Spanish then, so I didn't get the joke. It was Christmas, and we was going to meet my mama's parents. I kept asking what I should call them. My mama kept shushing me, saying we'd find out when we got there. Her hands kept touching me, smoothing down the ruffles of this pink-and-white dress she bought on consignment. Never did figure out what to call my mama's parents. When we got to the condo, they weren't there. We waited outside almost all day—me begging to go in the pool and her saying "Later"—'til the doorman told us we had to leave. He had this big, fleshy face with droopy cheeks. They drooped even more when he spoke. Even though his eyes were sad, he smiled at us. Think that might have been my very first pity smile. My mama put a hand over her forehead and peered up at the windows. "Guess they don't want you, either," she said. I was so mad about not getting to go in that pool, I ripped those ruffles right off that dress. My mama had to grab me, hold me down, else I was gonna tear that dress in half. I remember her hands pinching me tight, her sunburned arms on mine, like crushed tomatoes on top of golden butter.

Doc layers green-blue jelly over me. My pale skin reminds me of my mama's. Another reason I prefer to be tan.

"Is it too cold?" Doc asks.

"Nah." I shake my head and stop squirming. Little Angelo gives me a kick. He's not cold, either. I been feeling him more and more. But there's nothing like watching him. Arms swinging, legs kicking, the little pooch of his stomach, the smooth slope of his head, all bright white against the black of the screen. I almost make a joke. I almost ask Doc whether darker-skinned babies are harder to see because of that black screen. But he'd probably take it the wrong way. Think I'm some kind of a racist. I let out a snort, thinking about what his face would do if I had the balls to say it. Doc tips his head toward me, his eyes still on the screen. He's sweeping the wand up and over me, looking for Angelo's best angle.

"What was that?" he asks.

"Nothing." I snigger again. This time, he glances at me. Half his mouth lifts. It's the look a rock star gives a fan if he thinks she's hiding a camera behind her back.

My lip itches. I flex and unflex my toes. "Um. So how's my Angelo look today?"

Doc turns back to his machine. He bows his head to the controls. He takes some measurements. "His heartbeat is strong. His movement appears good. Nothing unexpected so far."

My breath fizzes like air from an underwater balloon. I curl my toes again. It's quiet in the room with just the two of us. No tapping from Heavenly's nails. No picture-snapping from Teri. No smacking of Yaz's gum.

"Um. I been drinking lots of milk. Three times a day. That's good for him, right?"

Doc nods his head.

"And I eat lots of peanut butter. For Angelo. For the protein."

Doc nods again.

"I rub that cocoa butter on my skin. Every night." Abuela said it would prevent stretch marks.

Angelo kicks off with both feet. His little body flips up through the black fluid. The motion on the screen reflects off the two rectangles of glass in front of Doc's eyes. Doc's stopped nodding. His brow furrows behind his eyeglasses. I wrap my fingers around the sheet that covers my pants. Does Doc see something bad?

"No cocoa butter," Doc says. "It has caffeine in it. Caffeine that can be absorbed through the skin. It could cause a fetal arrhythmia."

No idea what that means. But by the way Doc's talking, I don't want Angelo to get it.

Doc glances at me again. "A heart rhythm problem. It's usually not significant, but the uneven heartbeat can make other doctors nervous. I don't want them making you nervous before I can check him and reassure you. So it's best to avoid the risk altogether."

Doc's right. Angelo and me, we got enough problems. I wipe my nose with the sheet and snort. I'm gonna dump that tub of cream down the trash chute when I get home. Abuela got it for me back when she wanted Angelo. Back when she thought he'd be healthy. But I'm pissing mad at her all over again. I take the corner of the sheet and rub it hard over my upper lip.

Doc's typing some numbers on the screen. He puts the wand

back in its place. He reaches to the side and covers me with a towel. An actual towel. Like one you'd use after a shower. And it's warm.

Doc's eyes are on the fist that's clenching the gel-smeared sheet. My fingers are as white as my belly. I loosen them. I drop the sheet, take up the towel, and wipe myself off. "These new?"

Doc lifts a finger to his lips. Half his mouth curves up again. "I passed through the inpatient floor on my way up. We've got little ovens for blankets and towels there. I keep telling them we need some on this floor."

I frown down at the towel as I scrape gooey stuff off my skin. I'm not used to people—grown people—going out of their way for me.

"Everything looks good with the fetus, Ms. Pujols."

"Mari. You can call me Mari."

I think he nods. I'm still not looking at him. I wait for him to say what I know comes next. *See you in four weeks.* Instead, he sighs.

"Mari." He says it like he's testing the sound of it out. He doesn't say it the way other white folks do. *Mary.* As in Mary and Joseph. He says it like I do. *Mar*—like to make your *mark*—*ee. Mar-ee.* "I met your grandmother, the other day when your family came. I'm just wondering . . ." He rolls his chair away from me. He leans back, folds his hands in his lap.

I grit my teeth. I know what he's going to say.

"What about your parents?"

Yup. Knew it. I've kicked the dirty sheet to the floor. All I've got is the half-wet, half-warm towel to grab hold of. Doc thinks I can't do this. I can't take care of a baby with problems by myself. Maybe he knows I've kept the keeping of Angelo a secret. But instead of saying something like, *Can your parents help you?*, all Doc says is, "Would you tell me about them?"

Doc's face is bare. There's no furrow or frown. He waits.

"They're not around. They're not a part of my life." That's all he's gonna get. He doesn't want to know about my papi gettin' busted for dealing. About my mama skippin' town. Even if I knew where she was, I wouldn't go after her. I'm nothing to her. So she's nothing to me. There's no way I'm sharing any bit of this baby inside me with that lying *cuero*. She don't deserve Angelo. She don't deserve us. I'd sooner kill us both than go groveling to her. I press my belly through the black knit fabric of my shirt. I don't mean that. I wouldn't do that to you, Angelo. It's just . . . you don't have a grandma, okay? Not that one.

Doc sees me looking at my stomach. He doesn't say anything. He just sits there, watching me.

I could tell Doc my mama's dead. 'Cause she is. To me. To Angelo. But that would get me more questions. What I really want is to leave.

When I get up, Doc stands. At the door, he puts a hand on my shoulder.

"You're doing great. Really. This baby is lucky to have you."

I turn and leave quick. I punch the elevator button over and over 'til it comes. Outside, cold air attacks my ears, my eyes, my lips. A woman next to the subway entrance calls out she's got churros to sell. I feel the change in my pocket. When I ask her how much, she answers in broken English. My "*Gracias*" makes her eyes crinkle. She turns, bends into the steaming metal box beside her. There's a tiny baby on her back. Wrapped up tight. Kept close. He's sleeping. Bet his dreams are good. Full of warm mama and fried pastry smell.

I walk toward St. Nicholas Avenue. My teeth sink through the crisp of the churro. My tongue tastes the sweetness of sugar and cinnamon and then it's burning, the molten dough stuck to it. My eyes water. I turn my face to the wind and let them.

# TWENTY-NINE WEEKS

I sit on the third-floor landing of our building, waiting for my breath to slow. Though I'm getting bigger—finally—it's still not hard to hide. Abuela's size-twelve clothes make it easy. But I can't run up five flights no more.

Mr. and Mrs. Rodriguez were in the mail room, bundled up like there's a blizzard outside. It's like forty and sunny. But that's old folks for you. Mr. Rodriguez was trying to get the mailbox open. His wife was hollering at him to hurry it on up. It's a good thing they didn't have the mail yet, 'cause she would've been hitting him with it otherwise.

I went to our box quick and checked it. Empty. I'm overdue for a letter from my papi. Way overdue. Last one I got was in summer. I slammed the door so hard, the Rodriguezes stopped their bickering and stared at me. Like I was the one about to take off my husband's head with a holiday catalog. I huffed out and took the stairs. Wasn't going to share an elevator with those *locos*.

I unzip my coat and tug the sweater away from my armpits. I climb the last two flights to our apartment. Someone's cooking *habichuelas*. The smell of garlic and sizzling green peppers gets my tummy way too excited.

Abuela's home when I get in. I'm counting another one of the baby's kicks. He's kicked twenty-two times since I left school. I don't stop to think it's way too early for Abuela to be off work. She and I have traded only single words since the hospital. Most ain't been pretty. We been avoiding each other like we *perros y gatos.*

She's sitting at the kitchen table. Gato is in her lap. She's stroking him hard, the way he loves, flattening his ears to his neck. Toto's boots aren't at the door. He's the one who's usually here by now. My stomach flutters. But it's not from baby kicks.

"Maribel, how you feel?"

My insides drop. Abuela hasn't asked me that since she thought I had a healthy baby inside me back in September. Angelo joins in, kicking up a rhythm like a little Loso.

My bag slides off my back. It thunks to the floor. I want to grab my belly. But I don't.

"I'm fine," I say.

Abuela's not looking at me. Gato's purring like a leaf blower. "You have something you want to tell me?"

"No." I turn to go to my room.

"Not so fast. *Ven acá.* Come."

My fingers get all stiff. I don't like being ordered around. Ignoring is one thing. But I'm not going back to the way things were when I first started living with her.

Gato pushes his face against Abuela's hand. He's angry she's let off petting him. Abuela's fingers are bare. Her rings are off. The mug that says *Juan in a million* that she only uses to soak her jewelry sits on the counter with a bottle of Tide. They're in the spot Papi's envelope usually is. I've got a letter written. Telling Papi about Angelo. I wrote it right after I changed my mind. When I got back from the hospital. I've been waiting for Abuela to put out the envelope. She hasn't yet.

"What do you want?" I ask it through my teeth. I want to yell it. The memory of her telling me to get rid of my baby hangs like a half-bitten nail begging to be ripped off.

Abuela stands. Gato falls to the floor. He dashes away, runs over my foot.

"You have something to say?" Abuela's voice gets louder with each word. She steps closer.

I go to move back. But I'm against the door. I want to hug my belly so bad.

"Really?" I say. I can't help pour on a bit of sauce. My lip itches like mad. I rake my teeth against it.

Abuela comes in front of me. Grabs my sweater. Rips it upward, exposing me.

I expect her to scream. To stomp. To hit the wall. That's what she usually does. But she doesn't do any of that. She stares, her milky eyes searching mine. She makes a face like I've thrown dirty laundry water at her.

"What you done?" Her voice is a hiss.

"What have I done?" I'm screaming at her now. "I saved my baby—your *nieto*. That's what I done!"

I grab my bag from my feet. I stomp to the bathroom to pee. I head to my room. It's always a mess. But today it looks like a tropical storm hit it. Clothes from my dresser lie on the floor. Papers, the ones I was hiding in the bottom drawer, the ones from Doc, scatter across my bed. The letter to Papi sits on my nightstand. I bet she read that, too.

Quick, I grab up socks and underwear, the pants that still fit me, and three sweaters. I take Doc's papers, shove them in my bag. I leave the letter to Papi. She can have it. I also leave one of Angelo's pictures. I put it on my comforter, on top of the sand below the coconut tree. It's the one where you can see his perfect nose and his little fingers, despite the huge crease down the middle. I have a copy. A perfect one. She can have the wrinkled one. I want her to remember what she wanted me to throw away.

I storm to the bathroom. I pee again. Now that she knows I'm pregnant, I don't need to hide that from her anymore.

Abuela's still standing in the hallway when I head to the front door. She doesn't say anything. Her anger swirls like dead leaves, plastic bags, and Styrofoam coffee cups caught in a breeze on the city sidewalk. But mine, mine is hurricane-force wind that will rip off your roof, lift your boats and throw them football fields inland.

I don't say anything either.

I shut the door behind me.

are wintery cold against my

knows his mama's touch. He

all be good.

Teri's turned around. She's

straight hair tucked behind bc

and down then left to right ove

say nothing.

Teri's unlatching the locks before I ring the bell. She must've seen me out the window. From the second floor, she can see the whole street. She's always in her room at her desk when she's home. Her brothers and their friends aren't easy to be around.

Maybe she was heading downstairs to let me in. Her building is bigger than mine. But it still doesn't have a doorman or even a security guard. I don't have a key to the front entrance. But I grabbed the door when some *chopo* was leaving.

Teri frowns at the green Whole Foods bag, the one we snatched when they were giving them out for free. One handle is ripped, so I hold it in front of me, lumps of clothes balanced on my baby bump. My school bag's on my shoulders. She reaches for the cross at her neck but doesn't ask what happened. She brings me to her room, leaves me on her bed. She comes back with an extra pillow and a peanut butter sandwich. She goes to her school-loaned laptop and pretends to do homework. Her mouth fidgets all over the place. Her nails are in her teeth, but she doesn't chew them. They're too pretty for that, French manicure with a lilac base, the same color as the walls of her room.

Yaz does Teri's nails for her. (

salon. And that's on account

A door opens somewhere

"¡Óyeme, chan!" "Diache, she's

have you seen her ass?" I can

More than two at least. The

The refrigerator opens and cl

I wait to breathe until one

The front door slams shut.

Teri's sitting on the very e

she might fall off it. Her hand

fingers aren't moving. Maybe

She's not looking at me.

either. She's looking out on

Not now. Just brown buil

picking through a pile of ri

them. Teri's waiting. Mayb

explain why I'm in her room

looking like a cat ready to sc

I love her right now 'cause

I lie down on her bed, s

horns, sirens, and the stomp

neighbors fog my head. The

him. It's almost the beginni

# THIRTY-ONE WEEKS

The room's warm. Mrs. Heppersmith's talk of the Great Depression is tiring me out. My eyes close. Heavenly's boot strikes my chair, jolting me awake. "*Cuero*," I whisper.

"Love you, too," she whispers back, her eyes on the front of the room. She's sucking a lollipop, looking bored. She's wearing a white top with sequins on it. The bottom edge has this cool angle. Ter told her it looked just like the shirt some model wore the other night on this reality fashion show.

The teacher's old-lady voice goes on and on about something called the Dust Bowl. Makes me want to rub my eyes and throw water over my face.

Last spring, we had English in this same room. We was supposed to be talking about a book, the one about that farm where the animals decide to be people. Instead, I told my girls about Abuela's reaction to the baby news, how she'd said the baby was *como agua de mayo*. They was all squawking, making fun of her. Heavenly had whipped out her lipgloss, slicked it over her lips. "Your favorite lipstick." She held it up between two fingers. "The one you thought you lost but find just when your hot date arrives. *Es como agua de mayo.*" Yaz took her gum from her mouth and chucked it at me. "Gum, when you have bad breath and that hot date is going really well. It's like water in May." The gum got stuck in my hair. But nothing was going to ruin my mood. Not even the teacher, Mr. Romero, who was onto us by then. He was pushing through the chairs in the aisle, his bushy mustache thinned, mouth getting ready to yell. Teri whispered her joke before he got to us. "Scissors. For when you got gum in your hair. Like water in May." That girl actually had nail scissors in her bag. She was using them to get out that gum. We was laughing so hard Mr. Romero gave both Yaz and me detention. Even though Hev and Ter didn't need to, they waited for us that afternoon. We came up with a bunch more waters in May 'til Yaz made one up about Toto and Abuela. "Viagra. When your sugar mama come home ready to party. It's like water in May!" She was joking, but still. Gross.

"Listen," I said. "If I ever get me some thirty-year-old boyfriend when I'm forty-five, and it turns out he needs Viagra to get it up, I'll be trading him for a new one!"

Yaz gave me one of her huge hugs where she squeezes my butt like Bertie does and her boobs mush my face.

"Come on, Mar," she said. "Your boyfriend won't never need no Viagra, no matter how old you are. You'll always be your same sexy self."

I swatted her off me, laughing. She was still joking. But it felt good anyway. To be called something I knew I wasn't but wanted to be.

Heavenly passes her lollipop slow in front of my face. The fake cherry smell draws me back, makes my stomach grumble. I slap at it, trying to get it from her.

"Shhh," Teri scolds from behind.

When Mrs. Heppersmith's back is turned, I toss a wad of paper over my shoulder. *Un segundito* later, it whacks me in the back of the head. Dex, who's repeating the class from last year, is glaring at me. Guess I didn't hit Teri. Dex looks ridiculous, all six feet five inches of him squeezed into the normal-size chair and desk. It's hard to take someone seriously when rolls of his stomach fat spill out from under a shirt that says *Wanta Bachata?* I bare my teeth and turn back around. I don't look to my left. Yaz sits there. She's been staring at me all class, all day, all week. But I'm ignoring her. Me and her, we're done. Even if she used to make the best jokes. Even if she used to tell me things that weren't true just because I wanted to hear them.

The second hand of the clock just passes six. I position my book on the edge of my desk. It teeters, but I hold it until the minute hand crosses eleven. I let go. The text slams to the floor. Mrs. Heppersmith jumps and turns to scowl just as the bell rings. A bunch of people laugh. We're all packing up, so she can't even tell whose book it was.

"Nice," Heavenly says as we walk out. She looks a little less bored.

I nod, giving her a grin, forgetting not to look at Yaz's seat.

But Yaz is already gone.

eavenly drops her tray onto the table. Pizza, fries, two packs of Oreos, a Diet Coke, and an apple juice. I'm playing with a crumpled straw wrapper, dripping water on it to make it grow larger. Like a worm inching back to life. That tray has way too much food for Heavenly. Jo-jo spoils her but, come on.

"Here, take whatever." Hev slides the food toward me, snagging the Diet Coke and a fry.

Yaz squeals. Even from across the cafeteria, I know it's her. She's sitting with Teri and Sangi. Some boys, Vin and José, lean against their table. José keeps taking Yaz's apple and putting it under his shirt.

I scrub at my upper lip. Like I care that Yaz is getting some action. Like I care that Yaz is laughing. When she thinks I lost a baby.

Teri's smiling sideways at Vin. He doesn't notice. He shouts and jumps up to catch the apple José throws. Teri's smile follows Vin. She's pulled her hair back today. I told her it looked pretty that way, away from her face. Teri sees me looking and waves. I don't wave back. Don't want Yaz to think I'm waving at her.

"Come on, eat something, *flaquita!*" Heavenly shoves the tray again. She pulls up the sleeves of her red sweater. It's cropped, showing off curves above and below it. The color matches her lipstick and nails. I stare down at what I'm wearing. Baggy pants and a sweatshirt I borrowed from Teri. They don't even match. And my nails. They haven't been this stubby in years. I grab the juice, mumble thanks. Not sure how I feel about this. About Teri figuring it out and telling Heavenly. I mean, they know. They must. The apple juice is a dead giveaway.

As long as she don't tell Yaz, I guess I'm okay.

"Hey, baby."

I choke on juice.

"Can I sit?" Bertie doesn't wait for an answer.

Or Bertie. I don't want them to tell Bertie either.

I turn away from him, put the juice bottle on the bench between me and Heavenly. She's got it. Without even looking, she puts it on her other side.

"How you feeling?" he asks. His voice is low, like he doesn't want everyone to hear. He goes to touch my leg. I scoot away, bump against Heavenly's gray denim. Good thing the juice isn't there no more.

Bertie's eyes are white. And green. There's no red in there. Good. But there are plenty of words. Words he doesn't say with his mouth.

Bertie's tried this before. Pretended to care. If he cared so much, he wouldn't have wanted me to get rid of Angelo. He's not fooling nobody. Well, he may be fooling Teri. He's taken her to the diner a few times, bought her hot chocolate with Skinner's money, asked about me. Teri keeps at me to give Bertie a chance. She brings me little notes from him since I blocked him from my phone. But I know better. I rip them up without reading them.

I stare at the wall that's gray and dirty and flaking paint. I think how that's what Bertie is making me feel like inside. Making me remember what I almost did.

Angelo kicks. Right then. My *chinchin papi chulo* knows just when his mama needs a lift. I want to feel him with my hand. But I don't want to do nothing that'll look suspicious. I won't be able to hide it forever. But for now, I can.

Heavenly's looking at me, waiting for eye contact. When I give it to her, she raises her perfectly threaded eyebrow. *Want me to get rid of him?*

I close my eyes, rest my forehead on my fists. *Yes. Please.*

"Come on, Bertie. Let the girl eat. You know she not ready to talk to you."

Bertie's hand hovers over my back. Heavenly must be dirty-looking him because he don't touch me.

"I miss you, baby."

He gets up and leaves. I want to call after him, ask him if he misses Angelo, too. But I don't.

Bertie's walking to the exit, hands in his pockets, head down. Teri stands. She takes Bertie's arm as he gets close. Makes him sit next to her. He stares at the table, nods as Teri talks to his ear. Yaz is looking at them. Then she's looking at me. I turn around, show them all the hood of my dirty sweatshirt.

Heavenly cuts the pizza in half and hands me a slice and my juice. I take a bite and chew. Angelo feels like he's flipping over with excitement. Baby boy loves pizza.

I look at Heavenly and smile. She's looking down at her nails, maybe thinking what design to airbrush on them next. Even though I haven't told them my secret, I know my girls got my back.

I shut my locker and Yaz is there. She's freaky close. Her nails, silver with green question marks, pick at the buttons of her shirt. She sees me staring and drops her arm. Her rainbow bangle bracelets cling-clank on her wrist. I have a pack, too. We won them at a street fair in fifth grade. In between the bouncy hut and sharing a fried turkey leg and a giant blue Slurpee.

Yaz doesn't say nothing, which is good. I don't want her to.

I walk away.

"Mari, wait." Her hand touches my shoulder.

I whip around, throw an icy Slurpee glare at her. She takes her hand off me.

"Don't," I say, breaking my promise to never speak to her again.

I turn to go.

"I want to talk, Mari."

I pivot, arm sailing. I drive my fist into the locker next to her face. It slams shut with a sound like a car crash. Everyone in the hallway gets quiet and looks to see if there's blood.

Yaz's eyes are real big, mascara-lashes hitting cheeks and

eyebrows. She's twisting her lips around, mucking up her lipstick.

I point my fist at her, extend one finger. *Don't.* I say it with my stare.

She releases her lips. They're bitten and bloated under all that gloss.

*Okay.* She says it with her feet.

# THIRTY-THREE WEEKS

I want to lie in bed all day. I'm starting to show. My coat don't fit right no more. I can't take school. I can't take avoiding Yaz and Bertie and all the curious, feel-sorry-for-me stares. But Teri's mother's boyfriend works nights, so he's here all morning. I think about sneaking into Abuela's. But there's no way I'm getting into that building without Mrs. Rodriguez poking into my life. She is one nosy old lady.

Teri hands me a piece of folded-over toast with peanut butter as soon as we get outside. Our drill is she goes to the kitchen and distracts everyone while I slip out. I wait in the lobby, under the stairs, and we walk to school together.

Teri's still wearing her hair up. I told her she don't need no flat-iron this way, so she just blows it out. It gives it just the right wave. She's got this orange fuzzy scarf around her neck. We lifted it from her mama's closet. It's *manso*.

"You okay?" Teri asks. She had to shake me awake a few extra times this morning on account of I kept falling back to sleep. We turn onto St. Nicholas.

I give her a look, and she nods. She knows I'm tired of people asking me that. But she can't help it. Some people are too good for their own selves.

Sidewalk's getting crowded. School's next block over. I pay more attention to who's around. A girl up ahead has her hair, long, black, and glossy, twisted into a knot over her shoulder. I hang back 'til she turns, shows me she's not Yaz.

Teri opens her bag as we're walking up the steps to the entrance.

"¡Diache!" she says in her tiny voice that makes swears sound like a name she's giving to a puppy. "Forgot my essay. For the Griffin. Gotta go back."

I snort. "Don't want the Griffin to eat you!" I joke, but Mr. Griffin is pretty strict when it comes to homework.

Teri hands me a book. "Can you return this for me?" I take it as she turns and runs. I don't think she's ever not handed in an assignment. It's probably my fault seeing as I'm dumping my sorry ass on her bedroom floor each night.

I walk inside, shoving back against someone who shoved me first. I didn't even do the essay. I'm not afraid of no teacher. Even if it is the Griffin.

The library's quiet. Compared to the hallways. Compared to the sidewalks. Compared to Teri's mama's apartment. I drop the book on the counter and walk down one of the aisles to the back area with tables. It's empty. Desks and chairs are up against the walls, hidden by bookshelves that reach to the ceiling. Only one desk has a person at it. The guy's surrounded by books. I grab books off the nearest shelf and head in the opposite direction. I take the last desk, stack the books like stones around me. I put my head down. I sleep 'til the final bell.

Teri's waiting for me in the lobby, looking like she forgot a whole handful of the Griffin's assignments. Her hand is locked over the cross at her neck.

"Where were you?" she asks. "Don't you have your phone?"

I fish it out of my pocket. Ten texts. From Teri and Heavenly.

"Library." I grin. "It was awesome."

"This whole time? What were you doing?"

"Sleeping. Like I said, totally *chévere*."

Teri shakes her head. "Don't do that again, okay?" She takes out her phone to text.

"Fine. Next time I'm sleeping, I'll wake up to tell you guys I'm sleeping."

She wants to shove me, but she doesn't.

"Didn't you eat lunch?" she asks.

"Have you been listening to the words coming out of my mouth? I told you. I was sleeping."

Teri pulls a banana and a granola bar from her bag. "Here.

And this is from Heavenly." Apple juice. I take them and eat as we walk.

"You have to take care of yourself, Mar."

It's weird that she knows but we don't talk about it.

Angelo kicks, as if to yell at me, too. Guess he's hungry.

"Sorry, little guy." I pat my belly.

I walk half a block before realizing Teri's not next to me. She's back at the corner, standing next to a beat-up old Honda, looking at me like she's going to cry. Her fingers are touching the cross again.

"You didn't go through with it," she says as I get closer.

I shrug. I toss the banana peel into the recycle bin near the Honda's bumper and rip open the granola bar wrapper.

"What?" I ask, pretending not to see the tears in Teri's eyes. "Banana peels are recyclable, right?"

"Don't make a joke. I'm pissing mad at you." She grabs the ends of her scarf and twists them together.

"You mad at me? Why? What did I do?" A thick clump of hair has fallen out of her ponytail and is sticking to her lipstick, partway in her mouth. I go to push it off her, but she steps away.

"You didn't tell me. Me or Heavenly. We're on your side, you know. I've been letting you sleep in my room for weeks, sneaking you food, money."

"I don't want your money," I snap. It's true. The cash she hides in my bag, I hide right back in her dresser.

"Fine. I know you give the money back."

I glance at her, surprised. Thought I'd fooled her on that.

"But you should have said something, girl. Friends share. That's what we do." Teri brushes her ponytail behind her.

"And here I thought friends was just for giving you food and money and places to stay." That wasn't nice of me. But I can be a real *puta* sometimes.

Teri doesn't say nothing. She sniffs and blinks.

I finish the granola bar. I shove my hands in my coat pocket. It makes my belly stick out even more seeing as the coat don't close right. "I thought you knew," I say, looking down at the hump under my sweater.

"We did know, but we was waiting for you to tell us." Teri takes out her phone.

"Who you texting?" I don't like how my voice gets real high. I don't want her telling Yaz. I don't want her telling Bertie. Don't want Angelo to be the reason Bertie comes back. He's done what I asked. Left me alone. He and Teri still talk. I see them sometimes around school. But the little notes stopped coming. Wish I'd kept them. Maybe I'd open them sometime. Read what he had to say.

Teri keeps hitting her phone with her thumbs, ignoring me.

"Who you texting?" I say it again. I squeeze my hands so I don't grab her phone away.

"Heavenly." She throws the name at me.

"What you writing?"

She shows me the phone.

You were right

Heavenly's response comes back as I'm reading.

We having a baby! :)

W e don't say anything the rest of the walk home. Even when we get into the small elevator that always smells of old pizza boxes, we don't speak. The elevator groans to the second floor. I think of making a joke. Maybe something about stale cheese farts. But I can't think of nothing.

Teri's brother is standing near the front door when we get in, hands stuffed into his too-tight jeans. His hanging around waiting for us isn't unusual. Unless he's got a friend, he's always hanging around, looking for someone to bother. But him following us into Teri's room? That be unusual.

"How you girls doing?" He says it like he's an Italian mobster. He lived in Santo Domingo for his first ten years, but he's obsessed with *The Sopranos*.

"Flaming idiot," I mumble, turning my back to him.

"What you say?"

"Fine, we're fine!" I smile at him. Since I've never done this before, it confuses him.

"Nah, I think you said something." He looks too big for Teri's room. Like he wouldn't ever fit in her bed. Like if he leaned on her desk, it'd crack in two. He's wearing a T-shirt. Which is funny, 'cause it's cold in here. Teri's mama keeps the heat off, relies on the neighbors' radiators to keep us warm. I get it. Good way to save money.

"What do you want, Carlos?" Teri flops down on the bed and glares at the ceiling. She's tired out from our fight. She's not like me. She don't like confrontation. Her fingers flit over the end of her ponytail, pulling the strands straight. I sit by her shoulder. I don't take my coat off.

Carlos goes to the door and looks down the hall.

"What are you doing?" Teri asks at the same time I say, "Who are you looking for?"

"Mami. Y Pedro," he answers closing the door. I stand up. I don't like being shut in rooms with boys I don't want to have sex with.

"Mami won't be back until nine. Her shift ends at eight-thirty. Every day. Remember? And Pedro's probably with Leeza. Like he always is." Carlos has their mama's brain genes. Not much going on up there. With either of them. Teri's mama is a medical assistant at the hospital. She's why I don't let nobody but a doctor or a nurse touch me when I go there. Luckily, she's in colorectal and has nothing to do with me. We joke about how all she does is wipe old people's asses all day. Part of me feels bad making fun of Teri's mama. At least she's still around, working, bringing home food for her kids. Teri and Pedro, they take after their papi. They're smart. Smart enough to split from this place or spend as little time here as possible. Only reason Teri's home every afternoon these days is on account of me. And it's not like Teri's papi is totally checked out either. He runs a car service in DR. Every summer, he flies Teri and Pedro down to visit him. Teri got lucky in the parent department, even if she got the *mala pata* with her half brother.

"Come on, Teresa, why you have to talk to me like that? I'm no *pendejo*, you know? I sees things. I hears things." He looks at me as he says this. He crosses his arms. His T-shirt looks like it's gonna rip. Like someone stuck it in the dryer too many times.

I grab one of the pillows off Teri's bed. It's purple with lace all around. I hold it against me so I can turn and face him. I don't like how he's talking.

"I know she been sleeping here," Carlos says. "Every night."

Teri sits up real quick.

"Yeah, Mari, you think you so smart, huh? So tough, huh? How come you no with Bertie no more?"

"That's none of your business, dipshit." I say it with a smile.

"Yeah, well I heard you was *botao*. He threw you out. 'Cause you wasn't puttin' out no more."

My fingers dig into the pillow. Bertie wouldn't say that. Even if it was true.

"*Tú sí eres baboso,*" Teri says. "You're crazy."

"Uh-oh. *¿Te vas a fajar conmigo?* You gonna beat me up?" Carlos is looking at me, his eyes all wide, pretend-scared.

I unclench my hands. I move the purple pillow down over my belly. If it weren't for Angelo—and Teri—I would beat Carlos up. Muscles don't scare me. "Who'd you hear that from?" I keep my voice real sweet. My bet's on Skinner. Or one of his *manin.* The man's not dumb. Sure he knows I been dragging his name through all sorts of *ratreria* every chance I get.

Carlos loosens his arms. That ugly T-shirt still looks too tight. "Don't matter how I know. But I know."

Teri grabs up a small stuffed bear. Buttercup. Her papi got it for her for her tenth birthday. She's holding it in her lap. She's rubbing its nose over and over, even though the thread's all gone. The nose got rubbed off years ago. "What do you want?" she asks.

"I's just saying, it look like Mari need a place to stay." He shrugs. He sniffs real loud and his chin juts up. "She could stay with me. In my room."

"Carlos. No." Teri lets go of Buttercup. Her hand slices the air. I want to yuke.

"You want Mami to find out? That she been staying here? Eatin' all our food? 'Cause I'm gonna tell her. I tell her tonight." He's smiling like a kid who won a street-fair prize. Only he don't know it'll come apart and spill Styrofoam peanuts everywhere as soon as he gets it home.

"If she no want to be with me, she can always pay. Fifty bucks. Like at a hotel."

I'm about to rip the lace off the pillow. I want to scream that he's a dipshit *pendejo* and if I had money I'd be in a hotel and not their dirty, stinking apartment. But I don't want to hurt Teri. And screaming won't work. Not this time.

I take a breath. Calm myself down. Angelo is turning over inside me. He's as disgusted as I am. *Don't worry, baby boy. Mama's going to take care of this.*

"Okay." I say it slow, like I've been considering it.

"What?!" Teri's head jerks to me.

"Really?" Carlos grins. I want to smack that smile off his face so hard his teeth come with it. But that won't help anything.

"You can't be serious." Teri grabs my arm but I give her a look. *Wait.*

I lift my nose and breathe in. "*¿Qué grajo?* What's that smell?" I smell my armpit. I smell Teri. "Nope, not us." I look at Carlos. "Must be you." I say it real pleasant. I take the corner of my shirt, twist it in my hand. This makes my collar go down. Carlos is staring at me. His mouth is open. But not like Bertie. He is nothing like Bertie.

"Do you think you could take a nice, long, hot shower for me? You know, before . . . ?"

Carlos nods, real eager. He goes to the bathroom. This is going to be easier than I thought.

"What are you thinking?" Teri whispers at me as I beeline for Carlos and Pedro's room. Carlos really is a *pendejo*. He shares a room with his brother. I mean, come on. Where does he think he's going to hide me in here?

His phone is on top of his nightstand. He's an even bigger idiot than I thought. His password is *CARLOS*. Quick before he's out, I delete a bunch of contacts and post pics of naked-chest underwear guys on his social-media sites and "like" them. Teri's looking over my shoulder.

"You are so evil." She's trying not to laugh.

I go back to Teri's room, stuff my things in my ripped bag.

"Mari, no. Where will you go?" I knew she'd fight this. But there's no way I'm getting her in trouble on account of my trouble.

"I'll go to Heavenly's. She's already offered." Heavenly did offer. But seeing as Teri's mama is not as swift as Heavenly's, I thought Teri's was a safer bet.

"Are you sure?"

"Listen, Heavenly's mama hasn't had a boyfriend since we got rid of that last one. I'll be good." I pick up the purple pillow from the floor, put it on the bed. I scan Teri's room, making sure

I'm not leaving anything behind. Who am I kidding? All I got is the one small bag.

I head for the door. Teri stops me, her hand on the door frame. Her fingers cover part of a date scratched in pencil. *Teresa Vargas, 10 años, 105 cm, 11 de abril 2——*. I never noticed it before. Thought that was only something families on TV did.

"What should I tell Carlos when he gets out?"

"Tell him whatever you want. He's not that dumb. He'll figure it out. And he won't tell your mama."

Teri nibbles at her lower lip. "How do you know?"

"I changed the passwords on his accounts. And linked them all to my email. If he wants to know what they are, he's going to have to behave. If he doesn't, I'll post more stuff. Real guy-on-guy action this time. That you can tell him."

I hug her quick, slam the door, and make my way downstairs. I take out my phone, text Heavenly, then type Carlos's new password into my notes. Not that I'm going to forget it: *CARLOS*isaDUMBASS*!

# THIRTY-TWO WEEKS

**D**oc is quieter than usual. I watch the TV hanging from the ceiling as he tweaks the picture, colors swirling in my baby's heart. Angelo's cooperating today. Even I can tell. He's lying against me, untucked, chest up. Maybe that's why Doc is so quiet. He's finally getting good pics.

The wand moves over my round belly. I like this room. It's like a cave with the dim light, no windows, and soundproofed walls. A soap-scented, clean cave. And after sleeping on the floor for weeks, the exam table is downright luxurious.

"Could you turn on your side, please?" Doc is still staring at the machine. He doesn't pause to smile like he usually does.

"Must be some really good pictures," I grumble as I roll toward him. I'm almost eight months along. My belly's gotten real big. It's hard to turn over.

I can't see the TV without twisting my neck around. Doc's arm blocks the screen on the machine, so I can't see Angelo there either. I sigh but Doc doesn't pay me any notice. His hand flies over the keyboard, punching buttons, turning dials, flipping switches. His eyes are narrowed, concentrating. He looks so in control. I bet his life has been pretty surprise-free.

A gold band on his left ring finger winks at me as he reaches for more gel.

"Hey, you married?"

He glances at me. I get the well-fed-lion-sunning-on-the-grass smile. "I am," he says. He goes back to the machine.

"What's her name?"

"Sandra." He says this without looking away from the screen. His mouth is still mostly curved up, so I know he's not mad I'm asking. I bet she's beautiful. His wife. I bet she looks like a princess.

"How long you been married?"

"Almost three years."

*¡Anjá!* Three years. What was I doing three years ago? Nothing to do with marriage, that's for sure.

"Got kids?"

"Not yet."

"Must be time for some then," I tell him, grinning. "I bet your wife wants a bunch." Why wouldn't she? He's a doctor. He's *hot*. And he's nice.

Doc doesn't answer.

"Come on, you got this great job here at the hospital. You can afford a bunch, can't you?"

Doc puts the wand back on the machine. He holds a handful of wipes out for me. His eyes come to rest on mine. He gives me a smile that doesn't get anywhere near those light gold-and-blue eyes.

"I'll meet you in the conference room when you're cleaned up."

I put my hands behind me, struggle to push myself up. "Conference room? Why? What's wrong?" Nothing good ever happens in that room.

"There are a few more things we need to discuss." He gets up from his chair and moves to the door.

"No," I say sitting up farther. The sheet falls off me to the floor. I'm not going back in that room. "I want you to tell me here."

*Please don't let there be anything else wrong. Please.*

Doc is watching me. He looks at my bare legs and then at the sheet on the floor. I don't have access to laundry like I used to, so I didn't want to get my pants all sticky. Doc bends and picks up the sheet. He covers me with it. He takes hold of the rolling chair and spins it to face me. He sits down. He turns his hands over and runs his palms together. That's when I know it's bad.

"Mari, something else has happened. To the fetus."

"Angelo," I whisper. "His name is Angelo." I'm staring at the bumps of my knees under the white cloth. I can't take the expression on Doc's face.

"I know," he says softly. "We're trained to only use the term 'fetus' until they're born. In case something happens. It makes it less likely the mother will bond."

I snort-cough. "Too late for that." My fingers lie against the taut skin of my belly. It's still gooey. And the gel is getting cold. But I want to feel Angelo. "Tell me." I look at Doc.

"The blood coming back to his heart from his lungs is obstructed. The blood in his lungs can't get out. It's backing up and may be damaging his lungs."

"But he needs his lungs. To breathe." I haven't felt him move in a long while. But his heart was beating just now. On the screen. Wasn't it?

"After birth, he needs his lungs. Now, he's getting oxygen from you." Angelo kicks. Finally. Like he's agreeing with Doc. I let out a breath that's almost like a laugh. I hiccup and know I'm gonna cry. I won't do that in front of Doc. I slide off the table, shut myself in the bathroom. I tear off handfuls of paper towels, dunk them in cold water, rub them over me. I pull up my pants, splash cold water on my face. In the mirror, I look pale and tired. The skin above my upper lip is raw from where I've rubbed it too much. I smile, trying to change the way I look. But it just brings on tears. Why does everything keep getting worse? I slam my hand on the sink. Pain. Anger. Safer than tears.

Heavenly's sister, Destiny, is coming back from the DR in a few days. Her abuela's going on some trip and didn't want to bring the five-year-old along. So she's dropping her back with her mama. I don't know what that means for me. I grip my stomach. *And you too, baby boy.*

I don't like to think about after. When the baby comes. Before we knew about the heart, I thought about it all the time. How I'd have this perfect little person with me always. Sleeping in my bed, snuggled against me. How I would be the only person who would make him stop crying. Make him feel safe. And I would be the one he'd love most. Sure, he'd love Bertie, too. Bertie would have made a great papi. He was always talking about the places he was gonna take our baby. Yankee Stadium. Little Red Lighthouse. Times Square during the holidays. But the baby would be mine. Would live with me. And Abuela was going to help.

Ever since I found out about the heart, I don't think about where we gonna live after. Because maybe he ain't gonna live. I don't want to jinx us. Turns out, we're jinxed already.

Doc is still sitting on the stool when I come out. "I'm sorry, Mari," he says in his too-nice voice. "Can I ask how you've been doing? Before I told you this? You've been coming alone to all your appointments, without any of your cousins or the baby's father. Would you like to speak to our social worker about anything?"

Oh ho ho! He is not going to get me to go there.

I shake my head. I don't look at him. I hoist myself back onto the table. I glare at him when he tries to help.

"Draw it for me. The thing with the blood and the lungs."

He pulls pens out of his white coat pocket. He takes a clipboard from the counter. There's no more paper on it. He opens a cabinet, rips off a piece of paper towel from a new roll. He starts to draw.

"It's a known complication of HLHS. See this hole here? Between the two top chambers of the heart? Every normal fetus has this hole. In HLHS, this hole is needed to allow the blood coming back from the lungs to pass to the right side of the heart, so it can go out to the body. Normally, this blood would go out the left side, but in HLHS there is no left side."

"Okay. The hole is important. So . . . ?"

"The hole is supposed to close after birth. In your case, the hole is closing now. So the blood is stuck with nowhere to go."

He hands me the paper. Scribbles of red circle inside the small room of the heart and head back to the lungs. Only blue blood is coming out of the heart to the body. There's not even purple blood, because the red and the blue aren't getting to mix.

"So what do we do?"

"Some centers offer fetal interventions for this. To widen the hole while the fetus is still inside the mother." He frowns.

"But you don't think I should do that."

He glances at me, like he's surprised I figured that out. As if reading people's faces isn't my specialty. As if I didn't have years of training with my mama, not to mention Abuela. "You would be high-risk, because of your age. The procedures are not always successful. And not many have been performed. They're still considered experimental. But it's your decision. I can put you in contact with someone from one of those centers if you would like to speak—"

"No." My arms circle what's left of my waist. I don't want anyone experimenting on me or Angelo. "What else you got?"

"After birth, we can open the hole. We have to do it fast. Babies can die within a few hours if we don't get it open. You would need a scheduled delivery, so we can have the cath lab ready with all the necessary doctors and nurses. For you, that would mean a cesarean section."

"You gonna cut me open to take out the baby?"

He nods. "So we get the baby when we're ready for him. To maximize his chance of survival."

My mama had one of those with me. She hated the scar. She was always showing it to me, so I could see what I'd done to her.

"Okay, so you cut me open, take the baby, open the hole, and he's fine?"

Doc's mouth tightens. "Even if we open the hole, he might not make it—if his lungs are too damaged from the backup of blood during the pregnancy. We try to measure the damage to the lungs in utero, but it's not always accurate. And the risk of his three surgeries goes up because of this."

"Because his lungs might be damaged. And you need healthy lungs for that last surgery—the Fontan—to work."

He smiles, lion eyes all kind and warm again. "Yes, that's right. You've been paying attention."

"What do you think I've been doing?" I don't mean to be all snappy at him, but I can't help it.

Doc looks down at his hands again. He holds on to his smile 'til it fades.

"Mari," he says quietly. "There's something I have to bring up. I don't want to, because I think I know what you're going to say."

"What now? You gonna tell me this baby is going to explode inside of me and blow all of us up?" What could possibly be worse than what he's already said?

He doesn't accept my offer of a joke.

"You're thirty-two weeks pregnant. That's too far along for us to offer termination. But there are a couple of centers in the country that perform terminations at this late stage. For situations like these. Where the fetus's chance of survival is very low."

He's right. He shouldn't have told me that.

Doc's watching me with those patient eyes. "I'm sorry, but it's my job to give you all the information. Even if the information makes you uncomfortable."

"Uncomfortable?!" I stand. "Uncomfortable?!" I'm shouting. Doc stands, too. I barely come up to his chest. I poke him with my finger, pushing him away from me. "This ain't uncomfortable! This be mad!" I yell, pointing at my face. "You think I come this far to just give up? I told you. I need this baby." I don't tell him how now I need him more than ever. How he's really all I got left. "I'm gonna fight for him. I'm gonna fight."

"Okay." He's smiling his half smile again. But it's so sad I have to look away. "Then I'm going to fight with you."

My phone buzzes. It's under my pillow. I'm lying on the floor next to Heavenly's bed. It's only ten. Heavenly's not back from Jo-jo's, but I'm exhausted.

I take out the phone thinking it's Heavenly texting she's on her way. But it's Yaz.

I miss you :'(

I think about what Doc told me. About Angelo. I haven't shared it with no one yet. The first person I thought of as I was leaving the hospital was Yaz. She would've listened. She would've gotten angry with me, gone with me to do something stupid to let out all that anger. Like bash in some trashcans or knock off some side-views from the cars in the park. I wish Yaz hadn't done what she did. It's like she wanted Angelo gone, too. She had to know what Abuela and Bertie would think, how they'd react. Instead of sticking by me and keeping it between us, she went ahead and made me hate her.

My phone buzzes again.

Can we talk?

I stare at the phone, thinking what to do.

Please???? :) :) :)

The thing is, I miss her, too. I miss her hugs, her peppermint gum, her crazy glitter nails, and how I can tell what sort of mood she's in by the color of her lipstick and the loudness of her laugh. I miss that she can tell what sort of mood I'm in just by looking at me.

The door flies open.

"Hey." Heavenly drops her coat and hat on the bed. Her cheeks are flushed. From the cold or from Jo-jo, I don't know. She unwinds her purple-and-gray scarf from her neck, pausing to untangle an earring. I lie back down on the pillow, pretending I didn't almost bite my fingertips off just now. Every time that door opens, I think it's Heavenly's mama coming to throw me out.

I slip the phone beneath me.

"Who were you texting?" Heavenly lies across the bed. Her head sticks over the edge to look down at me. Her feet kick the cot her mama put out for Destiny.

"No one." I roll over and stuff a pillow between my legs. "'Night."

The next day, I ask Teri and Heavenly if they wanna go to the diner. I have something important to tell them. I remember the way Teri looked when I told her about keeping Angelo. How her forehead got all these wrinkles I'd never seen. How she wouldn't look me in the eye. My girls have gone all out for me. Letting me crash with them. Hiding it from their mamas. Keeping my secret. They're the closest thing Angelo and I have to family. They deserve to know.

I leave the school library in the middle of last period. Everyone else is still in class. I wait for Ter and Hev at the deli two blocks away, the one owned by a Korean family. Hardly anyone we know goes there. We walk down Broadway together. Some white-haired *viejito* teeters on a ladder in front of a locksmith store, stringing green and red lights over the awning. The butcher next-door advertises Thanksgiving turkeys that are free-range or pre-brined. I don't know what that means. The only turkey we ever ate was frozen from the supermarket, purchased the day of on special. It was past midnight by the time we had dinner. The thing was cooked. But just barely. Toto was the only one who finished his. Probably 'cause he has to share Carmen's bed and didn't want to be out on the couch. Can't say I blame Abuela for not wanting to repeat the experience.

Heavenly has my arm. She's pulling me across the street as the light goes yellow. We pass a group of guys hanging in front of a lottery shop. One of them must've scratched off a win 'cause they're hooting, "¡*Qué cheposo!*" and high-fiving. Santa and snowmen and reindeer peer at us from Rite Aid's windows. Holiday candy's on sale. Two for six dollars. The idea of chocolate wakes my stomach. It wakes Angelo. I slide my hand under my belly, remind him where we're headed. But I can't help looking inside for those bright plastic bags of foil-covered candies. Fake evergreen streamers, huge yellow bells, and ornaments hang from the cookies-'n'-cream ceiling. That's what Yaz and I used to call it. Those white foam tiles flecked with bits of black made us think of vanilla and crushed Oreos. Once, when we was in the store giggling about it, we got so hungry we stole a pint. Snuck it out under Yaz's shirt, ate it on a bench by the river, passing a spoon we'd snatched from Starbucks back and forth.

Teri swings the door to the diner open and waits for me to go first. The warmth of the restaurant hits my face, making my cheeks feel like they're right up against a space heater. My fingers are strips of ice against them. Our usual booth is open, but I head for the back. Sitting by the window seems like asking for trouble, no matter it's too early for Jo-jo or Bertie or Yaz to be here. The smell of roasted chicken, fried potatoes, and plantains makes Angelo go wild. The two of us, we're always starving. I asked my girls to meet me because I'm gonna tell them what Doc told me. I asked them to meet me here, at Reme's, because I've been dying for their breaded fried steak and I'm hoping one of them brought cash to cover it. I know that makes me a big, fat *puta*. But I figure they've known me for years. They know I'm a *puta*.

The fake red leather of the bench squeaks as I slide my fat ass over it. Didn't use to make that noise. But my ass didn't used to be this fat. Didn't even used to have an ass. I poke my belly. "It's your fault," I tell Angelo, but I'm smiling.

My girls slide in opposite. Hev unzips her silver puffer coat, tucks it behind her. She folds the fur collar in so it don't get dirty. Underneath, she's got this fluffy vest with tassels hanging down. It's cool-looking, but it sheds. Hev's lips purse as she picks gray fuzz off her black turtleneck. Teri's sitting straight-backed, her plain-sweatered shoulders pressed to the seat, hands under her jeaned thighs. She's watching me, but not watching me, you know? Her eyes going from my face to my bitten stubs of nails to the table, back to my face again. She still wears her hair up even though I'm not there every morning to give her confidence about it. I'm glad. She looks more grown-up this way.

"*¿Pero dónde está el mesero?* I'd die for *un cafecito.*" Hev flicks a final fuzz from her arm. She glances at the kitchen.

Teri pushes a menu toward me. "You want anything to eat?" She doesn't like that I've been skipping lunch. But what else am I gonna do? I'm not parading myself into that cafeteria. Anyway, I've gotten used to my five-hour naps in the library.

I don't take the menu. But Hev does. She brings it right up under her nose. I take the edge of the plastic-covered paper, pull it back down to the table.

"You found yourself your own doctor yet?" I ask her. "For these?" I point to my eyes.

Hev blows out her lips and snorts. Her open palms frame her face. "This ain't made for no glasses."

I glance at Ter. "You been taking notes for her in class?"

Teri turns the menu toward me. "Same as I do for you. Now order something. I'll pay."

I don't say nothing more. Teri gives me a smile. But it's one of those mouth-only smiles. She's sitting on her hands again.

The waiter comes. We order two coffees, one apple juice, and a *bistec empanizada.* As he's walking away, Hev calls out for an order of *maduros.* I love those sticky, sweet roasted bananas. Hev looks at me and winks.

"So," she says, smoothing down the tassels of her vest. "*¿Qué lo qué?*"

"Yeah." Teri brings her hands to the top of the table. She laces them together. "What's up?"

I scratch at my lip then tell them what Doc told me. Teri's head is making mini up-and-down movements, like one of those bobbleheads on a car dash. She does it when she's concentrating hard. Her mouth is a tiny open circle. She's squeezing her fingers tight. Hev's staring down at her coffee. She drags the spoon around and around. It clinks against the mug. She hasn't even put any sugar in it yet.

My steak comes. I lean back, shift against the hard plastic. The food looks real good. Smells good, too. But I'm not hungry anymore.

Hev mutters something. She grabs her bag and starts to rummage. She slams her phone on the table. Next comes her wallet. Her keys. Makeup. She wads a tissue into her fist. She's shaking her head. Like she's angry at the bag. Like it lost something or ate something really important.

She wraps the tissue around her finger. She looks to the ceiling and holds real still as she swipes the tissue under her eye. She opens her eyeshadow case, brings the mirror close, blinks a bunch of times. She mutters again. I thought she was swearing, but it's a prayer. She's praying.

Teri doesn't move. Her hands are in front of her, fingers

tangled. A tear falls from one eye. It drops down her cheek. She sniffs real loud. She takes a breath, sits forward. She notices I'm not eating and tilts her head at me. Her bottom lip wobbles. "*Pero*, Mari," she says. "*Por favor.*" She untangles her hands, pushes her open palm toward my food. "Eat."

I take a breath, too. I hate that it's not steady. I grab a fork. I grab it so tight it feels like a knife. I spear a chunk of gooey banana. I shove it in my mouth. There. Now I can't talk. Can't cry.

"*Todo 'ta bien.* Everything will be okay." Heavenly's looking at my belly. At my hand on my belly. I'm dragging it around and around, circling Angelo like Hev's spoon was circling her coffee cup. I hadn't even noticed I was doing it.

"When are you gonna tell Bertie?" Teri's voice is quiet. More tears leak out her eyes. Her hands are at her neck, massaging the cross.

I spear another *maduro* quick. I shake my head.

"Mari. You have to," Teri says. Heavenly turns to her. "You know, he still asks about you." Teri wipes her cheek.

I swallow. The bite scrapes on the way down. I should have chewed more. "When?" I ask, clearing my throat.

Heavenly lifts her eyebrows. She's still looking at Teri.

"Like every day. I see him every day."

Teri talks with Bertie every day? *¿Qué?* What? "What you been telling him?" I take up the knife.

"I tell him you need time. I haven't told him about Angelo. That's for you to tell."

I jab the knife into the steak. I saw off pieces.

"It's not fair to him," Teri says. "You're not being fair to him."

Hev puts a hand on Teri's arm. She's staring at her. It's a look I would give.

Teri frowns at the table. Her hand takes hold of the gold cross again.

I shovel a bite of steak into my mouth. I don't want to say anything. If I do, it won't be good.

Teri pulls her purse toward her. She takes out five twenties. Lays them on the table. It's way too much for the steak and plantains.

"I know it's your choice. But he gives me money. Makes me promise to use it on you. For you."

I stop chewing. I want to spit the meat into my napkin.

"Does he know?" I say, my mouth still full.

"Like I said, I haven't told him about the baby. But he's not stupid, Mari. He knows something's up. He knows you're not staying with your abuela no more. He knows you're skipping class. He's worried about you."

I grab my glass of juice, force myself to swallow. If he's so worried, he could find me. He could tell me that himself. I know I told him to leave me alone. But that was over a month ago.

I look at the food on my plate. It's getting cold. It doesn't look or taste good anymore.

Teri and Hev are both watching me. Teri's chin is jutted out a little. Her hands are back under her legs. Hev is looking at me like she's trying to tell me something. Like she's begging me to listen to what she can't say right now.

Teri offered to pay. But really it's Bertie who's paying. I don't want to eat food from Skinner's plate.

I should scream at Teri. For tricking me. For taking Bertie's side against me.

Angelo kicks. Hard. I gasp and my hand goes to my waist.

"You okay?" Hev is on her feet. She's reaching across the table for me.

Teri's crying again. But it's just tears. She's making no noise.

"I'm fine," I say. I lift half my mouth, give them a smile like Doc's. One that says *I'm a rock star and everything's gonna be cool even though you're freaking out over there.*

I make myself eat the steak. I make myself not scream, not talk. Because it's what Angelo needs.

I did what I came to do. I told my girls. That's all I'm going to do. That and take care of Angelo.

It's been three weeks since daylight savings. But it's still dark when we stumble up the steps of school. Bet the sun, still hot and toasty in his bed, hasn't even thought about the East River. It's too quiet without all the students. There's just a distant police siren and the shrill brake of a paper truck stopping at the bodega across the street. First period don't start for another forty minutes, but Heavenly wants the time on the sewing machines in home ec. She's been making Jo-jo something. Says it's his Christmas gift. She won't tell me what it is. Normally, I'd be flaming she's not sharing. But I've been so tired lately, since I barely been sleeping. I keep waking up. When I'm sure everyone else is still out cold, I get up, pull my blankets from the floor, and head into Heavenly's mama's kitchen. She's got a window in there, a narrow one. With a view of the George Washington Bridge. You can see it better at night, all lit up, the black ribbon of river below. I borrow some of the hand lotion on the counter by the sink. I rub it over my belly as I whisper to Angelo, telling him how beautiful the bridge is, telling him I can't wait to show it to him when he's born.

"See ya at lunch?" Heavenly's backing down the school hallway. I can't get over how weird the hall looks empty like this.

"Maybe," I say. She knows she won't. I haven't been to the cafeteria in weeks. It's getting harder to hide this belly. It's why I didn't fight the idea of going to school so early. I've been pretty careful. I never take my coat off where people can see me. But mostly, I been hiding. In the library. Where Bertie never goes. Where no one who knows me would think to look. Plus, I get to catch up on my sleep. I cover my yawn with my coat sleeve. Today, it feels like I could nap for twelve hours straight.

The bar across the library entry doesn't open when I swipe my ID. I back up and read the sign. Says it opens at seven. Just like I thought. I try my ID again. And again. I duck under it—not easy with my big belly. I stomp over to the counter that's usually staffed by three teachers. 'Cause of the hour, there's only one there now. A black woman with gray hair and glasses and a name tag that says *Ms. Tayler* looks at me like she's never seen me before. She's wearing a dress that reminds me of Mother Goose. It's all bright-colored patchwork, knit together with stitches you can see.

"Card's not working." I flick it on the counter. The woman's humming to herself. I hate when folks do that. Don't she know that makes her seem psycho? As if the mismatched buttons zigging down her front—a yellow round one like Big Bird's egg, followed by a puke-green square one and a red oval one—weren't suspicious enough. Library Lady picks up the card and swipes it through her computer.

"Maribel Pujols?" she asks.

"Yup."

"Says you've been expelled. So you can't come in here." She smiles at me. Like this is good news.

"What?!" I glance to my space. I can't see it from here, but I know it's behind all those books, waiting for me.

"You've missed more than ten days of classes. They sent you warnings in the mail."

Mail. I wonder if Abuela even bothers opening the letters or if she just trashes them. She knows my cell number. She knows my friends' cell numbers. She could've tried calling or texting. Could have done me the decency of letting me know what was going down.

I go to snatch my ID card back, but Psycho Library Lady holds it out of reach.

"Sorry. I have to keep this. When the admin offices open at eight, you need to go get this all figured out." With her other hand, she unbuttons and rebuttons the Big Bird egg. I look away. I don't want to know what kind of bra she's got hiding under there.

I gather my coat around me and hunch forward, trying not to

look too much like a pregnant lady. If I'd known about the ten-day rule, I would've gone to class. But I'm not going into some office and begging for a second chance.

"Okay. I'll go to the offices," I lie. "But can you at least let me wait in here?" I lean back. Let my coat fall open. Hopefully, this Ms. Tayler won't be here all day. Hopefully, she's got some other class to teach. Hopefully, it's not Hev's home ec class or Jo-jo's gonna have an interesting Christmas.

Tayler eyes my fat stomach then glances at the entrance. She taps my ID into a little box and lifts a padded shoulder. "Go." She's staring down her nose through her glasses at the file box. She flicks her hand at me. Toward where my desk is hiding. "Just can't take any books out. Not until you're all sorted."

I give her my practiced smile. When I get to my desk, I look at the books I've stacked around it. I pick one that's kinda thin, not too heavy. I peel the security sticker off and press it to the underside of the table next to me. I slide the book into my bag, put my bag on the desk, put my head on my bag. After my nap, I'm outta here. They can kiss my pregnant ass good-bye.

# THIRTY-FIVE WEEKS

It's too early for me to be out. Darker even than when Heavenly dragged me to school that other morning. But Destiny wakes painful early. She can't see me sleeping on the floor. Five-year-olds can't keep secrets.

I huddle inside a blue puff coat that's zipped all the way up. Carlos's coat. I lifted it from his locker when I left the library that day I found out I was expelled. *Pariguayo.* He shouldn't have threatened me. His locker wasn't even locked. Dipshit. Why does he think they call it a *locker*?

My shoes mark the snow dust on the sidewalks. My breath is a white cloud. But I'm warm. In this coat. Plus I've got a heater on the inside.

Some days, I walk for a few hours. Sit in Dunkin' Donuts and drink ten-cent cups of hot water with milk. Walk some more 'til the library opens up. The one on St. Nicholas closes late Monday and Wednesday, so I hang out there. On days when Heavenly doesn't need her unlimited, I ride the buses or the subways. It gives me a place to sit out of the cold. I like the bus. I look out the windows, watch folks hurry by, bags loaded up, heads ducked. Watch dogs sniff each other and piss on steps and hydrants and trees. Feel neon signs blink words like PIZZA and BAR and COFFEE into the back of my brain. Watch mamas with strollers pull bundled-up children like balloons behind them on the sidewalk. But Angelo, he likes the subway best. He gets all quiet, listening to the *rumble-jumble* of the wheels on the tracks, the shouts of the riders. "Move in!" "Hold that door!" The rhythm and the swaying, the jerks and screeching stops? He loves all that. Puts him to sleep like nothing else can.

Today, I'm thinking the library. But it don't open 'til ten. Never thought I'd spend so much time with so many books. I've even started reading some. Mostly to Angelo. He likes picture books best. Our favorite is that one about the baby bird who falls from the nest and goes around thinking everything it sees is its mama. And they all say, no, we're not your mama, and it's kinda sad, but then, finally, the real mama comes back.

The sun hits the buildings. Yellow-gold light reflects off hundreds of windows. The sidewalks lighten enough for me to go in the park. Won't do that when it's pitch out. I'm not that crazy.

I take hold of the staircase railing. Cold metal bites through the holes in my gloves. I slip on the bottom step. Frost on stone is like butter in a baking pan. But I don't fall 'cause I'm holding on real good.

The trees look cold without their leaves. But they don't complain. They watch over the asphalt pathways that fork and weave and twist like their own bare branches.

Feet pound behind me. Guys in sweats and cleats swarm, talking, joking in Spanish. Mexicans. I can tell from their accents. Soccer. They're going to play soccer. They head for the field. But one, then two more, stop. They turn to me.

"*Órale, ¿qué haces aquí?* What are you doing here, pretty thing?"

I shove my hands in my pockets, lift my chin. "None of your business." I sass it back.

The two who didn't speak laugh and punch the one who did in the arm. "Eh, Ernesto, *que pegue tienes con las mujeres.* You're such a ladies' man."

Ernesto grins a mouth full of gold teeth. He's new to New York. Or hasn't made enough yet to replace them.

"*Una mujer tan guapa no debe estar aquí tan sola.* A good looking girl like you shouldn't be here all alone."

I yell at him, "*¡Vete pa'l carajo!*"

One whistles. "*¿La blanquita habla español? ¿Dominicana, eh?*" I'm used to this. Unless I'm standing with my girls, folks don't assume I know Spanish.

I turn and walk away.

"*¿Mande? ¿Qué me dijiste?* What did you say?" Swear words

are different in each country, but he knows what I meant. Even if he pretends he doesn't.

Gold Teeth takes my sleeve.

The wind whistles at us. The giant trees bend and hiss.

My pulse is singing in my ear. He is not allowed to touch me. I shrug him off. I whirl around, fist high. I get him in the chest. His coat is thick. The punch barely reaches him.

He laughs. He takes my arm again. His friend takes my other arm. They back me up against the stone wall.

*No.*

I twist around. Curse at them. *¡Chopos!* I kick. My shoe lands between Gold Teeth's thighs. He groans, drops my arm. Another one grabs me, hard. It hurts.

Gold Teeth straightens up. He undoes his pants.

My heart claws at my throat. *No. No! This is NOT going to happen.* Angelo. I have to keep Angelo safe. I kick out again, swearing louder.

He takes out his *güebo*. He starts to pee. In the snow by my feet. Drops of yellow hit my shoes.

I spit at him, hurl curses at his face.

His friends press me into the huge stone bricks. He steps forward. It's still in his hand.

"Are you too much of a coward to do it like a man?" I scream. "You need yo homies to hold me down?"

He stops. He grins and gestures to his friends to release me.

I duck and run, hands up under my belly.

My hood snaps back, choking me. He pulls me against him, presses himself into me. I can feel him, through the coat. I gag and stab him with my elbow. He grunts, releases my hood. I double over, stomp his foot on the bones. He yells and pushes me. I stumble. I fall forward. I cry out, thinking only about the baby. I wrench myself sideways, land on my hip. Hands pull me up, turn me around. Gold Teeth's face is in my face. His hand gropes for the bottom of my coat.

"*¿Te gusta peliar?* You like to fight?" He finds the coat zipper, tugs it up. My coat opens like a Ziploc bag.

"No!" I scream. He slaps the side of my mouth.

Bodies come between us.

"What the hell, man?"

Gold Teeth is pulled away from me. Someone punches his face. He lets me go. I fall. On my butt. I'm shivering. My hands find my stomach, press into it. *The baby, the baby.* Is he ok? I can't feel him move.

Soccer guys surround me. They push the two that held me down against the wall, hands on their necks, holding them. Someone is punching Gold Teeth again. And again. Until he doesn't get up.

Punching Man turns, shoulders slumped, fists bloody. Sweat

drips from his low hairline. "Mari?" he says. "Oh my god, it *is* you."

Toto. It's Toto. He steps toward me. "Are you okay?" He stops. "You pregnant? But I thought . . ."

Abuela didn't tell him.

He heaves a breath in. He's staring at the ground, blinking hard. He's holding out his arm, as if he's thinking of punching Gold Teeth again. He looks back up at me. "Why did you leave?" he asks.

I shake my head. My face is wet and numb. "Because she didn't want him. Because he's not perfect." *Because she didn't want me. Because I'm not perfect.*

My hands slide across my belly feeling for the baby. I don't feel anything.

I close my eyes. I'm still shivering. Maybe I'm sobbing.

I feel a little kick against my finger.

Toto rubs a hand over his face. "She said you left. I figured you upset. Because of *el aborto.* I figured you with Bertie. He said he'd take care of you." His hair sticks up like clumps of wet fur. "I didn't know you still with the baby." He turns to Gold Teeth, sinks his cleat in his side. "*¡Culero!* She's fuckin' pregnant!"

Hands help me up, hold me, testing to see if I can stand. I can stand. I'm standing real strong now.

"So he's your friend, huh? Nice friends, Toto. Real nice.

I hope he's legal, because if he's not, he's going right back to where he came from after I tell the cops all about how he tried to RAPE A PREGNANT LADY!"

"He no do that. He just trying to scare you," one of the other guys says.

"You need a doctor." Toto's standing real close. He doesn't let me get near Gold Teeth. I'm ready to punch and smash and bite and spit all over again. Angelo's moving now, kicking away as if he's trying to get at Gold Teeth, too.

"Forget this guy. No more fighting, Mari. You need to go to the hospital." Toto reaches for my face. I jerk back.

"No." I shrug off the hands on my arms even though it hurts. "Baby's fine. He's kicking like crazy." Toto watches my hand as I circle my belly.

"I can go with you," he says.

I step away from him, from them, from this stupid park and their stupid soccer game. My right hip hurts like hell and my knee's all banged up. "I'll go. By myself."

I head up the ramp, trying not to hobble like an injured person. Don't really care anymore if I look like a pregnant person.

The trees are all quiet again. The wind's gone flat. I press my palm into the iron rail, squeeze my fingers around its coldness. I will not let myself fall.

"Mari?" Toto calls after me. "You gonna go to the cops?"

I eye him, look at the rest of the guys. Some of them look worried. I bet a lot aren't legal. Gold Teeth is still down. His head is back, eyes closed, mouth bloody.

"You gonna tell Carmen?" I ask. I don't want Abuela to know about this. I'm already a disgrace. No need to hammer it in.

Toto looks surprised. Before he can say what I'm afraid he's gonna, I add, "I'm fine where I'm staying. I'm not coming back. I won't tell *la hada* about your *friends* if you don't tell Carmen."

I turn my back on them and head to the street. The guys are murmuring. I don't want to know what they're murmuring about.

I sit in the waiting room. I don't have an appointment today, but I said I'd go to the doctor. Don't know why I didn't think of coming to hang out here before. It's better than the library. Clean, comfy sofas all done up with matching cushions. Views of the Hudson. People wait here all day, going in and out of appointments. I totally fit in, seeing as I'm pregnant. Don't matter my age. No one here's gonna ask me why I'm not at school. And there's food.

I put down the preggo magazine I'm reading. I stand, slowly, and stretch my arm. My back and shoulder ache. I'm gonna be bruised all up and down to Sunday. I take baby steps to the fridge for another juice. Swipe my fourth pack of cookies. Head back for the chair in the corner, the one behind the column where no one can see me.

"Ms. Pujols?"

*Coño.* The lady at the front desk saw me. I've been here so much, she knows me. I make eye contact but don't say nothing.

"Who are you seeing today?"

"Dr. Love." I say it without thinking.

Front Desk Lady's eyebrows scrunch up. "He usually sees patients up here on Mondays and Thursdays. Are you sure you have the date correct?"

*Coño.* And *coño.* Now I'm gonna have to go. That's what I get for being greedy. But Angelo really likes the cookies and juice. I sling on my coat. Pain cuts up my side, making my eyes water. I don't want to go back to the library. I just want to stay here. Where I can sit and be warm and not move for a while.

"Hold on, honey. Let me page Dr. Love for you. You don't look so good—if you don't mind me saying."

I hate when people feel sorry for me. Plus, I don't want to see Doc. Not like this.

I head for the bathroom still not looking at Front Desk Lady. I try to wash dirt off my cheek. It doesn't come off. 'Cause it's not dirt.

I slip out of the bathroom, planning to head down the hall for the back exit. But Doc is here. Waiting for me.

He's smiling. His usual. It only takes a second for shock to slam his smile to the side.

"Mari? What happened?" His lips flatten. His fingers curl. It makes me think of claws. I've never seen angry lion before.

I look at my feet. "Nothing," I choke out. *I will not cry. I will not cry.*

"Stephanie, is 1202 available?" Doc calls over to Front Desk Lady. She answers and he takes my arm. I try not to wince. He notices and lets go.

"Mari." He whispers it, like a scolding. Then, in his regular doctor voice he says, "Follow me."

He shuts the door behind us. Out of habit, I turn to the exam bed. It's way high.

"Talk to me," he orders. "I knew something must be wrong. You never mix up your appointments."

I lean against the table. No way I can climb up with my knee all busted.

"Who did this to you?" Doc crosses his arms. He studies me, all outraged and suspicious.

Is it crazy that I want him to touch me? That I want to feel the weight of his hand on my shoulder? I imagine him doing it. I imagine leaning into him instead of the table. I imagine telling him. Telling him everything that's happened. He would say it's okay. He would say I'm safe now.

I don't say nothing. I go to clench the exam bed but stop because the paper crackles too loudly.

Doc shakes his head. He takes a chair and pulls it close. He sighs. "Did you fall?" His voice is quieter now.

I nod.

"Can you feel the baby moving?"

I nod. I close my eyes and grit my teeth.

He leans back. His chair rolls a few inches away from me. "That's good. But let's just check by ultrasound to be sure. Hop up." He hands me a sheet and powers on the machine. While he's turned away, I try to pull myself onto the table.

He turns back too quick. "Oh, Mari." He says it like I let him down. His gold eyes track me behind doctor glasses. He leans over and takes the control for the bed. He lowers it as low as it can go. So I don't have to climb. I sit and pull my legs up.

"You can't keep doing this to yourself," he says, turning back to the machine. "You have someone else to think of now."

I try to figure what he means. Doing what? I thought I'd been doing a good job of coming to all my doctors' meetings. Eating the right things. Drinking the right things. Finding a warm place for us to sleep. I've been doing the best I can.

Behind him, my name is white on the black screen. The cursor blinks at the end of a number, where he left off typing.

My number. The one that has all my records for this hospital.

"No more fighting, okay?" His mouth is tense, like's he's trying not to growl. He drapes the sheet over me. He hits the button to raise the bed.

He read about them. He must have. Three ER visits over two years. Stitches. A broken hand. Stitches again. I never ratted on nobody. Didn't want trouble for Heavenly or her mama. Always said it was from fights at school. Other girls getting at my man or taking my stuff. Wasn't true 'til the day that boyfriend left Heavenly's mama for good. But fighting other girls never landed me in emergency. Girls are smarter. We know when to jump out of the way.

Sometimes a lie is easier to believe than the truth. This is one of those sometimes.

I did it for Heavenly. I've done it for Yaz and Teri, too. Someone messes with my tribe, they mess with me. I'm small, but I can be mean. Real mean. Everybody knows that.

Doc squirts on the jelly. He goes through the list of questions he always asks. About pee and weight gain. He lays the wand on me, gentle, so I don't feel it. And there's Angelo. I see his little head for a second before Doc zooms in on his chest. Angelo's heart looks strong to me. Doc strikes a bunch of buttons, his hand moving over the keyboard faster even than Heavenly's when she's texting. The sound of my baby's heart comes on loud. It sounds strong.

I close my eyes. I'm not going to tell Doc he's wrong. What he thinks happened is better than what really did. I don't care what Doc believes. I know there's someone else to think about now. That's why I'm doing all this. My baby's heart may be ruined, but as long as he's got a chance, I'm gonna fight. 'Cause that's what I've always done.

Angelo moves and I feel it. He loves me. Even if I'm mean. Even if I'm a fighter. He's not going to leave me neither. I'm not gonna let him.

# THIRTY-SIX WEEKS

The train rockets into a curve. *Clackety-clack, clackety-clack.* My butt slides along the seat. I clutch the armrest to keep from sliding more. My other hand checks my pocket for Heavenly's unlimited. I've never taken it out of the city before. I feel again to make sure it's there.

We just left Dobbs Ferry. Six more stops. I've memorized them all. The names are weird. Make me think of white folks swinging golf clubs—Glenwood, Irvington, Philipse Manor. Who was Philip anyway? And Dobbs? Must have had a freakin' big ferry if the whole town was named after it.

We go around another bend at full speed. The tips of my fingers whiten against the brown vinyl. I like the subway better.

It's cold out. Arctic effect or some *vaina* like that. Just in time for the holidays. Chunks of ice block up the Hudson, piling over one another. Good day to be inside. Hardly nobody out. Only cars. Waiting behind flashing lights. Waiting for the train to pass.

My arms rest on my big belly. Angelo's kicks are so strong, I don't need my hands to feel them no more. Even in my sleep, this boy wakes me. After Christmas, Doc's gonna give me a date for that C-section. I can hardly wait. I want to meet Angelo. See him with my own eyes. Hold him in my arms. I'd be lying if I said I wasn't nervous. Nervous about having him taken away from me. Nervous about what will happen to him. About what will happen to us.

The conductor calls for Ardsley-on-Hudson. I close my eyes. Five more stops. Doc told me I had to think of others besides myself. So I got to thinking about how Papi hasn't had any visits from me ever. Because Abuela'd never take me. I know she said he don't want visits. But maybe he'll feel different now that I'm grown. Maybe I should've written him. Told him I was coming. Abuela was the one who always sent our letters. But I could've looked up the address. Just as I looked up how to get there and checked to make sure they'd let me in. Having Angelo makes me an emancipated minor. So it don't matter that I'm not yet eighteen. I wiggle in my seat. Try and find a position that doesn't make my butt fall asleep. I'm nervous, but it feels good to be nervous about something that's not Angelo.

Last time Papi saw me I was three. According to Abuela. I don't look like no three-year-old no more. Papi shouldn't be too surprised by my state though. I wrote about Angelo. Just like I told Yaz. Didn't tell him about Angelo's heart until that last letter, which he probably didn't get. I doubt Abuela sent it. I didn't want to tell him before. He has enough to be depressed about being stuck in there because his crap lawyer made him confess to doing stuff and selling stuff that a whole lot of other fools were doing with him.

But Angelo's excited to meet his abuelito. I know he is.

"Next stop, miss."

I sit forward, watch Ticket Man shuffle down the aisle. My stub's in his hands. I reach for my unlimited, mad I dozed off. I try not to think about how much the ticket cost. Or about the ring of Papi's I pawned to make the fare. Abuela had given it to me a while ago. It's not like it wasn't mine. But I was hoping to save it. Maybe give it to Angelo one day.

The train slows, like it's catching its breath. We pass through a tunnel of concrete walls and barbed wire. Bridges swoop by overhead. Papi's in there. Somewhere.

Winter air circles my neck, slaps my cheeks as we get off. There are a couple of taxis, but Angelo and I are gonna walk. I duck my head into my coat—Carlos's coat. I keep the river to my right. Pretty soon, the concrete walls and barbed wire come back into view. I walk, not stopping 'til I'm standing in line at a window, giving my papi's name to the woman behind the glass.

"ID, young lady."

I hand over my NYC ID card along with the note from the hospital social worker. Turns out she was good for something after all. I add a picture of Angelo for good measure.

"I'm an emancipated minor." I open my coat to show her.

Her baggy eyes almost close as she holds the letter at arm's length. Her mouth moves as she reads. Clumps of coral lipstick jump from her lower to her upper lip. She gets on the phone. Someone else comes into the booth. They talk. He looks at my papers. He looks at me. When he leaves, her microphone voice says, "Wait over there."

Angelo and I sit on a bench. The line of visitors is crazy. It's Christmas Eve, so I didn't expect different. It's perfect, really. This way, Angelo and I get to spend part of Christmas with my family. We don't have to force our sorry selves off on anyone else's family. Not that Heavenly and Teri didn't offer.

The line is almost gone when a door off to the side opens. A man in a uniform comes over.

"Miss Pujols?" he asks.

I stand up. It takes me a few seconds. I fist my hands, getting ready to argue, but all he says is, "Come with me."

Twenty minutes later, after going through security checks and locking away my sweater and coat, I sit in a room. It's just like on TV. There's a desk with a phone. I touch the scratches on the plexiglass in front of me, wondering how they got there. Maybe it's old. Back from when they let you keep stuff like pens and keys in your pockets.

Next to me is a big black man. He's talking to somebody on

the other side who has to be his brother because he's just as big and black. There's a tattoo on his neck. Signs say you can't wear anything gang-related, but there's nothing to be done about tattoos, I guess. The woman on my left reminds me of Bertie's mama. Her hands are trembling something fierce. Maybe it's because she's a junkie not used to going so long without a hit. Maybe it's because she's nervous.

I take my hands from my belly and sit on them.

A door opens. Must be for her. She's been waiting longer than me. And the skinny black dude that comes toward us looks nothing like my papi. He walks with a lurch. Like something long ago got broke in his legs and never got fixed. He's got no hair. Whether it was shaved off, pulled out, or fell out, I can't tell. But I'm staring trying to figure it out.

He stops in front of me, squints at the number written on the desk. The chair shrieks when he pulls it out. Even through the glass I hear it. The woman beside me jumps. Baldy's grinning, looking between the two of us. He's got a gap between his front teeth. It's so wide, a whole other tooth could fit in it. He leans over, squints at her number, shakes his head. He lowers himself into the chair in front of me.

Real quick, he scrapes the chair forward, looking at my neighbor. She jumps again and he laughs. His knees bow wide-open. The jumpsuit bags around his legs, making them look like sticks. His fingers drum the inside of his thighs. He's still grinning. He catches my eye and runs his tongue over his lip.

There must be some mistake. This man looks nothing like the boy in Abuela's photo frame.

I take a hand out from under my butt. I grab the phone. He does the same.

"You coming to claim something, baby? 'Cause I be in here nine long years. No way I be responsible fo' that." He puckers and blows a kiss to my belly.

"Are you Luis Pujols?"

"*Sí*," he answers, cracking his jaw.

There's probably more than one Luis Pujols at Sing Sing. The DR is filled with Pujols.

"Luis Francesco Echevarría Pujols?"

"*Sí, soy yo.*" He leans back. "The one and only." He runs a hand over his head, slowly, from forehead to neck. Like there's still hair there. His eyes dart to my neighbor. She's adjusting her bra. His hand comes back to his thigh. His leg sways open.

This can't be right. Angelo doesn't move. He doesn't believe it either.

Nine years. He said nine years. But the last time he saw me was . . .

"*¿Quién eres?*" he says. "Who are you? Not that I care too

much. I'll take a visit from a pretty white girl any day, even if she is knocked up."

I swallow and look at my belly. I swallow again, looking for anger, hoping to feel something other than the flat emptiness of disappointment.

"Mari." My throat is dry.

"Eh?" He shifts forward, rests his head on the hand holding the phone. He traces a heart on the plexiglass between us. He winks at me.

I suck in a breath. I hold my mouth closed until I can speak. I feel like I'm going to be sick. "Maribel Lucy Pujols."

His face is still as he looks at me. No more lip-licking. No more grinning winks. I'm looking, too. I'm looking real hard. For something of me in there. I don't see nothing.

"*Coño, hijo de la porra.*" His arm slams the wall. "What kind of fucking shit joke is this?" He shoots up. He mutters something that may be my mama's name. He jabs a finger at me. "You no supposed to be here. She made me a promise." He chucks the phone. It smacks the glass in front of my face and hits the desk. The woman next to me shrieks.

"Why? Why?" I repeat it, even though I don't know what I want to say. Even though his phone is hanging, maybe on the ground, the curls of the cord pulled straight. Even though he's walking away. Pounding on the door.

*Why do you look so different?*

*Why did you never come to see me, when I was a kid, before you got locked up?* A three-year-old wouldn't remember her papi. But a six-year-old would.

*Why didn't you read my letters?* Because I know he didn't. That man wouldn't have. I know guys like him. Guys like Heavenly's mother's boyfriend. I had believed my papi wasn't one of them.

A guard opens the door. My papi is walking through it. He stops. He looks over his shoulder at me. He hand-chops the air like he's hacking a piece of meat. He says something. I can't hear him. But I see his lips move.

*I never wanted you. You are nothing to me.*

Mari, is that you?" Mrs. Rodriguez shouts at me from the mail room. I ignore her and duck into the elevator.

The whole way back, I kept thinking about my papi. The one in my letters. Not the one in Sing Sing.

Toto's shoes, but not Abuela's, are on the mat. It smells like Christmas in the apartment, all piney and peppermint. Gato comes out from under the tree. Pine needles are stuck in his fur. He rubs them off on my legs. The TV's on in Abuela's room, the sound real loud.

I pick up the shiny metal frame that's in the living room. The one on the chipped plaster mantel above a bricked-in fireplace. I stare at the picture that's supposed to be my father. A boy stares back at me. He looks more like Bertie than the man I just met. Espresso skin. Freckles sprinkled like sand blown over a beach towel. Hazel eyes squinting in a smile. His grin has the same wide gap between his two front teeth. As if he'd had three front teeth and one fell out. Or got knocked out.

*I never wanted you.*

I put the picture back. Facedown. I go to my room. I toss a

whole bunch of Toto's stuff off my bed, take hold of the head-board, and heave it away from the wall. I put a hand on my throat. My stomach hurts. I still feel like puking. I touch behind the headboard for the break in the plaster. The one I made with my foot when I caught Toto in here two summers ago. I find it. Inside are the envelopes.

I open them, read the letters. I know what they say. I've read them so much I've memorized them. *Cariño. Nenita. Princesa. My only daughter. I think of you always. I love you. I am the only one who loves you. More than life itself. Your Papi.*

I'm not reading for the words. I'm reading for the handwrit-ing.

Back in the kitchen, I grab papers off the counter. Bills, catalogs. Abuela's scrawl is on the edge of one. I hold Papi's letter to it.

*Carajo.* I am a fool. A real, live fool.

I stuff the letters in the garbage.

I'm out the door so fast, no one hears me. Not even Mrs. Rodriguez.

I can barely breathe as I come up from the subway. It's 4:25 and night already. The air is so cold, it burns on the way in. But I gulp it. And think about water. And not yuking.

There's a shadow of a person on Heavenly's stoop. It's too short to be her, so I stop. The person walks toward me. I step back. I think of turning and running. But I know I can't. Not with this baby. Not when everything inside me hurts so bad.

"Mari? Is that you?"

For a second, I'm dreaming. "Mrs. Rodriguez?" I say, not realizing how stupid that sounds.

"No." Yaz. It's Yaz. She comes closer. Her hand lifts. She does her stupid side-to-side wave. The same one she's done ever since we were kids.

"Wow. You got big," she says. She widens her eyes as if to make it funny. She chews her lip as I say nothing.

"Listen," she starts and stops. "Hey—*¿estás bien?* Why are you breathing like that?"

I open my mouth to ask, *Breathing like what?* I hurl onto the sidewalk.

Yaz jumps back. I hurl again. Soaking my shoes and my coat. Carlos's coat.

Yaz's arm takes mine. She holds me up. "Mari? Mari?" She's speaking like I can't hear her. "What's wrong? Tell me what's wrong!"

I shake my head. Yuke again. I can't stand. I can't be standing.

Yaz is yanking me up. Her phone is in her other hand. She's yelling into it.

Warmth spreads down my legs. Like I've pissed myself. It gushes again and again as I puke, emptying everything, all the hate, all the hope. Everything.

I find Yaz's fingers, grab on to them.

"I think my water broke."

The ambulance takes the corner fast. I retch into a plastic container. The medic holds it so it doesn't drop. My legs are wet and shivering. Warm liquid comes out of me in small bursts, soaking my seat.

*It's not time yet. It's not time yet.*

There's an IV in my arm. The oxygen mask is on top of my head. The medic keeps trying to put it over my nose and mouth, but I keep needing to puke.

*It's too early. It's too early.*

We stop. The back doors wrench open. Big guys with masks and gloves grab at the stretcher and haul me out. The green of their scrubs shows below their winter coats. Medic Man jumps down with us, his hand high with the IV bag. He's shouting, giving them information. But I'm looking for Yaz. They left her on the street. She promised to meet me here.

They wheel me right through Emergency. We're on the elevators going up. A nurse meets us as the door opens, leads us through a waiting room, through another door.

"Yaz? Yaz?!" I shout. I don't see her.

"Shhh, it's okay. Just relax and sit back," the nurse says. "Does she speak English?" she asks Medic Man, looking at my chart. My name tells her I'm Dominican, even if my face doesn't. He nods to her.

"Of course I speak English, you stupid sack of sh—" I yuke again. Medic Man is good with that yellow plastic bin. He catches it. Only there's not much left. I'm puked out.

They bring me to an area that looks like the ER, only everyone here is pregnant. Two fancy white chicks with diamond studs and blond blowouts stare at me over their bellies. They look way more pregnant than I do. Their Brooks Brothers coat-and-tie husbands pull their curtains closed as we go by. I'm still retching, but nothing's coming up. In between retches, I'm yelling—for Yaz, for Doc. They need to get Doc. If Angelo's coming, they need to get ready.

"I'm sorry, we don't have anyone named Dr. Love here. Was that your OB at your regular hospital?" The nurse, whose skin color is the same as Abuela's but she wears a bindi on her forehead, smiles at me like she's being helpful. I want to bite that bindi off and slap her 'til she gets some sense.

"This is my regular hospital! Look in my—" Medic Man is gone, so I puke on the floor. I guess there was something left.

"Sujita!" someone at the desk calls out to her. "Read off the patient's number so I can put her on the board."

Nurse Nimwit grabs my wrist for the bracelet Medic Man put on me in the elevator. She reads out the number.

"Okay, okay, relax, relax," she says. "I will give you some medicine for the vomiting, and then we will get you out of these clothes and into a gown. Then the doctor can come examine you. Do you know your due date, missy?"

"You need. To call. My doctor. Dr. Love." I'm lying back. I'm concentrating on breathing. The pain in my stomach is getting worse.

"Yes, yes, after Dr. Simon checks you, she will call the referring doctor to update him or her. Now what is your due date?"

I would punch her if I had any strength. "January twenty-fifth."

She takes a card out of her pocket. "Let's see, that makes you thirty-six weeks. Not so bad for around here. Maybe an early Christmas present, right?"

I want to scratch that dumb smile off her face. "You don't understand. My baby. He's sick. He needs special attention. You have to tell them. They have to get ready for him."

"Many of the babies are sick, missy. They wouldn't be here otherwise. And we are always ready. You just rest while I go find the doctor." She pats my shoulder.

The pain comes. I tuck up as much as I can. I turn to one side. Then the other. I stretch my legs, kick off the blanket. I'm hot. Too hot.

Someone peels off my old clothes. They move me from the stretcher to a bed.

Nurse Nimwit comes back with a machine. She tries to wrap belts around my waist. She says it's to check Angelo's heartbeat. I try to stay still—I want to hear it, too—but I can't. I turn. I puke over the other side.

"There, there," the nurse says, sliding a disc first one way and then the other over my belly. No sound comes on. "Oh, it looks like you are having a contraction now. We have to wait for the contraction to finish before listening for the heartbeat." Her smile is so limp it looks like it may fall off her face. Still no heartbeat sounds. My fingers twist the sheet. I bite off my groan. I don't want to show them how much it hurts.

"Is this Ms. Pujols?" A lady doctor comes behind the curtains. The nurse nods. "I'm Dr. Simon. I need to exam you, please." She asks questions as she does it. When did my water break? Have I been sick? Have I eaten anything I'm not supposed to or traveled out of the country?

"Please," I say. "Call Dr. Love. He's my baby's doctor. He needs to know."

"She's eight and zero. This baby is coming," she says to the nurse. "Get neonatology down here. I'm sorry, Ms. Pujols. Is Dr. Love an OB?"

I stiffen. Another wave of pain. The girl doc repeats her

question. But I can't talk. I squirm sideways, clenching my jaw. I'm heaving for breath. Panting like a dog. But I don't care. I'm not gonna scream like those other ladies.

Lady Doc doesn't wait. She's almost out the curtains when I gasp, "Heart."

"Excuse me?" She turns. "Did you say 'heart'?"

I nod. My breathing is coming back. The pain is fading. "The baby. He has congenital heart disease. HLHS. Restricted foramen." I pant it at her, using the words I heard Doc say to Goldie. "Dr. Love. He knows. Talk to him."

# BIRTH DAY

I need pediatric cardiology on the line. NOW! Where is neonatology? Call Dr. Chai. He's going to want to be here for his. How come the patient's not on our list?" Lady Doc is shouting.

"She's too early. She's only thirty-six and zero. She wouldn't hit the list until next week," someone says.

The curtains rip open. Doctors and nurses circle me. They wheel me out, down the hall, into a bigger room.

"Ms. Pujols, I'm Dr. Singh from neonatology."

"Ms. Pujols, I'm Dr. Chai from maternal fetal medicine."

"Ms. Pujols, I'm Dr. Tarfield from anesthesiology."

They all look the same in their blue outfits.

A machine is rolled next to me. It's different from the one Doc uses, but it has a wand.

"Ms. Pujols, I'm Dr. Gupta from pediatric cardiology."

*No.* I shake my head. She is not my baby's heart doctor. She's petite, and dark-haired, and a girl. And she has an accent. I do not trust people with accents.

"Where's Dr. Love?" They've given me medicine, and my words don't sound right.

"Dr. Love is not here tonight. He has the Christmas holiday off. I am the on-call fellow. But Dr. Stevenson is my attending. You met her in the beginning, remember? Her name is on your first report."

Not her. Anyone but her. I can only deal with Pudgy Purple if Doc is here.

The petite doctor makes a sound like water trickling over pieces of glass. Is she giggling?!

"You should have used Dr. Stevenson's name when you arrived." She chuckles. It makes me want to hit her. "Everyone knows Dr. Stevenson. She's been here *forever*. But Joshua and I, we just joined the fetal service this year. Not all the OB doctors and nurses know us yet. So that is why there was a bit of a holdup."

Joshua. That's Dr. Love's first name. It's written on the reports.

I don't care that Dr. Love is young. I don't care that he's been doing this fetal work for only a year. He's the best doctor I've ever had. And he cares about me and Angelo.

I gasp as pain punches my gut. "Call Dr. Love." He doesn't know. If he did, he would be here. He promised he would be here.

"I'm sorry, I know it is hard. It seems like you have bonded with him." Petite Doc has the wand on me. She's looking at her screen. "I will do my best to fit his shoes."

I'm hyperventilating. Angelo bounces up and down on the screen on account of my breathing. *"Fill," not "fit,"* I want to scream it at her. It's the same type of slipup Abuela always makes.

"Unfortunately, I can't seem to get any good pictures at this point. The baby is very far down. He looks eager to come out! But we have the images from Dr. Love's scan last week that showed your baby is at moderate risk for pulmonary hypertension."

I grab at a bin and vomit. I don't understand what she's saying. I only understand Doc. He says it so I can understand.

"He's going to die?!" I'm afraid to ask it. But I'm also afraid not to.

"Hopefully not." She's being cheerful. She's trying to be nice. But I can't take it. Her attitude is like a lie. How will I know if her words are lies, too? And my face reading is all off. Everyone seems happy. Like they're smiling even when they're not. What did they give me? This is why I don't do drugs. Even when I'm in control, bad things happen.

"We've called in the team from the catheterization laboratory. They should be ready within a few hours. Do you think you can keep this baby inside you until then?"

She's asking me?!

"But it's too early. Dr. Love said—" I grunt and roll to the side. The pain comes again. A nurse sticks something into my IV.

"Tut-tut," Petite Doc says. "There is nothing we can do about that now. Dr. Love is right. It would be preferable for the baby to be born full-term. But we have to assess the situation we face and handle it." Another nurse moves her out of the way to give me a shot in my arm. I hardly feel it.

"Let us think of something positive." Petite Doc is still talking. I wish she'd shut up. "Now you will no longer need a cesarean section. So no scars. A positive, correct?"

I'd take a million scars if it meant things would be better for Angelo. If it meant Doc could be here.

"Are you finished? Can we get in here?" A man doctor asks.

"Oh yes. Certainly, Dr. Chai. Let me get out of your way. Ms. Pujols, I will see your baby in a little while. I will see you after we have attended to the baby. Do not dwell on the negative. Think only positive thoughts. Okay? Bye-bye for now. And good luck."

"Ms. Pujols." The man doctor is talking to me. He is very tall. I can't make out his face from down here. "Do you have someone special you want to be here with you?"

I'm sleepy. So sleepy. "Dr. Love. I need love."

Someone in the room snickers.

"I'm sorry, Ms. Pujols. I mean a family member. Is anyone here for you?"

I wait for him to stop swaying. He doesn't.

I want to go to sleep. The pain. It's coming again. But I don't care about it anymore.

"There's a Ms. Gonzalez in the waiting room. She's been asking for you. Is that who you would like with you?"

Yaz. "Yes," I say. I black out.

I'm screaming.

A cool hand holds mine. Charcoal-lined eyes stare at me above a blue mask.

"¡Dale, Mari! ¡Dale!"

I'm in a familiar room. It's like the room where they tried to take Angelo from me. A room I ran out of.

They're going to take him from me now. He's coming. I can feel it. I can't protect him anymore. It feels like giving up.

Someone yanks my leg. My knees are at my shoulders.

"Ms. Pujols, you need to help us. We can't do this without you." It's the voice of the tall doctor. The room is full of bodies. I don't know which is his.

"Mari, come on. You have to. You're almost there." The cool hand squeezes mine.

Pain rips me with its teeth.

I don't want to scream. I don't want to be here. I want to be in the dim room. Where it's quiet. With Doc. Where he can smile at me with his lion eyes. Where we can check in on Angelo. Where we can see he's safe.

"Push!"

Hands shove my knees higher.

"Ms. Pujols. Listen—do you hear that sound? That's your baby's heart rate. It's dropping. Your baby is in distress. He needs to come out."

I hear it. Frantic beeping. Then slow. Like it's going to stop.

"Push, Mari," Yaz says. "You have to."

The pain comes again. Ferocious pain. The pain is pissed.

I'm not ready. I'm not ready to let him go. He could die. He's the one who's supposed to love me. To take care of me. And I want him. I want him so bad. I always wanted him. He has to know that.

I don't push. It doesn't matter. The pain does it for me.

"*Ay, chichí,*" Yaz whispers.

The pain is gone.

A baby cries. A yowling of outrage.

"Mommy, take a look at your baby." The doctor holds him up. A nurse holds my head up.

He's tiny, and dark, and squirming. He's covered in muck and blood. He yowls again. He's pissed.

"Hi, Angelo," I whisper.

And I'm scared. Because I can't not love him. And he might leave me. Even if he doesn't want to.

I hold my arms out to take him even though they're shaking and weak.

"Okay, baby off to pediatrics." A waiting blue ghost takes Angelo.

"Wait," I croak. "Wait!" I shout. But my voice is dead.

Blue ghost zips out. Angelo's howls get fainter until I can't hear them no more.

My heart is clattering. It wants to run after Angelo.

"Let's get you cleaned up." The doctor is working on me.

"I want to hold him. Why can't I hold him?" I can't feel my legs. If I could, I would run after my baby. Snatch him back. Deck Blue Ghost in the face.

"Your baby is very sick, Ms. Pujols. The pediatricians are attending to him now."

But what if that's it? What if I never get to see him again?

Fingers push sweaty hair off my forehead.

"You did it, Mari. Amazing. You're my hero." Yaz's mask is around her neck. Purple glitter lipstick marks the white inside part of it.

I take a breath. I don't speak. All I'm thinking of is Angelo. How he's in some room. Maybe fighting to breathe.

How can I fight for him when I'm not even with him?

Yaz takes out her phone. "*Ay, ¡qué papi chulo!*" She shows me a pic of Angelo looking smudgy and angry. I didn't realize she took it.

I can't speak. Because I'm crying.

M s. Pujols?" Tall Doctor stands. "You're all set. Congratulations on your baby." He looks at the clock. "And merry Christmas."

It's 1:34 a.m. That means I did it. I held on for at least a few hours. All the doctors should have had time to get here.

A nurse helps me into a clean gown. They put me in a new bed and wheel me to another room. The hallway is real quiet. No babies crying.

Why hasn't anyone come to tell me what's going on with Angelo?

Yaz is still holding my hand.

A nurse comes in, introduces herself as Judy. She looks about as excited to be here as I am. I ask about Angelo, but she says I have to wait for the doctors. She doesn't know anything. She eyes Yaz and tells us my visitor can stay for only another twenty minutes. When she's gone, Yaz kicks off her shoes and lies down on the bed next to me. She offers me a piece of gum and takes out her phone.

We look at Angelo's picture.

"You believe you made that?" she asks me. Her breath is minty.

I shake my head. I run my hands over my belly. It's still pretty round. But it feels all empty.

Her phone buzzes from a text. It's from Heavenly. I grab the phone and scroll. There are about forty texts from Heavenly starting from six o'clock last night. There's a bunch from Teri, too. They came to the hospital and waited. Yaz was keeping them updated. They stayed 'til Angelo was born, but they were told they had to leave. Only one person was allowed back to visit me. No one can visit Angelo.

"Can I send it to them?" Yaz means the pic.

I nod, hand the phone back.

"Anyone else you want me to text? Bertie, maybe?" she asks.

Our eyes meet. *Does he know?*

She tilts her head and looks at the ceiling. *He knows.*

"Fine, go ahead." I sigh.

I had my reasons for hiding the secret of Angelo. Good reasons. I could deal with Hev and Ter. They didn't bother me much. They figured out real quick I didn't like talking about the baby. But there was no way I was gonna be dealing with crowds at school asking me why I didn't go through with it. Asking if I was scared. Asking what I was gonna do if my baby died. Like I said before, a girl pregs at school? Not news. A girl pregs with a baby that's got only half a heart? That news be *big*. Some of those *chicas*, they'd be all crying, mascara marking up their cheeks, pretending to feel sorry for me. I hate pity. But there'd be some who'd be glad about it. Thinking the *galla* got what she deserved. Part of me knows they'd be right. But still, I'd have to fight them. Because they'd be saying they're glad Angelo's gonna suffer. They'd be saying it's okay for a baby to suffer for something his mama did. And that's not right. That's not right at all. Even if that's what's gonna happen. I promised Angelo I wouldn't do any fighting that wasn't for him. That fighting would have been for me.

And then there's Bertie. I couldn't deal with those hazel eyes looking at me, asking what I done. I didn't want to be searching them for red. Wondering what he been up to and if it's good for him. I had to think of Angelo. There's only Angelo and me. Bertie didn't want Angelo. He doesn't get to ask me those questions anymore. Even if he's only saying them with his eyes.

"I didn't tell him." Yaz is typing and doesn't look up. "Just so you know it wasn't me this time."

I reach for the glass of crushed ice water by my bed. I take a small sip. I wince as it goes down. "Who told you?" I ask. 'Cause I feel like she knew before yesterday. I feel like that's why she was coming to check on me.

Yaz is still texting. She works her gum between her tongue and her teeth. "No one." She shakes her head. "I saw you. 'Bout a month ago by Reme's. From a block away, I could tell. You wasn't walking like yourself. You was waddling." She lets off playing with her gum to grin.

I wonder if that's how Bertie found out. Wonder if he was checking up on me. Wonder if he was trying to take care of me the way he told Toto he would.

"Hev and Teri texted back." Yaz leans on me so I can see her screen.

Teri texted congrats with a slew of smileys and a he's sooooo cute. Heavenly sent a picture of her mouth, teeth showing, shiny lips stretched wide.

"You know Bertie beat up Carlos?"

I shake my head and glance at the door. When is someone going to come and tell me how Angelo's doing? I press my hand to my belly. It's all crampy, like it's wondering where Angelo went, too.

"Teri and Hev didn't tell you?" Yaz pops her gum. "Yeah, I figured they wouldn't. I saw you was wearing Carlos's coat. He musta done something to piss you both off." Yaz snickers. Her phone buzzes. I glance at it, wondering if it's Bertie.

"Hev wants to come see him. And she wants to know who the godmother is."

I shift in the bed. Everything is sore. My legs still feel funny, like jelly legs. And I'm still so freakin' mad. If I weren't so wiped, I would be out of here. I'd be in the hallways, looking for doctors. For someone who could tell me what's going on with my baby.

"So can she come tomorrow—I mean today?" Yaz is looking at me. Waiting. She's excited about the baby. Excited we're friends again.

I shrug a yes. Yaz types. "How about the godmama? Who's it gonna be?"

Godmama? If the doctors fix him and I get my baby back, no one is going to take him away from me again. So they better not be thinking of taking him on any excursions. Not unless I'm going, too.

But if he's gonna have godmamas, he's gonna have three. "Teri, Heavenly, and you. Together."

Yaz keeps typing. She's trying not to smile too big. She's having trouble keeping the gum in her mouth. "I can't believe you had a baby on Christmas, Mar. That's like too perfect. Best Christmas present Bertie could ever give you. Way better than that necklace."

She's talking about the loopy chain with plastic papayas and mangos strung on it Bertie gave me that first year. It was from DR. Something his mama would've worn. Not me. But we'd only been official for a few months, so I didn't care much. It's not like he knew me well. Not like he knows me now.

I don't want to talk about Angelo like he's a present Bertie gave me. I made him. I kept him alive. He's more my son than Bertie's. Bertie didn't even want him. "I got to pee," I say instead. I try to lift my butt.

"You don't got to get up for that. You have a tube in." Yaz holds up a clear hose that's under my legs. Yellow liquid slides down the inside of it.

*Ewww. Gross.*

Yaz is watching me. She laughs. "I know, right?"

The door opens. A small woman comes in.

"Ms. Pujols?" She takes the blue cap off her head. Long strands of dark hair fall out. "Remember me? I am Dr. Gupta from pediatric cardiology. I'm here to give you an update on your baby."

FINALLY.

Petite Doc looks from me to Yaz and back again. She's not really smiling. But she's not frowning either.

"Tell us!" Yaz gives the bed a shake with her legs.

"I want to be sure it is okay to speak freely in front of your friend. Is this your girlfriend?" Petite Doc asks.

"Yeah, she's okay," I say.

Petite Doc looks real serious all of a sudden.

*Why does she look like that? What happened to Angelo?*

"Will you be coparenting the baby together?" she asks. "Mommy one and mommy two?" She points at each of us.

*What?! No.*

Yaz laughs. She flings her arms around my neck and makes smoochy sounds. "She thinks we're *pájaras!*"

I don't feel like laughing.

"She's my *friend*." I say it real slow since Petite Doc don't seem to understand too well.

Petite Doc looks confused. Maybe it's because Yaz is still trying to smooch me. "Well, may I speak in front of her?"

"YES!" Yaz and I shout it at the same time.

"We have confirmed everything that Dr. Love told you before. Including the critical obstruction. The baby is very sick. We are going to take him to the cath lab now. I need you to sign these papers to give us permission to do the procedure."

Yaz isn't joking any longer. She's sitting real quiet.

I bite the side of my tongue. I blink 'til I'm okay. "Is he breathing? Dr. Love said his lungs might be damaged."

"He's intubated on a ventilator. He needs us to relieve the obstruction in his heart."

Petite Doc goes through a long list of bad things that could happen to Angelo during the procedure. The most important one is that he might not make it, even if the procedure is successful. I sign the sheets. Like I have any other choice.

"Can I see him? Before he goes?" There's that feeling again. Like the emptiness inside me is growing.

Petite Doc makes a sad face. "Unfortunately not. He is too

sick. He is already down being prepped. Even if you did not sign, we would be going ahead with the procedure. As it is an emergency, we technically do not need your permission."

"Then why ask for it?!" I throw the papers at her. Why did she bother me? To tell me Angelo might die. As if I don't know that already.

"Ms. Pujols. I am very sorry your baby is sick. But please, do not punish the messenger. We are here to help." She stands and walks out.

"It'll be okay," Yaz says as the door clicks closed.

I glare at her. "You can't say that. You can't lie to me. Not ever again. Okay? If you do, that's it. We're done."

Yaz looks at me, her face real still. She nods.

Nurse Judy comes in. She points a crooked finger at Yaz in a way that reminds me of Abuela. I grind my teeth together.

"Guess I gotta go." Yaz stands, hikes her jeans up. I hand over her phone, glancing at the screen for a text that hasn't come. Yaz grabs her coat.

"Mari? I hope it'll be okay."

I nod, but I'm not looking at her.

"Call me in case . . . In case anything. I'll come back if you want. They won't be able to keep me away."

I nod again. I feel like only speaking nastiness. So I'm not going to say nothing.

I stay awake. I want to be awake in case something happens. At 5:45, someone comes in to check on me. An OB doc. She asks me if I have any pain, if I've gotten out of bed yet. She checks me and tells me to rest. She doesn't know anything about my baby.

At seven thirty, a big man in white scrubs brings me a tray of food. I'm starving but also nauseous from nerves. I try to sit up. I can't. I find the control, make the bed upright. I pull the table with the tray closer. Lumpy oatmeal, a rock-hard bagel, and a dish of icy pineapple. I make myself eat.

A nurse that's not Judy comes in. She takes out the pee tube and helps me to the bathroom. I take a shower. It's hot. So it should feel good. But I don't feel much 'cause I'm rushing, thinking about Angelo, thinking about how maybe one of the heart doctors is going to come update me but I'll be in here instead of out there. The nurse stands in the bathroom waiting for me. I think she's afraid I might fall. She gives me this weird underwear. It's all fishnet in the front and back but a diaper on the bottom. "For the blood," she says.

The clock says ten when I'm back in bed. The sheets and

blankets have been changed again. I want to know what's going on with Angelo. But I'm afraid to ask. I only want to hear if it's good.

I look for my phone. Maybe talking with Yaz or Heavenly or Teri would keep away bad thoughts. I use a clipboard to swing open the closet. There's a plastic bag at the bottom filled with my stuff. I get up real slow. I feel like a truck ran me over. I look in the bag. Carlos's coat is on top. It's pretty wrecked with puke and uterus water on it. My phone's in the pocket, but it's out of juice. I put it on the table, hoping Yaz or Heavenly or Teri will bring a charger. I find Heavenly's unlimited, too.

Back in bed, I pull up the covers and stare at the clock.

"Mari."

My hand's on my belly. I feel Angelo kick. I'm in the sonogram room. I must have fallen asleep while Doc was taking pictures.

"Mari, I'm sorry to wake you."

Doc is next to me, but he's on the wrong side. He's always only on my right. Why is he on my left?

"Congratulations on the birth. How do you feel?"

The clock on the wall says five. A new tray of food is on the counter by the sink. I push hair from my mouth. I start to yawn but stop myself.

"How's Angelo?" My voice cracks.

Doc looks for a chair. There's only the big lounger at the foot of the bed. He drags it closer and sits.

He looks different. He's in a sports coat. His hospital ID half hides behind an expensive-looking tie. Heavenly's catcall whispers in my head, "*Qué caché-caché.*"

I pull my gown more closed around me.

Doc's looking at his hands. He twists his wedding band around his finger. I don't want to think why he isn't answering my question.

"He's sick," he says. "Angelo's sick. But he's still with us."

"Did they do the procedure?" I stare at his ring. It's pure gold.

"Yes. The whole team came in. They were ready. They knew they'd have to answer to me if they weren't." He gives me half a smile. But it's not the rock-star smile. It's like he's worried what I might think of that. I believe him though. Those other docs who work with him probably were afraid of him. I remember how he looked when I showed up with all those cuts and bruises. Angry lion was scary. "It went well," Doc says. "A technical success. Which is amazing considering his size."

"His size?"

"He's small. Since he was born a few weeks early. Sometimes we can't do the catheterization on premature babies because our equipment is too large. But Angelo's bigger than most babies are at thirty-six weeks. You did a good job there, mama." He bumps my arm lightly with his elbow. "You got him as fat as you could."

I put my hand on my arm. Where his elbow touched it. I can't take credit for that. Heavenly—and Jo-jo—Teri's mama, they were the ones feeding me this whole time.

"But we're not in the clear yet. He still needs our help to breathe. He's on the breathing machine, the ventilator. We'll give him a couple of days to recover from the procedure. And then we have to do the first surgery."

"The Norwood."

He smiles. "Yes, the Norwood." He runs a hand over his head. The gold ring disappears in the golden strands of his hair. "Listen." He reaches out. His fingers touch mine. "I'm sorry. I'm sorry I wasn't here. I promised you I would be." He leans over his legs. His whole hand takes my hand. His skin is warm. And soft. "How are you doing?"

I'm staring down at the blanket. At his hand holding mine. My whole arm feels warm. And safe. *Angelo's not dead. He's sick, but I knew he would be.*

"Fine." I bite my lip to keep away tears.

"Have you seen him yet?"

I nod. "When he came out. They showed him to me."

"Would you like to see him again? I can take you to him."

I look at his face to make sure he's not teasing. Though he

should know me well enough to know that type of joke would earn him a jab in the shoulder.

His eyes are steady, more blue now than gold. No teasing. "Come on, I can bring you right now."

Doc opens the door. There's a wheelchair waiting. He helps me into it and pushes me down the hallway out to the elevators.

"You can go see Angelo whenever you want. The NICU is always open to parents and grandparents. You just can't sleep there. And until you're more mobile, your nurse will have to call Transport to take you."

"I thought that's why I have you?" I'm joking. But I wish I wasn't. I wish he could stay here the whole time Angelo has to.

"As long as I'm here, I'm happy to serve as your transport, madame." He bows and wheels me into the elevator.

We get out on the ninth floor. We're in the children's section. The walls, floors, and ceiling are all colored with shapes—stars and circles, triangles and squares.

"I want to warn you, Angelo looks different than he did yesterday. He has a tube in his nose. To help him breathe. He has two special IVs, one in his groin and one in the stump from his umbilical cord. To give him medicine and monitor his blood pressure."

Doc hits a metal panel in the wall. A light blue door swings open.

I've never been here before. To the NICU. I know it stands for neonatal intensive care unit. It's the place they put all the really sick new babies. I had an appointment for a visit, but it was going to be after New Year's. None of us knew Angelo would come so early.

It's quiet. I don't hear babies crying. Just machine sounds. And adults talking real soft. There are no individual rooms. The space is all open. There are nurses and doctors. And families. Lots of families. I can't hardly see the babies. There are plastic boxes on stands. The boxes have round doors in them. A nurse has her arm stuck through one of them. But I still can't see a baby. Just a stuffed animal—a teddy bear—in the plastic box.

I can't believe I'm about to see Angelo. He had his procedure. And he's alive. I focus on that. I don't want to think beyond that.

We turn into a different section. Doc stops at a place to wash our hands. Finally, I hear a baby crying. Don't know why that makes me smile, but it does. Even though the baby's cry is different than on TV. It's breathy. It's different than Angelo's was yesterday. Is it Angelo?

The hallway ends. This area is bigger. Instead of just three or four, there's room for about seven babies. I can see the babies here 'cause they're not hiding in plastic boxes. They're in the open. Lying faceup on little square tables. Doc tells me this is where all the babies with heart problems are cared for.

"Aren't they cold?" Don't know why that's my first question. But seeing their tiny bodies, naked except for their diapers, makes me shiver.

"No. They have heaters. On top. You'll see when we get close. It's quite warm."

The baby that's crying is having his diaper changed. His little legs jut at the air like he's angry. His chest is covered with white bandages. The nurse wraps him up and pops a pacifier in his mouth. She hands him to a lady in a rocking chair. She looks kind of old, but it must be the baby's mama. She's in a bathrobe. Fluffy pink slippers are on her feet.

I look at each baby. I want to recognize Angelo before Doc tells me it's him. A mama should know her baby, right? I think I spot him in the corner. That baby's got a tube in his nose and a big machine by his table. But then a family goes over to him. A pink card is taped above the baby's head, to the thing that must be part heater, part light. *I'm a girl*, it says. Definitely not Angelo.

Doc turns the wheelchair and backs me into a space one over

from the diaper-change baby. Next to a table with no family. I should have known this was him. Every other baby's got family here. It's Christmas, so where else they gonna be? I shouldn't have been sleeping. I should've been here earlier. With my son.

A blue card is taped up top. *I'm a boy.* It's one of those cards like you see on restaurant tables, telling you the specials. The folded over portion is sticking up. Since I'm right below it, I see *Angelo* is written inside. Doc sees me looking.

"I went ahead and wrote down his name for you. Figured you wouldn't want the nurses all calling him Baby Boy Pujols."

"Thanks." I mumble it. I should look at my son. But I'm afraid. I can only look at his foot. His itty-bitty toes. They look too much like real baby toes. So I stare at the machine next to him. At the dials and colors and tubes. It whirrs and hisses, like a robot trying for language. It lets out a sudden, piercing *ding-dong*, like an out-of-tune doorbell for a deaf person.

"You must be Ms. Pujols. How are you feeling, sweetie?" A woman in blue operating-room clothes touches a button on the machine. The noise stops. She's smiling, but she's not really looking at me. She's looking at Angelo, straightening the tube coming out of his nose, twisting the top off it, disconnecting him from the machine.

"Wait— What—?!" I sputter.

"Maggie is going to suction his tube. Take out the extra water and secretions," Doc says. His voice is calm. "That's why the ventilator alarmed."

Nurse Maggie makes eye contact for a chip of a second. "That's right, sweetie. Don't want those secretions getting into his lungs." She sounds very awake. And cheerful. Guess she don't mind having to work on Christmas. She's from the South, based on how she talks. She takes a long, thin straw—like a plastic mouse tail—and wraps it around her gloved finger, then sticks it down the tube in Angelo's nose. Angelo looked like he'd been sleeping. But he bucks. He opens his mouth to cough, to cry, but no sound comes out.

"There, there. That's right. Let it out, let me get it all out," Nurse Maggie baby-talks to him.

Doc asks her a few questions. Medical stuff. Poor Angelo looks like he's about to puke up a lung, but the nurse thumps his chest. She hooks Angelo back up, still cooing at him, before turning to me. "I'm Maggie by the way. Your baby's nurse." She bats her eyes at me. She'd been doing that to Doc, which I thought was because she's got no wedding ring, and he's, you know, Doc Hottie. I was starting to have unpleasant feelings about her. But maybe it's just her thing. Her eyes are pretty. A greenish brown. But her nose is crooked. Like she ran into a pole without looking. Maybe that's why she does the eye-blinking thing. To get you to notice the part of her that's the prettiest.

"I'll be here another hour or so. I'll introduce you to the over-night nurse before I go though, don't you worry. You have any questions? About your son?"

Why would I ask her with Doc standing right here?

"No? Well that's all right. It can be a bit of a shock to see them at first. But pretty soon, I bet your head will be crawling with questions. So don't hold back, okay? I'll be right over here doing some paperwork for now." She goes over to a counter in the middle of the room with big plastic folders and computers. She sits down at one of the monitors and starts typing, still smiling. My cheeks hurt just looking at her.

"You're lucky," Doc says, real quiet now. "Maggie is one of the best. Hopefully, she'll stay with Angelo through the Norwood. So be nice, okay?"

I look at him like, *When have I ever not been nice?*

"Just don't say anything nasty to her. If the nurse doesn't like a family, sometimes she'll request a change. I know she sometimes sounds a bit goofy, but trust me on this"—he tilts his head toward Maggie—"her, you want."

I turn back around and focus on Angelo's foot. He's not moving any longer. Maybe he fell back to sleep. It's hard to believe this little foot belongs to my baby. And that yesterday it was inside me. The skin on the bottom of his foot is lighter than on the top. Little calves lead to little knees. He doesn't look as dark as I remember him. Maybe all the gunk on him yesterday made him look different.

There's a bandage, on the top of his left leg, a cotton square covered with plastic wrap. A bit of blood is on the white of the cotton. I don't like that. A toothpick-size tube comes out from under the cotton. It runs and runs then loops until it disappears in a walkie-talkie box that's attached to a pole. A bag drips clear fluid into the other side of the box. He's wearing a diaper. It looks fresh. Good. It's multicolored, like something you might get in a Mickey D's Happy Meal. Not so good. Other babies have the same kind though, so I guess the hospital just got a weird batch. Above the diaper, a belly sticks out. It rises and falls with the sounds of the breathing machine. Another bandage is taped to his belly button. Two tubes come out from there. They go into other walkie-talkies connected to other bags of clear liquid. Then there's his chest. Tiny baby nipples that look like brown dots from a paintbrush. Perfectly curved shoulders with wisps of hair on them. And then his head. Chubby chin (from Bertie). Bow-tie mouth, pink and perfect (from me). His lips are parted. A bubble is forming between them. He's got two little ears that are folded and creased. They're not too big at all. A mass of dark hair is combed back so it looks like a cap. And then there's his nose. The tube comes out one side, lifting his nose up and back. White tape wraps around the tube. The tape stretches to his cheeks. It makes it hard to see his face the way it's supposed to look with all the parts put together.

"Do you want to touch him?" Doc stands next to me. He's looking down at Angelo, too.

"Can I?"

"You're his mother. Of course you can."

He holds a bottle of sanitizer out for me. I rub it in, but I don't know where to go from there.

"You can hold his hand," Doc says.

I shift forward in my chair. Doc lifts and lowers a clear plastic wall on one side of Angelo's table. It looks like something meant to keep him from rolling off. Not like Angelo could even do that if he tried. I put my hand on the white sheet. I push it forward until my finger touches Angelo. He moves. He takes his hand away from mine.

"Put your finger in his palm. He'll grab on."

I don't believe Doc, but I give it a try.

Teeny fingers hold on to me. I can feel Doc smiling behind me.

My nail, my needs-to-be-filed, ragged, no-polish nail, looks so big next to Angelo's. It takes three of his fingers to cover it. His grip is strong, man. Real strong. This kid wants to live. He's not going to give up. He's a fighter. Like me.

I can't believe it. My baby, *my son*, is holding *my* hand. Like he's never going to let it go.

❧

"*Hola*, baby mama!" Yaz bursts into my room. She's got flowers, and chocolates, and balloons. Teri and Heavenly are behind her, all glitter-shadowed eyes and lip-glossed smiles.

I stayed with Angelo for a while. 'Til I had to pee. And change that disgusting disposable underwear before I leaked blood over everything. Doc brought me back to my room. I felt bad about keeping him from a Christmas dinner or something. But he said not to worry about it. That he was around anyway. He promised to be back tomorrow.

Teri looks like she just came from church with her long blue dress. Heavenly looks like she just came from downtown with her red satin mini and heels. Yaz just came from her bed. Her nails aren't even done. Don't think I've seen them plain like that since the fourth grade.

"How you feeling, girl?" Heavenly kisses me on both cheeks while giving my body a once-over. "You don't even look like you had no baby."

"Merry Christmas," Teri sings, leaning down for kisses, too. "Seriously, Mari. What happened to your baby bump? It's like ice in a glass in Santo Domingo."

I rub my hands over my stomach. It's not as flat as before getting pregs, but way flatter than yesterday. I don't like that it feels so empty. I wish Angelo could be here with me instead of upstairs on his little platform bed.

"You all sore?" Heavenly asks it like she's interrogating me.

I shrug. "Not so bad."

"They give you those crazy panties? For the bleeding?" Heavenly's older cousin, Serena, had a baby six months ago, so Hev considers herself an expert.

I pull up my gown to show her. She and Yaz howl like animals.

Yaz reaches out and plucks the elastic band that sits way above my belly button. She snaps her gum. Peppermint, like always. "*Pero* Mari, it's so big. And so see-through! It's like for a sexy grandma or something."

"I know, right?"

"How's the baby?" Teri asks. Her hands are together like she's praying.

"Good," I lie. No sense in getting into all the gritty with them. "The docs did the procedure. Now we wait for the surgery."

The three of them look at one another. They're not laughing anymore. Teri sighs. She puts her hand on my arm. Yaz plunks the flowers on the table. She ties the balloons on a chair. One of them says *Little Man* with a picture of a baby wearing plumber overalls and a red cap.

Hev reaches behind her into a bag. She pulls out a small package wrapped in blue. "Here. This is for you."

The tissue paper crunches and tears. It's a sweater coat. A coat sweater. For a baby boy. Patches of blue stripes alternate with a blue teddy-bear pattern. There's a hood. Teddy bear ears are sewn onto it. Each button down the front is different. A navy teddy-bear head. A red paw. And a green baseball.

I run my hand over the lining. It's soft fleece and red like the paw button. My lip itches, so I lick it. I wish Yaz would offer me a piece of gum right now. Instead, she whistles.

"You made this? I mean, we all knew you had taste. And that you could work it, girl. But this . . ." She runs her bare-nailed thumb over the stitching. "*Manso*, this be like something Narciso Rodriguez would do. You could sell this. For money."

I nod my head. If this were for sale in some fancy baby boutique, I wouldn't be able to afford it.

Teri touches one of the little ears and murmurs, "*Qué mono.*"

Heavenly is watching me. She's trying to be all cool, but her long lashes keep moving, giving her away. "You like it?" she asks.

"I love it." And I mean it. That Ms. Tayler must have been a pretty good teacher, even if she was a psycho library lady.

"Couldn't tell you I was making something for Angelo," Heavenly says, explaining why she lied about it being Jo-jo's gift. "Was gonna give it to you for Christmas. So I had it ready. And yeah," she says to Yaz, "I know I could sell it. I know it's good. Mar and Angelo wouldn't have deserved it otherwise."

Heavenly snatches the box of chocolates and eases into the lounger Doc left by my bed. She hooks a shiny heel into the plastic bar that's supposed to keep me from rolling off the blankets and onto the floor. "We proud of you, girl." She lifts her chin at me. "You did it."

"I didn't do nothing," I grumble. "Except let him get born a month early."

Heavenly snorts. "Yeah, you didn't do nothing. Except grow him and keep him safe this whole time. All by yourself. And after that *chopa* Carmen—"

"Tch, tch." Yaz smacks the top of the candy box, cutting her off. Heavenly gives her a look of death.

"The baby's good now," Teri says. Her fingers are working the end of her braid. "Let's focus on the good."

Heavenly wrestles open the box of chocolates, draping the yellow ribbon over my head. She goes to throw a chocolate at Yaz's head, but pops it in her own mouth instead.

"Mmm, I love caramel." She makes a sound like she's having sex. Teri whacks her. Heavenly rolls her eyes and shows me the box. "Have one."

I wave it away. "Maybe later. Thanks, Hev." I'm still holding the sweater she made for Angelo. I'm pretty sure I never had anything so fancy when I was a kid. Won't find this in no consignment store. Clothes like this are kept, passed down. "And thanks, Yaz." I gesture at all the stuff she brought. "You didn't have to."

Yaz's smile is like her nails. Stripped-down simple. It bothers her that she doesn't have something special that she made for Angelo. Not that I care. Her being with me yesterday was better than any gift she could have got. "Wasn't just me. Was all of us." She plops down on the bed and grabs my dead phone. She takes a charger from her pocket and plugs it in.

"Thanks, *guys*," I say.

"You know, there is one thing I'm kinda sad about with Angelo." Yaz tucks the phone beside her. She turns to me, her hands up like she's holding a sandwich. "Saw these freakin' *chévere* baby pajamas the other day. Had My Little Ponies all over them. Even your fav, Pinkie Pie." She raises her eyebrows and pooches out her bottom lip. "But . . ."—she leans back, shaking her head—"I figured it was too girly for your little man. If only he'd been *una hembra* after all." The names of those ponies come out under her breath. She's looking at the ceiling, pointing at imaginary stickers. But she's also looking at me, waiting for my smile. I give her one, even though I don't feel like smiling.

"So it hurt, huh? A lot?" Heavenly's smacking her teeth, sucking the last of the caramel off them. "I heard you was screaming like a model kicked off the runway."

*What?!*

She swivels her eyes to Yaz, who's taking up half my pillow. "Yaz filled us in."

"Not us. You!" Teri shouts from the bathroom. She's doing something with running water. "I didn't hear anything!"

"That's because you were the good girl who went to church this morning. How's your boyfriend, by the way?" Heavenly calls back.

Teri comes out. She's holding the flowers in one hand and a pink plastic water pitcher in the other. Her eyes are real big. Her lips are parted. They're quivering like she's looking for the words to say.

"Padre Andrés?" Heavenly's licking the chocolate off her fingers so the name comes out funny.

"Oh, Father Andrés!" Teri lets out her breath. "I thought you meant—" She glances at me. "Never mind." She swipes the air, tilting the flowers upside down. "Father Andrés is good. I asked him for a special prayer for you and the baby, Mari."

I nod my thanks as Ter turns to the counter, fussing with the flowers. Yaz drapes her leg over her bent knee. Her foot bounces up and down.

"I didn't tell them everything, you know." Yaz is twirling her hair with her finger. Her nails still look so funny being all bare like that.

"How come we didn't get to be in there with you?" Heavenly asks. She pokes a chocolate open. "I like the nature channel. I wanted to see, too."

Yaz kicks her. "That is so gross, mami. You touch it, you gotta eat it."

"Since when do you watch the nature channel?" I say as Heavenly downs the poked candy.

Heavenly chews. "I watch it with Jo-jo."

"More like you make it with Jo-jo." Yaz bounces on the bed, grinding her hips into the air. Heavenly swats her.

"Don't be crass. What Jo-jo and I do? That be making love."

"Ooooooh!" Yaz hollers. The springs of my bed creak as Yaz jumps more. Her phone slides toward me. I want to check it for texts from Bertie. But I'm not going to.

"You just jealous." Heavenly licks chocolate off her red-and-white-striped nail. She's gone all out for Christmas. She's like a *Playboy* elf. As if men don't pant after her enough already.

"Yep." Yaz sits up. "Just like you jealous of me getting to see Angelo before you."

Heavenly ignores her. "Speaking of love, did Doc make an

appearance?" Her voice always gets real husky when she says his name.

I nod.

"When?" Yaz asks real quick. She gives Heavenly a look. Teri looks over her shoulder at me.

"An hour ago. He just left before you came."

Another look.

"What?" I say. They both shrug. Teri turns back around, jabs a flower stem into the pitcher. Yaz picks up my phone and tries to turn it on. Heavenly looks real close at the chocolates. They both still got a thing for Doc. I blow out my sigh.

"So when can we see Angelo?" Teri plunks my water pitcher on the rolling table. White and blue daisies stick out of it.

"Anytime."

"Great!" Teri claps. Her face lights up. For a moment, she don't look so nervous.

"Can we go now?" Heavenly puts down the chocolates.

"Yes, now?" Teri says.

"Sure." I hit the button for the nurse. I keep my face real stiff. I don't want them to see how scared I am. Angelo doesn't look like a normal baby. I knew that before I saw him. But it was still a shock.

I feel fierce all of a sudden. Like I need to protect him. I don't want people thinking Angelo looks funny or that he's too small. He's my Angelo. He's perfect the way he is. Except for his heart.

"What's that for?" Heavenly's looking at the red button in my hand.

"To get the nurse." Yaz sits up, all smug. Heavenly pushes Yaz's forehead with her hand. Yaz falls onto the pillow, cackling.

When the nurse comes in, she gives Yaz a stern look that shuts her up. "How can I help you?"

I tell her I want to see my baby. Half an hour later, we're in the elevator with some dude who doesn't speak. At the reception desk, a woman calls out to remind us only one visitor with a parent at a time. Heavenly takes my hand. Yaz and Teri go to the waiting room.

"Hey, I been meaning to tell you something." Hev stops us right in front of the door. "And it's not 'cause I expect you to come with me. I know you're gonna have your hands full. But I made an appointment." Hev sucks her lips into her mouth. I must look confused because she keeps going. "For my eyes. You so strong, Mari, all for baby Angelo. Figured it was time for me to be strong, too. Just don't say nothing to anyone else."

I give her a nod and squeeze her hand. She knows I won't.

Maggie's not here anymore. Another nurse is here instead. She comes over to make sure we both use the hand sanitizer after washing our hands and tells me there've been no changes. The other mother is still here. The one with the pink slippers. I thought her baby was a boy, but the card on the baby's bed is pink.

She sees me looking at them. "Would you like some Christmas cookies?" A fancy tin sits on the counter with the computers. "Please, help yourselves."

I nod to thank her as the transport guy rolls me to Angelo's spot.

Angelo is the same. Tiny, under a bright light, with tubes.

I look at Heavenly. I can't feel my hand because she's squeezing it so tight. She's staring at him, her eyes real wide. She blinks. Real quick, she wipes a finger across her lashes.

"Mar, he's beautiful," she whispers. Like she's afraid of waking him. No matter the machine two spaces over is acting up like it has a clog.

I squeeze her hand back.

"I know."

# DAY TWO

The elevator is taking too long. I'm shivering. I wish I had a robe. Like the mama with the pink slippers.

I woke at five thirty. When that OB doc came to check on me. Seemed like a good time to go check on my baby. Didn't want to wait for the wheelchair guy, so I'm walking over myself.

The elevator finally comes. I hit nine and stand in the corner. No one else gets on.

The receptionist desk is empty. I go on back. I know the way.

The hallways inside are still dark. The only lights come from the babies' beds. It's nice like this. Quiet. Reminds me of the room with the sonogram machine. I don't see families. Only a few nurses feeding babies.

I turn the corner. The area where Angelo and the other heart babies are is all lit up. There's a crowd around one of the beds. There are so many doctors and nurses I can't tell which baby is in trouble. A plastic bag is handed up and over heads. A lady in a short white coat grabs it and runs it down the hall. Her feet slap the floor. She doesn't look at me as she passes.

"Epi, one to one thousand," someone says. It's not a shout,

but it's close. A nurse standing by a red cart hands something to another woman in blue.

I take a breath. And then another. *Please don't be Angelo.*

It's foolish to wish. It's foolish to pray. God has never listened to me before. Why would he start now?

No one notices me. I creep forward until I can see him. My baby. It's Angelo they're crowded around.

His color is off. He was pale before, but a pinky pale. Now he looks gray. Like his skin is turning to clay.

A doctor is standing above his head. She has her hands around him, like she's gonna pick him up upside down. Her thumbs are pressing his chest in. She's counting. His chest goes in so far it's almost touching his spine. She's going to break him. The lady doc is going to break him. The tube in his nose is not connected to the machine. It's connected to a blue balloon. Someone else—a guy—is squeezing it. His head is bobbing like he's counting, too.

The monitor beeps, shrill, nonstop. A nurse hits a button, once, twice. She smacks it. The alarm goes off. But the red lines that used to show my baby's heartbeat, his breathing, his oxygen levels—all the readings Maggie showed me yesterday—they're flat.

"Blood gas result, seven-point-one, twenty-four, eighteen, forty-five!" A woman shouts it next to me.

A phone slams down. "Dr. Moses is here. They're prepping the OR." A different lady doctor stands at the counter with the computers. She shakes her blond ponytail off her shoulder. Her mouth is an angry slash in her face. It's Goldie. "Give another round of epi. Anesthesia's on their way up."

What does that mean?

Goldie sees me. Before she can say anything, a blur of blue goes between us.

"I'll take over respirations." It's Maggie. She takes the balloon from the guy who's been squeezing it. "We need to switch out compressions. You're looking tired, sweetie." She's talking to the doctor whose hands are around my baby's chest.

"Ms. Pujols." Goldie is speaking to me. But I can't take my eyes off Angelo. Off his little, stone-gray body. His chest caving in. His closed eyes. The bandages around his umbilical stump are oozing blood. "Your son has had a cardiac arrest. We're going to take him to the operating room to put him on ECMO, the heart-lung machine. I need you to sign this consent."

I remember Petite Doc and the cath. In an emergency, they don't need my permission.

"Is he going to die?" I look at her then. Afraid if I don't, she might lie and I won't be able to see it.

Goldie looks back at me. She doesn't blink. "He might. But not if we can help it." Her eyebrows are pulled close. Her jaw is set. "I need you to tell me if this is still what you would like us to do. To try to save your baby."

I don't understand the question. Who would say no to that?

I nod. I say it out loud, in case a nod don't count. I reach for the pen and papers she's holding out. "Yes. Please. Please save him."

I'm sitting in the rocking chair by Angelo's empty bed. Maggie keeps coming to check on me. She only has one other baby to care for since Angelo's not here, a baby that's due to go home in a few days.

Pink Slipper Mama comes in. Only she's not wearing the pink slippers. She's in street clothes.

"Hi." She waves to me as she finishes washing her hands in the sink. "Good morning, Amelia," she burbles at her baby. "You are just too cute. Yes you are. You are Mommy's cute little munchkin." She makes faces and blows a kiss. The baby's eyes are open, watching. But the baby don't make any sound.

"Did your baby go for surgery?" Pink Slipper Mama is looking at me.

I nod. I don't want to speak. Not right now. Not to her.

"That's good. I'm glad even with the holiday they were able to take your baby so quickly. Amelia had to wait five days for her surgery. But now that's behind us, isn't it?" She's gone back to using her baby voice. "And maybe today they'll take the rest of your tubes out. And we can go home for New Year's? Right, Amelia?"

She looks over at me again. "What's your baby's heart problem?"

I'm not going to say anything, but Maggie is watching me from across the room, where she's reorganizing a supply closet. I don't want her to think I'm rude.

"HLHS." I use the fancy word. Maybe Pink Slipper Mama won't know what that is.

"Oh, that's what Amelia has, too!" She says it like it's a luck thing. "She had her Norwood with Dr. Moses. Is that who is doing your surgery?"

Goldie had used that name. I don't know if Angelo is having his Norwood or if he's just getting that EC-thing though. I nod.

"He's the best, you know. Out of the three of them, he has the most experience. Would you like a croissant?" She goes over to her purse, takes out a white paper bag. "I got a few extra. Sorry, I didn't bring you coffee. I didn't know if you'd be here so early. Do you drink coffee?"

I shrug-nod. God, is she a talker. But I am hungry.

"Here, take one." She points the bag's opening at me. I stick my hand in, grab something warm and crusty, and pull it out. Maggie's not looking at us anymore.

"Dr. Moses says we'll be able to take Amelia home soon. It's amazing, isn't it? That they can take these teeny hearts and fix them." She pulls her rocker to the other side of Amelia's bed so it's next to mine. "I'm Helen by the way." She holds out her hand.

"Mari," I say, shaking it.

"Mary?"

The woman's as white as they come. Freckles. Blond hair, but it's gray at the roots. She's got a diamond ring that's more grape than raisin.

"Mari as in Maribel. My dad's Dominican," I say.

"That's pretty. I like that." She sips her coffee. She stares out over the beds of diapered babies. "I never thought I'd be here." She says it like she's surprised. She leans toward me, like we're friends or something. "I never thought I'd be a mother, much less a mother to a baby with special needs. Howard said he didn't want children. Until we turned forty and all of a sudden he was like, 'Honey, let's have a baby!' Two years and four rounds of IVF later, here we are. Well, here I am. Howard's at work. I took a leave from the firm, so they're not expecting me back until April. A nice long maternity leave so Amelia and I can get to know each other. I've been waiting for you for a while, little miss." She brushes the top of the baby's toes with her hand. "A long time indeed. How about you?" She rocks her chair, takes another sip of coffee, and looks at me.

I'm still chewing. I'm trying hard not to think of how good it tastes, all buttery and soft on the inside, crunchy on the out. The crap that comes on the hospital tray isn't even food compared to this. "Pretty much same thing," I say, swallowing. "Except I'm fifteen. And we didn't do that VF thing. But I've waited a long time for Angelo, too." Like my whole life. I can't remember a time when I wasn't lonely.

"Angelo is his name? That's darling. How did you decide on that?"

"He's my angel." I take another bite real fast.

Helen reaches across the space between us. She puts her hand on top of mine. "Angelo will be okay. You'll see. Dr. Moses is going to take care of him."

I don't look at her. I don't want to see the lie on her face. I just chew and swallow.

"Mari, someone's out front to see you. Are you up for visitors?" Maggie holds the phone against her shoulder, waiting for my answer.

"Sure," I say, looking over at Amelia's bed. Howard, Amelia's dad, came for lunch. He brought a whole mess of sandwiches from the deli. Enough for the nurses and some of the parents. I think Helen has taken on fattening me up as a personal goal of hers. She kept telling me about how important it is to eat so my body can heal. I took a chicken parm just to make her happy. I'll eat it later. Ever since the pastry, my stomach's been in a tangle. Still no update on Angelo. And Maggie's called down a couple of times.

I'm expecting Yaz. She told me she'd be here in the morning. But Yaz doesn't come around the corner. Heavenly and Teri don't either.

*Coño.*

My *visitor* shuffles forward slowly. He looks at a notecard in his hand. He looks at the numbers of the bed spaces on the walls. He's wearing dress pants, not jeans. He's got on a white button-down. His mouth hangs open. He looks like a Catholic schoolboy who lost half of his uniform. Except he's still got his earring in. No matter it's a gold stud instead of the ring. And his Yankees cap is on his head.

Bertie stops when he sees me. I wonder what he sees. A deflated girl in a gray hospital gown. Fear sits on my back like a nasty bird, hunching my shoulders. At least my hair is clean.

Bertie lifts his hand. *Hi.*

I lift my hand back at him.

He doesn't come any closer. He looks around the room at the different beds. He looks at the card in his hand. The card is shaking.

I feel like I gulped a plum whole, pit and all. And it's stuck in my throat. I want to swallow, but I can't.

What if he missed his chance to meet Angelo?

I stand, my hands fisted. I go to reach for my belly but stop. I feel so empty, so hollow. Not to mention scared. But also mad. At Bertie. Still. That he wanted me to get the abortion. That the baby he gave me might not live. That he let me walk away and didn't come after me. Not hard enough.

When did he figure out I was still pregnant? Why didn't he call? What happened in Riverside Park—what *almost* happened—he could've prevented that. I could've been staying with him instead of Heavenly. If he'd only come after me. If he'd only apologized. I could've been safe. Bertie never would've let me go to Sing Sing. I never would've found out the truth about my papi. I never would've found out the truth that nobody in my family loves me. Except Angelo. Who might die. Who might already be dead.

I'm across the room in three steps. I shove him, hands on his chest. "THIS IS ALL YOUR FAULT!"

"Whoa!" Maggie is between us. "I said, whoa! Step back there, young lady."

Howard has Bertie's arm. But Bertie's not going to do nothing. Except look like he's gonna cry. He wants me to beat him up.

"This is Angelo's father, I presume?" Maggie's pretty eyes are pissed. They're poking holes in my forehead. Thin red hairs have loosened from her hair bun. "Nice to meet you. My name's

Maggie. I'm your baby's nurse." She's still glaring at me while she shakes his hand.

Bertie's voice is all high and weird. "My name is José Humberto Valdez. Folks call me Bertie."

"Bertie. Nice name. Now, it looks like you two have some talking to do. I'm going to put you here in this room." Maggie opens a door I thought led to a closet. Two green couches patterned with circles and squares face each other. Two armchairs sandwich a coffee table. "Do you need a chaperone or can you be civil?" She stands in the doorway, hands on hips.

"It's okay. We be good." Bertie ducks his head looking for my eyes.

I cross my arms over my chest and flop down on a couch.

"That means yes in Mari speak," Bertie explains to Maggie.

"Okay, but I'm not going to warn you two again. Any other outbursts, and I'm going to have to call security. It's not safe for the babies for you two to be acting like babies."

"Yes, ma'am," Bertie says as she shuts the door.

We don't say nothing to each other. Bertie sits on the other couch. He grabs a pillow. It has designs with shapes on it, too. He puts it behind him, then changes his mind and shoves it away.

His eyes don't look at me. But it's not because he's hiding anything. He's staring at the checked linoleum, but I can see the white parts of his eyes are white. There's nothing bloodshot about them. Good.

"So where is he?" That's the first thing he asks. "He's not out there."

"How do you know?" I say. What does he know about what his son looks like? He's never seen him yet.

"All them babies out there look white. Don't see no baby that looks like it come from me. Unless there's some other secret you been keeping." He waits for me to look at him. But I don't. Bertie knows I wouldn't lie about something like that. "Also," Bertie coughs, trying to make it seem like his voice didn't break, "there was a space next to where you was sitting. Like where a bed used to be."

I glance at him, annoyed. Bertie's not usually observant. "Angelo's in the OR."

"The what?"

"The OPERATING room." I say it like he's an idiot. I want him to feel like an idiot. For all he's done to me.

Bertie leans over his legs. He smooths down his eyebrows with his thumb and readjusts his baseball cap. "So you named him Angelo after all, huh?"

"What else was I going to name him? Some *alelao* like José or Humberto?"

"I don't know." He shrugs. His fingers are tapping his

knee. "Sometimes you change your mind." He fake coughs again.

He's waiting for me to look him in the eye.

"Why didn't you tell me?" he says finally. "You should've told me."

"You didn't want him." I hurl the words at him like fists. I wait for Bertie to say something back. But he doesn't. He's not looking at me no more. He's looking at the goddamn floor. Like he don't want me either.

"I always wanted him," I say. "I needed him. I NEED HIM." I cover my eyes with my hand, trying to make it seem like I have a bad headache. But really, I don't want him to see me crying.

Bertie stands. He moves to my couch. His arms hold me. I want to push him away. For some reason, I don't.

"You might get your wish." I'm hiccuping between sobs. "He might die. He's gonna die. Because you didn't want him enough. Because you didn't want him like I did."

"Shhh. Don't say that. We don't know what's going to happen. And I did—I do—want him. I love him, Mari. I haven't even seen him and I love him. You don't know. You just don't know." He takes a breath. When he lets it out, I feel it on my neck. "I didn't want our baby to suffer. Just like I don't want you to suffer. It's an unfair choice I had. Either way, someone I love suffers."

"Angelo's suffering?" I say. "He's a baby. He ain't gonna remember none of this."

Bertie doesn't let me go though I try to pull back. "Just 'cause he don't remember, don't mean there's no suffering. I see those babies out there. With them needles and tubes. You can't tell me they're not suffering. But now that they born, there ain't nothing more to do than let those doctors try and save them."

He holds me until I calm down. He's wearing the cologne I gave him for his birthday. The one Yaz and I picked out at four a.m. after sampling the entire store during one of those Black Friday sales where they open at midnight. We smelled like perfume for days.

Bertie moves me side to side. He starts to hum, so soft I feel it before I hear it. I think it's "Suavémente." But then I catch the tune. Luis Vargas. "Volvió el dolor." Bertie doesn't sing about the man who was betrayed. He only sings about the pain and about how he still loves her. We're still on the couch. Rocking to the thread of his voice. Bertie doesn't just dance, he can sing, too.

"How did you find out?" I ask when I can talk without hiccups.

"Teri's brother," he says.

I didn't realize Carlos knew about Angelo. "He told you or he told everyone?" Carlos has a big mouth, but I thought my threats would hold.

"Let's just say I beat it out of him."

Just like Yaz said. I wonder if Teri's mad at him for it. Carlos is a *pendejo*, but he is her brother. "Why did you do it? Beat him up?" I say.

"He was mouthing off about you. Bragging about your rack. I mean, I knew you was staying over at Teri's. I thought you was still angry with Carmen. Just like you was angry with me. But I knew there was no way you would let him see you. Figured he was being a perv. Spying on you in the shower or something. Then he goes and says he only ever saw your rack through clothes. That you was so big—bigger than he thought you was—he couldn't help notice." Bertie's talking like he has a sour taste in his mouth. "So I figured it out. I knew you still had to be pregnant. I asked Teri. She didn't deny it. You know her, she don't like to lie. Then, 'bout two weeks ago, Toto called. He told me straight up."

"When?" I clear my throat. "When did you first find out?"

"Week after Thanksgiving."

"And you didn't say nothing?"

"*Qué no,* I was waiting for you to come tell me yourself. Figured you had a good reason for waiting."

"Yeah. I was mad at you."

Bertie screws his mouth up to the side. "I know. Figured that was part of it. Figured you needed time. Didn't think you'd wait 'til after he was born."

"Me neither," I say, real quiet. "But he came early."

"Babies can do that."

I sit back on the couch, so I can see all of him better. I want to tell him he should have come. That I was mad at him, but he should have found me anyway. That I wanted him to. Instead, I ask, "You tell Toto you're here?"

Bertie holds my gaze. "Not yet."

I scrunch up my nose, trying to get at my lip. It's driving me crazy. I go to scratch it, but Bertie takes my hand. I look down at his fingers pressed around mine.

"He still might die, you know. Angelo could still die."

Bertie nods. His eyebrows pull his forehead over his eyes. "I know. But I'm not gonna leave. Not 'til Angelo is safe. Either here or in heaven. I can't do more than that. We just have to leave it up to God and the doctors, like my mama says."

I wince. "Don't you go bringing her into the conversation."

"You know you gonna have to deal with her. For Angelo's sake. Can't have too many people loving a baby or praying for a baby, Mar. She's his abuela. She have a right to come see him."

I don't want to share Angelo. With Yaz, or Heavenly, or Teri. Not even with Bertie. And now Bertie's saying I have to share him with Cacata Mama? Angelo's a part of *me*. He's here on this earth on account of me. For me to love. And for him to love me. Not anyone else.

I rake my teeth over my lip. I chew it a few times. I think about what Dr. Love said about Maggie. Bertie might be right. But I'm not going to say nothing.

There's a knock. "You lovebirds make up yet?" Maggie peeks her head inside. "Oh good, looks like you did. Now, here's the deal. They're finished in the OR. Angelo's on his way up. We'll need some time to get him settled out here, so you guys need to wait in the lounge outside."

"Can't we stay in here?" Bertie asks. This surprises me, 'cause I was going to ask the same thing. "We won't bother no one. Promise."

Maggie eyes us. Bertie puts on his Catholic schoolboy face. "You'll stay here 'til I come get you?" she asks.

Catholic Schoolboy nods.

"All right," Maggie says, "but if I catch you sneaking out . . ."

"We won't," Bertie says.

Maggie leaves us. A moment later, she's back. She tosses something at Bertie—my chicken parm—and puts two cans of soda on the table. "Helen and Howard thought you might be hungry."

A crowd of people and beeping machines pass behind Maggie. A baby bed is in the middle of it, rolling by real slow. I feel a pulse in my gut. It's Angelo. It's got to be.

"Got to go," Maggie says. The door swings shut behind her.

When Doc brought me to the NICU the first time, he warned me Angelo wouldn't look the same. I was prepared. I wish Doc was here now. Because I don't know what to expect.

An hour after she leaves, Maggie comes to get us. Bertie kept looking at his watch the whole time. Even while he was downing the chicken parm.

A bunch of people are still around Angelo's bed. Not as many as this morning, but enough to make me wish I hadn't eaten. Goldie's there. She's standing by Angelo's feet, her arms crossed in front of her as she stares at the monitor on the wall. Her eyes drop to a bag hanging off the side of the bed. The bag is filled with bloody water. One of the tubes coming from Angelo feeds it. Goldie frowns. A machine the size of three baby beds put together chugs beside her. A man in blue sitting on a stool watches the machine.

My lip is doing that itching thing again. I hold my hands together behind my back so I won't scratch it. I'm afraid to look too close at my son. I don't want to know where the tubes are coming from. I don't want to see his face. Bertie's staring straight at him. His face is whiter than usual. But at least his mouth is closed.

I blow out a breath.

Angelo doesn't look like himself. He doesn't look like a baby. Or a doll even. He looks like some freak horror-movie creation, something possessed.

For one, he's puffy as hell. His arms and legs are twice as thick as they were this morning. He don't even look smaller than Amelia now. Before, I remember thinking Amelia could eat him up in one swallow. Now, he could probably take her.

His eyes are taped closed. There's something gooey on top of them. His mouth is open—like Bertie's usually is—and his lips are smeared with the same gooey jelly. The tube that was in his nose is still there. Only now it looks small because Angelo's face is so blown up. His hair is matted down. Like he was sweating or something. Bandages cover his chest, from one side to the other. They're white except for the middle part which is damp and pink. The bandages are taped down at the top and bottom, except for where the tubes are. There're three of them. Tubes. They have the same pinky fluid inside them. There're other tubes coming out from his chest, too. Some so small they look like black strings. Some so big they look like vacuum-cleaner hoses. Tubes come out from the top of both his legs. And one comes from his diaper. The fluid there is orangish. Don't look nothing like regular pee.

"Mrs. Pujols?" Goldie is speaking to me. She's still got that frown on. "Mr. Pujols?" She looks at Bertie. He shakes his head.

"Valdez. We don't have the same last name," he says.

Goldie looks at him like she's looking through him. She turns back to me.

"Your son is on ECMO." She says it like *heck no*, and points at the machine and the man on the stool. "Dr. Moses completed the Norwood, but he wasn't able to come off the bypass machine, even with the chest open. Hopefully, in a few days, we can come off ECMO and then close the baby's chest."

I understand only half of what she's saying.

Bertie's looking confused. "Wait—his chest is OPEN?"

Goldie nods.

"Can't germs and shit just get in there?"

"Bertie, watch your mouth." Maggie is emptying bloody water from one of the bags, but she's been listening.

"Sorry." Bertie looks around, like he's wondering who heard him. Helen's in the rocker on the other side of Amelia's bed. Her hand's on Amelia's little foot, holding it. She's reading but looks up and gives me a small smile. I don't think she heard Bertie.

"Your baby is on antibiotics to protect him from infection. But yes, having an open chest is an infection risk," Goldie says. "We didn't have a choice. When Dr. Moses tried to close his chest, your son's heart stopped beating." She marches over to the container of orange pee. She lifts the pee tube, getting what's in the tube to fall into the container.

"And that thing, that problem with the hole and his lungs getting blocked up? Is that all good now?"

Goldie answers him in a sharp voice. "It may still be a problem down the road. But for now, it's not a major player in what's going on."

I'm looking at Bertie, wondering how he knew about that.

"Any more questions?" Goldie asks. I can't see her face, but I bet she's still frowning. She doesn't sound happy. I hope it's because she has to talk to us. I hope it's not because of the orange pee.

"What do we do?" Bertie says.

"Just be with Angelo," Maggie says at the same time Goldie says, "Stay out of our way." They give each other not-too-friendly looks. Makes me wish Doc was here. Again.

"Why don't you take a seat?" Maggie says. She motions with her head toward the rocker. It's been pushed all the way across the room. Bertie nods and goes to get it. He drags it over. Goldie whips her head around at him, looking like she's gonna scratch him 'cause he came too close. Bertie pulls the chair back a few feet.

"Mari?" He gives me the seat. Helen's in the same type of chair, her feet up on a stool, a book balanced on her knees. Without saying nothing, Bertie disappears around the corner. I'm about to get pissed, wondering where he went, when he comes back. He's got a footrest in one hand and a magazine in the other.

"Here," he says, sliding the stool under me. He hands me the mag. It's covered with photos of celebrities. The kind Abuela always goes nuts over. "This one okay?"

I shrug and take it. My stomach's still angry about the croissant since its primary job now is to be nervous and not digest stuff. And I'm still mad at Bertie. Don't know when I'm not gonna be. But it's not as if I don't notice he's trying.

Bertie takes a few steps toward Angelo's bed. "This okay?" he asks, hands up like he's surrendering.

Goldie shoots him a nasty look but Maggie says, "That's fine. Right there is fine."

Goldie and Maggie do their thing. Bertie watches Angelo like he's watching over him. He watches Angelo like I would.

Someone puts a blanket over me. That's what wakes me up.

"Sorry." Helen's lips bunch up real close, like she's nervous. "You looked cold. It's cold in here." She wraps her arms around her like she's giving herself a hug.

My eyes find Angelo, worried something's happened and that he's cold, too. The heater coils above him glow orange like coals. He's still practically naked, but he's not cold. Otherwise, he looks the same. Maybe more puffy, but I could be imagining it.

Bertie's still standing there. Like a statue. Watching our baby.

"Are you hungry?" Helen asks, all hopeful.

"Nah." I shake my head. "Thanks for this," I say. I lift my hand under the blanket at her. The blanket is soft. And *warm*. Like the one the doc gave me that time.

"There's a little oven filled with them. Over in pod 720. You can take one whenever you like." Helen must be a mind reader. She goes back to Amelia's bed. She leans over the baby, kisses her forehead. Amelia's sleeping. She doesn't stir.

I stand. My legs are stiff. I roll my foot, stretching my ankle. I better not have been sleeping too long. "What'd I miss?" I say to Bertie.

He turns, looking surprised I'm up. He shakes his head and shrugs, then goes back to watching Angelo. Goldie's not here. The man on the stool, the one in charge of that machine, is typing on a computer.

"Dr. Moses came by and checked on Angelo." Maggie's got gloves and a mask on. She's holding that long plastic mouse-tail thing again.

*Coño.* I can't believe I missed the surgeon.

"What did he say?" I give Bertie a look like he's keeping something from me.

"I dunno," he says. He takes his cap off and smooths his hair back. "Something like, we'll have to wait and see."

"The first twenty-four hours are crucial," Maggie says. She smiles at the man who's come to tend Angelo's breathing machine and asks him about his day. She nods at his response, then disconnects Angelo's tube. The plastic mouse tail goes down inside my baby's throat. The machine yells at her. Which is good because then I don't have to. It's that same loud *ding-dong* noise from before. Bertie shoves his fingers in his ears.

"Sorry," the man at the machine says. He hits a button. The sound goes off.

When Maggie's finished, she comes to the garbage can near me to take off her gloves and mask. "We're checking his fluids—what goes in and what comes out—multiple times an hour. Dave," she pauses as the man near the heck-no machine lifts a finger and nods to us, "is running tests on Angelo's blood, so we can correct his electrolytes or give him more blood products as he needs it."

"Blood products?" The way Bertie says it makes it sound like he's talking about someone's private parts.

"Platelets, which your body needs for clotting. Red blood cells, which your body needs to bring the oxygen to all your other cells." Maggie enjoys explaining things. She reminds me of Doc this way. She takes up some dirty tubes and dumps them in a red garbage bin.

"Does Dr. Love know?" I ask when she returns. "That Angelo had his surgery?"

Bertie turns to look at me. He doesn't like Doc. Said he didn't like that the guy got to touch my pregnant belly. And he didn't like that we all called him Doc Hottie. This was before the fake abortion. I'm guessing he knows Doc and I had all those extra months together. Bertie's the jealous type. Not that he has any right to be. I don't even know what we—Bertie and I—are anymore.

"Dr. Goldstein updated Dr. Love," Maggie says.

I look at the clock. It's seven.

"You know Dr. Love isn't working these next few days, right?" Maggie gives me a sympathy smile. I hate those.

"Yeah, I know." I hug my blanket around my shoulders. It's not warm anymore. Maggie doesn't know about the promise Doc made to me yesterday. He's not on the schedule. But Doc said he'd come check on Angelo.

"Hey." Helen comes over to me. "I know you said you're not hungry, but Pam and I are going to order dinner. Can I get something for you guys? We were thinking pizza."

My stomach grumbles. Guess it's not mad anymore. But I don't have any money on me. I look to Bertie, but he's still staring at Angelo.

"My treat," Helen says. See? Mind reader.

"Nah, it's okay." I don't want her to keep giving us stuff. I don't like handouts. Even when I was staying with Teri and

Heavenly, I tried to make myself useful, which was pretty difficult. You try sweeping up a kitchen or vacuuming a living room in an apartment where you're not supposed to be.

"I'm ordering an extra pie anyway, for the nurses and residents. So if you have a preference, you should tell me."

God, she's pushy. Still, I don't budge.

"Do you eat meat? Pepperoni okay with you?"

"Thank you, that's real nice of you." Bertie turns around. "She loves pepperoni." He puts his hand in his pocket, takes out a wad of bills. "Here, let me pay." He holds out a twenty.

The inside of my chest gets all hot when I see the cash. Makes me remember the money he gave to Teri, the money he tried to give me. It's gotta be from Skinner. Bertie better not be in deeper with him.

"No, no." Helen backs away. "My treat. I offered."

"Please," Bertie says it like he's real tired. "Take it. She'll be mad at me otherwise." He tips his head toward me. "She already is."

Helen takes the money, but she doesn't want to. She goes back to give Amelia another kiss. She murmurs some mama words I can't hear, then waves at me and Maggie. She goes to look for Pam. Pam's baby has a heart defect, too, TG something, like TGIF. Helen told me Pam's baby was blue like a blueberry when she came out. They had to do some emergency thing to her little girl before the surgery, too. Only they did it right there in the NICU in front of everyone. I was thinking *TGIH—thank God it's her—and not m*e. My baby been through enough.

"Can I touch him?" I ask. "Hold his hand? Like yesterday?" I want to kiss my son like Helen kissed Amelia. I didn't do that yesterday, and now I'm upset thinking I missed my chance.

"Maybe later," Maggie says. "There's too much going on now."

"You got to hold his hand?" Bertie's whispering. Like he's embarrassed to have Maggie hear him.

I nod at Bertie. Makes me feel guilty. Maybe if I'd texted him instead of Yaz doing it, Bertie would've come yesterday and gotten to hold Angelo's hand, too.

"I gotta pee," I say. I hold the blanket up. "Can I take this to my room? Bring it back later?"

Maggie nods.

"I'll go with you," Bertie says.

"I don't need no chaperone." I snap it before I know what I'm doing. "How you think I got here this morning?" I wag my chin at him.

"'Course you don't." Bertie stretches his arms above him. "I'd just like to come with you is all."

Maybe he wants me alone again. Maybe here's where we iron it all out. What we are. Where we stand.

I hold on to the blanket like it's keeping me up. "Suit yourself."

I say bye to Maggie. Bertie follows me out.

The first thing I see as we go out those doors is a pair of boots sticking up in the air. The legs they belong to drape over the arm of one of the waiting-room chairs.

"Mari!" Heavenly shouts from a sofa. The woman behind the desk shushes her. Heavenly stands, giving the woman her back. She doesn't listen to people who are ugly or old as a general rule. Yaz scrambles out of the chair. Her boots land on the floor where they belong. Teri's still sitting, a book that's about fifty pounds weighing down her lap. She lets go of her cross necklace and closes the book as we come closer. BIOLOGY it says in black, bold letters. She's looking from me to Bertie and back to me again like she's nervous about something. Probably wondering if we're all patched up or if I'm still mad at him.

"What are you guys doing here?" I say.

Heavenly pushes her glossy curls behind her then plants a hand on her hip. "What do you mean, what are we doing here? Where else we gonna be? Didn't Bertie tell you we was waiting out here?" She's swishing her head at me.

I look at Bertie, but he's staring at the ground. Teri's looking at Bertie, too.

"Since when?"

"Like three, maybe two." Yaz's hands are in her butt pockets. She's rocking back and forth on her heels and then her toes.

"I didn't know." I glare at Bertie. Teri's still looking at him. She hasn't gotten up. Her fingers are wiggling all over the place like they don't know where to be. She must be nervous about Angelo. Or about me and Bertie.

"How's the baby?" Teri asks.

Bertie shrugs but doesn't say nothing. He's frowning at his shoe like there's something gross on it.

I swallow and look up at the lights. All three of them are looking at me with worry in their eyes. I don't want to see that either. "He had his surgery."

Heavenly claps. "That's good right?"

I nod, but say, "I don't know. He's on some kind of machine. It's doing the work of his heart and lungs for him, 'cause he can't do it himself."

Yaz lets out a whistle. "*¡Güay!* Doctors these days." She sways forward, then rocks back again.

"I was going to my room. Bertie was taking me."

"I'll go!" Yaz says, smile taking over her frown.

"Me, too. *Óyeme*, Bertie, *siéntate*. You don't look so good." Heavenly raises an eyebrow at him. "You look like you been mistreating your legs so much they going to run away on you."

Bertie nods. He takes a seat in one of the armchairs. His hand holds up his head.

Teri pushes the book off her lap and goes and stands next to Bertie. She reaches out, like she's gonna touch his arm. She glances at me. She takes hold of her braid instead. "Can I see Angelo?" Teri asks. "Bertie could take me, couldn't he? He's a parent?"

Bertie looks at her, his expression funny. Like he's annoyed and uneasy at the same time.

"Why don't you let the boy relax?" Heavenly says.

"Yeah, *déjale*. Leave him alone." Yaz stares hard at Teri.

Teri's working her hair, flipping the elastic band up and down. "Sorry, it's just, I really want to see him, too."

"*A mí me da igual*," I say. "If Bertie wants to take you, fine by me."

Teri looks at Bertie, but now he's not looking at anything. Maybe he's tired out after watching Angelo.

I just really got to pee. "Come on," I say to Hev and Yaz. They each take one of my arms and lead me to the elevator.

In my room, an enormous jar of flowers looks like it's going to crush the table it's sitting on. Roses. Red ones. And one of those yuppy thousand-dollar strollers with the big wheels.

I always made fun of those strollers. Because they're all over the fancy parts of Manhattan, even though they're made to go up into mountains. And you know those diamond-ringed mamas ain't taking no baby up no mountains. Maybe up a hill in Central Park, but that's it. The stroller's red. The bow's red, too. My favorite color.

"*¡El pipo!*" Yaz exclaims.

There's only one person could've come up with this.

"Heavenly!" I turn on her.

Heavenly's eyes are real wide, her eyebrows all caught off guard. "Wasn't me. Swear. Unless Jo-jo . . ." She marches over and swipes the card from the petals. She reads it. "Not Jo-jo. It's from *your* boyfriend." She snaps it in the air to me with her nail.

For an instant, I think she means Doc. Heavenly calls him that sometimes. Before I can figure out why my stomach jumped, I read the words.

*Thank you for having our son.*
*Let me back in? Please?*

Bertie signed his full name. Like it's some important document. My stomach is bouncing all over the place. I still can't figure out why it's doing that though. I bend over the stroller to get a good look. I don't want my girls looking too close at my face right now. The seat of the stroller's worn. The rubber on the handle is scuffed. But I don't care it's used. It's beautiful. I wouldn't have wasted my time making fun of it if it weren't. It bothers me how sometimes Bertie can know me so well, and sometimes, it seems he hardly knows me at all.

"How'd he get the money?" I demand, looking first at Heavenly, then at Yaz.

They glance at each other. "Maybe you should ask him," Heavenly says.

"It better not be Skinner's money. If it is, I'm not taking this stuff. He can have it all back."

"It's not what you think." Heavenly's shaking her hair, like she's trying to push it off her shoulders.

"He got a job," Yaz says. Heavenly smacks her arm. "What?" Yaz glares at her.

Yeah, I bet he got a job. Bet he and Skinner made it all official. So my baby's papi is going to be a dealer. Bertie knows how I feel about that. He knows what happened to my papi. I'm so steamed up, I'm seeing red all over the place, the walls, the chairs. I go do my business and think about taking a shower. Maybe it'll calm me down. But I want to get back to Angelo. It's been like fifteen minutes and already I'm nervous something could've happened. And now I got to confront Bertie. I stomp all the way back to the NICU. Heavenly and Yaz don't even try to talk.

"YOU!" I shout, pointing a finger at Bertie. He and Teri are both sitting on the couch, talking real quiet. I wonder why they're still not with Angelo. Bertie's head snaps up. Teri jumps away from Bertie, looking pale and like she needs to pee. Her hand flies to her pendant. I hope that's not because of the way Angelo looked. "YOU!" I say it again. "Have some explaining to do." The woman behind the desk clears her throat and taps a pen on her computer. Heavenly goes and puts her back in front of her, blocking her view.

"*¿Y qué?* You saw the stroller?" Bertie drawls like a Mexican. Like he's trying to pretend he's calm. Or maybe it's just that he's tired. "What, you don't like red no more?"

"Don't you give me that." I step right up to him. He's still sitting so my head's over his.

"Maybe we should go?" Teri asks.

"But I haven't gotten to see Angelo. I want to see Angelo," Yaz whines.

"Me, too," Heavenly says. "I ain't leaving 'til we see that little cutie."

"Oh, there you are!" Helen is back with pizza. Helen is smiling real big, but Pam's smile is so little, it's almost not there. She keeps looking from me to the others. She doesn't come close. But Helen comes right up and hands over one of the boxes. "It's so nice your friends are here. Here, take an extra pie, I got enough for everyone." She hands two to Bertie. "They like us to eat over on the other side of the elevators. It's a huge space. I left some soda there already." Her hand takes my shoulder. She gives me a squeeze. For some reason, I don't shrug her off. For some reason, I like that she's showing me she's there for me. This woman who's almost as old as Abuela, and who's got life all figured out—a job and a husband, an apartment. We couldn't be more different. But 'cause we both have babies with heart problems, at this time, in this place, we're the same.

Helen's off down the hallway, delivering pizza to hospital workers. Pam follows behind her.

"Who was that?" Yaz asks, looking like she's going to start making fun of Helen.

"Who cares. You heard the lady. Let's go eat!" Heavenly struts toward the elevator. Teri leaps up and runs after her.

Yaz watches Helen disappear. It's a good thing she doesn't talk smack about her, 'cause then I'd have to say something. "Here, give me one." Yaz takes a box from Bertie and follows them, giving us plenty of room to argue.

"So, *do* you still like red?" Bertie asks. He's standing next to me, waiting for me to turn and face the right direction.

I don't answer. My leg buckles as I spin around. Bertie's hand catches me. My body keeps forgetting it just had a baby the other day. "*Gracias*," I grumble.

"*De nada*," he says. I move my arm and he lets go. I wish I hadn't done that. I wish he hadn't let go.

"So you've got some job now?" We start walking to the elevators.

Bertie nods. "Familia car service. Teri's cousin been helping me out."

Not what I was expecting. "Orlando? But he's a driver. You don't have a license."

"Starting low. Manning the phones. Figured if I stick with it, by the time I'm seventeen, maybe they give me one of their cars. It's a good job. Pays well. Needed to do something to help you and the baby out."

I'm impressed. But also angry he's changing his whole life around like that for us. "What about Skinner? He mad at you?"

"Nah." Bertie says it in that carefree way that makes me think it ain't true. "Took a few months, but he understands. I told him I made a promise."

He did make a promise. To me. That by the time the baby came, he wouldn't be involved in that no more. I'm surprised he remembered. I thought it was one of those promises that wasn't meant to keep. Like when he used to get me to go back to his place, he always promised his mama wasn't gonna be there. But half the time, she was.

Bertie lifts his shoulder in a lazy shrug. "Got some stuff I'll have to pay back, but *to' ta frío*. Skinner even called. Yesterday. To give his *felicidades*."

Skinner knew about the baby coming early?

Bertie takes my elbow. Makes me stop walking. As if he knows what I'm thinking. "I didn't tell him. I'd just found out Angelo was born, too. I didn't even tell him you was still pregnant. Fact, last time we spoke was near Halloween."

Wait. Bertie cut it off with Skinner before he knew about Angelo? When he thought I wasn't pregnant no more?

Bertie's watching me. He looks kinda silly standing there: not smiling but not frowning either, the pizza box up by his face. Switch the Yankees cap for a Papa John's, and he'd be a delivery boy.

Bertie's long fingers tighten on my arm. Like he's going to pull me into a dance step and he's giving me advance warning. Instead, he lets me go. He lifts the pizza box higher. He motions for me to go ahead.

We get to the big room. Yaz, Hev, and Teri are chowing down at a table in the corner. Yaz gives me two thumbs-up and points to another room at the other end. She winks. It feels good to have her back in my life.

Bertie hasn't seen her, I don't think. But he leads me to the separate area anyway. He puts down the pizza box. He picks out the slice with the most pepperoni on it and hands it over. He removes pepperoni from his piece and layers them on top of mine.

"Sit down, Mari." He says it so gentle, my eyes get all teary. I squeeze them tight to make them stop and quickly take a bite of pizza.

I try not to think of my papi. Of what he said to me. Of what kind of man he is. But looking at Bertie, sitting there, chewing with his mouth open, I can't help but think of how my papi was probably in the same seat, eating pizza, fifteen years ago. I was born in this hospital, too. But maybe my papi never came to see me in the hospital. Don't make sense to visit someone you never wanted.

I pick up a piece of pepperoni and slide it in my mouth. I lick orange ovals of grease from my finger and thumb. I hold on to my breath, let it out slow so it doesn't shake. Bertie starts on a second piece. He gives me all the pepperoni from that slice, too.

I look back at my girls. Heavenly has the TV on some fashion show. She and Yaz are ripping on some poor contestant. Teri's watching Bertie and me. When she sees me looking, she gives a little smile. Bertie's chewing. He's staring at the plain cheese slice he's balancing on his fingertips.

It feels good having all my girls back together. It feels good having Bertie back, too. I didn't think I'd been lonely, what with having Angelo inside me and the promise of the baby coming. But I think I'd just gotten so used to being lonely all the time, I forgot how good even one extra friend can feel.

I take another bite. "When did you start at Familia?"

"Last week," he says.

"How'd you save enough for the stroller then? In just one week?"

"They gave me an advance. I asked them to. For the baby."

"What about school?"

Bertie slides his pizza to his other hand. He drags a napkin toward him. "I'll get my GED."

Bertie's no academic, but he loves school. He's so social, it's like food to him. He's like the opposite of me when it comes to friends. Seeing as I usually don't trust nobody, I only keep a few around me. But Bertie, he's friends with everybody. I can't see him sitting in some depressing office with chain-smoking, paunchy guys arranging carfares. I see him working the cafeteria, sitting on one of them tables, surrounded by his *manos*, wide smile infecting everyone around him.

"Teri said she'd help me," Bertie adds. "You know how she is with books." He coughs like he's nervous about it.

"She told you about the problem with Angelo's lungs, didn't she?" It had to be her. She's smart. She got it when I explained it to her.

"Don't be mad at her. I been stalking her, begging her to give me something. Anything. About the pregnancy. About you."

Oh, I know all about their meetings. I'm guessing Teri told him I know. "And you didn't just come and ask me?" I'm still fuming he didn't try harder to get to me.

His forehead gathers like my words have let him down. I scowl back at him.

"See," he says. "You still angry at me. I couldn't go to you. You might've been pregnant, but you still mean when you fight."

I rip off the end of my crust with my teeth. What he says hurts. Even if he's right.

"I didn't want to upset you," Bertie says. "More than I already did. You know, Mari, don't be mad, but I think you're afraid. Because of what your mama and your papi did to you. You're always so sure somebody you love is gonna leave. And I get it, I do. But I didn't leave, Mari. I stayed. I tried to stay. But you wouldn't let me. You was the one who left."

I take another bite of pizza. I don't want to say what I'm thinking. About Angelo, his little body mangled by nature and doctors. How now that he's outside of me, there's nothing I can do to protect him. How that scares me like nothing ever has. How I'd rather trade Bertie and get to keep Angelo. As if God is into trades. As if God even cares what happens to me.

"You gonna finish that pizza," I say instead. "Or you gonna

just make eyes at it all night? 'Cause I want to get back in there and be with our baby."

There. I said it out loud. Our baby.

Bertie looks up. His eyes are green, green, green with a little bit of brown. Like an island rainforest. No gray. And still no red.

Bertie lifts the pizza to his mouth. Yaz cackles and Bertie's tropical-jungle eyes sweep over to them. Teri's watching us again. Like she knows we've been talking about her. I give her a smile to show her I'm not mad. Not at her.

"He's still cute," Yaz says. "Even with all the pipey things and bandages."

"No he's not. You don't gotta lie to me. He looks freaky, I know." He's my Angelo. I'll love him no matter what. But that don't mean I'm blind.

"Angelo-oh-oh," Yaz sings.

I elbow her.

"What?" she asks. "Is there a no-lullaby rule here, too?"

"You're too loud. You'll disturb the other babies." I glance around the room. Since it's late, most of the lights are out. Helen's in the rocker, reading, her hand over Amelia's hand.

"I don't mind!" she calls out, not even looking up. "Amelia and I like singing."

"I don't mind, either," Dave the heck-no heart-lung machine guy says. He's taking blood out of one of the tubes.

Yaz rubs her triumphant smile in my face. *Seeeeeeee*, it says.

*Fine*, my glare says back to her.

Yaz starts with a Dominican one, her voice all hushed and fast. Something about an angel. I don't remember any lullabies. Even if my mama was the lullaby type, they wouldn't be songs like this. But I would've liked this one.

Next Yaz sings "Silent Night." In English. The words are cool and crisp. Like snowflakes tingling your skin, settling on your heart and melting.

Helen is looking at us, her eyes shiny like glass.

"Wow, you can sing," Dave says, pulling his mask down.

"I always told her she should try out for one of those TV talent shows, but she never listens to me."

"*Mari!*" Yaz hisses, cheeks getting all red.

"You should do it," Dave says. "I'd vote for you."

"Thank you," Yaz answers, turning away. It's so weird. The girl who loves loud jokes and laughter is shy about singing. I guess we all have our own things we're shy about.

The nurse comes back. Not Maggie, the other one. We don't like each other. But we've decided to get along. For Angelo's sake. Though I almost punched her for the way she yelled at Heavenly when she got too close to the bed.

The nurse taps the watch on her wrist.

Yaz gets the hint. "Good night, sweet angel!" Yaz blows Angelo a kiss and walks to the door.

I settle on a chair. Not the rocker. One that's higher up, so I can see Angelo better. My bottom is still sore, but it's nothing compared to my boobs. They're huge. And I thought they was big before the baby came. Bertie was even staring at them tonight.

"You should wear a bra. It'll feel better." Helen must have caught me rearranging myself. It's crazy how she can still sound so quiet and respectful and make herself heard from across the room like that. "Are you planning to breastfeed?"

I shrug. "Don't know. Haven't really thought about it." I didn't want to think too much about what was going to happen after the birth. I didn't read any baby books or anything, just pregnancy books. Thought it might bring more bad luck. To assume we'd get to this point.

"Angelo was born two days ago, right? So your milk may be coming in. If you want to keep it, you've got to take it out."

"How am I going to do that?" Angelo doesn't look near ready to drink.

"There's a pump for that," Helen says it like it's super natural for two women to be talking about breasts and milk. "They have a bunch of them in the rooms out back."

"You mean I'm going to be like a cow in one of them factories?"

Helen laughs. "Yes, exactly like a cow. It's not comfortable, but it's more comfortable than being engorged. And you do it for the baby. Mother's milk is supposed to be better for them than formula."

I know my mama didn't breastfeed me. She was afraid it would ruin her boobs. I don't remember what they looked like, but I doubt they were anything special. Mine certainly aren't. Even if they were, I can't understand how a woman would choose her looks over her baby's health. I mean, if I could give Angelo my own heart to make him better, I would do it.

"Can you show me how?" I ask Helen, nervous she'll say no. "To do the breastfeeding pump thing?"

"Of course." Helen stands. She puts her book on the rocker. *Baby's First Year.*

When we get back to the NICU, it's real late. Helen and I wash our hands at the sink.

"That's a lot for the first pump. Think of all the nutrients that milk will give Angelo." Helen nods at the bottles I'm holding. I tilt them back and forth. The weird orangish liquid sticks to the sides. It seems like a small amount to me. And it looks nothing like real milk. I thought maybe my boobs were defective. Helen says that the beginning stuff is different and it's especially good for babies. It even helps them fight infections.

Bertie's sitting in the rocker at Angelo's feet, fast asleep. I wouldn't have left Angelo alone to pump if Bertie hadn't agreed to stay. Howard's there, too, reading a paper. He and Helen hug. Arm in arm, they gaze at Amelia. The baby opens her eyes, and Helen and Howard lean in and smile and coo at her. Amelia stares up at them, doing nothing.

"How come she's not smiling back at you?" I'm scared for them that something happened to Amelia during the surgery. That maybe her brain don't work right. I'm scared for Angelo, too.

Howard starts to laugh, but Helen hushes him. "Babies don't smile until about six weeks. But you're still supposed to smile and talk and sing to them. It stimulates their development."

I nod. The woman is like a walking Wikipedia of baby information. The nurse takes the two bottles from me, slaps stickers with Angelo's name on them, and stores them in a small refrigerator behind Angelo's bed. Howard's stacking Helen's books, putting them in a bag. Each of them is about caring for babies. Amelia's so lucky to have Helen for a mother. You just know Helen would never leave, no matter how rough life got.

I go over to Angelo's bed, careful not to wake Bertie. The tubes are still there, swarming around him. Angelo has puffed even more. His skin's real pale. He kinda looks like a toasted marshmallow when it blows up real big. His lips are dry. He needs more jelly on them. Maggie would never let them get like that.

"Do you think I could touch him now?" I ask Dave. He seems nicer than the night nurse. He looks around for Gloria. That's the night nurse's name.

"I won't tell if you don't." He winks at me.

Real quick, I slather on some sanitizer and go to Angelo's side. His arms stick straight out, one of them on a board. His fingers are pudgy and swollen. I put my thumb in his little hand. He doesn't squeeze back. I try again, pressing harder. Nothing.

"He's sedated. So he probably won't respond to you." Dave is watching me. But he's smiling.

I nod, pretending I knew that. I trace the tips of Angelo's little sausage fingers. They're warm and soft, and still so tiny, even with all the swelling. I rise on tippy-toes and lean over, bringing my face closer to his. I keep my eyes off his chest with the bloody bandages and bloody tubes. The breathing straw is still pulling at his nose. His eyelids are puffy, the color of the skin even lighter there than on his cheeks. But his lashes are long and black. They feel like feathers against my finger. He gets that from Bertie. Mine are short and stubby. I take a deep sniff in, looking for his baby smell. All I find is stinging alcohol and antiseptic. There's none of the sweet scent Heavenly's cousin's baby girl had, that combination of baby shampoo, talcum, and newborn skin.

Bertie makes a noise, like his breath got stuck in his throat. He's sleeping with his mouth open. Big surprise. But he doesn't wake. He crosses his arms and turns in the chair.

Angelo lies there, warm and sleeping. The tube with the lip jelly is on the bed. Right by the board for his arm. I sneak some onto a Q-tip, like I've seen Maggie do. I spread it over his mouth, wanting to do something for him. Shouldn't mamas be helpful, too? Everything feels all backward. I should be the one caring for my baby. But all I can do is let them take him away from me and hope they give him back. It's harder. Doing nothing. Letting him go. The hardest thing I think I've ever done.

I put more jelly on the Q-tip and work on Angelo's bottom lip. His mouth moves. Like he's looking for something to suck. Maybe he knows it's me.

Dave chuckles. "Not too sedated, I see."

I bite my smile down. But my heart is swelling. Like it's a toasted marshmallow, too.


"There you are."

I open my eyes. I focus on Angelo's plump little hand, about five inches from my face.

I sit up, lick my lips moist, and stretch.

Goldie is staring at me. She don't look so good. She's wearing glasses now and her ponytail is all mussed up. "I've been looking for you."

The clock says 12:00. *Well you haven't been looking too hard, 'cause I been right here for the past two hours.* I want to say it, but I don't. Bertie's right. So is Doc. We need all these folks on our side. For Angelo.

Bertie's still asleep in the rocker. Goldie gives him a look like he smells something awful—which he doesn't—then comes over to me.

"You shouldn't be leaning on his bed like that," she says, her voice kind of nasty.

I take a slow breath, count to five. I lean back in my chair, cross my arms. It hurts my boobs, so I let my arms down. But I still stare daggers at her.

Goldie doesn't notice. She's checking Angelo, feeling his feet, listening to his chest. She picks up the tubes, helping the liquid drain out. She writes some notes on her clipboard.

"Dr. Love wants to speak with you." Goldie goes to the phone.

I sit up. I look at the clock again. Goldie's dialing.

"Um, isn't it too late to call him?"

She ignores me. "Hey, Josh, how's it going? . . . Sorry, no, nothing's wrong. Yeah, I know, I called on the landline so you could talk to your patient." Goldie has her back to me, but her voice is pretty loud. "BP is stable. In's and out's respectable. Still on pressors, no change there. Gave him some packed RBCs about an hour ago."

I'm not following what she's saying, but her tone is relaxed. So it makes me relaxed. Guess Angelo's doing okay. For now.

"Hey—how's Sandra doing?" Goldie's typing on the computer as she talks. The phone on her hip, some weird combination of a walkie-talkie and a cell, goes off. "Great, tell her good luck from me. PICU is calling about the transplant, so I've got to go. Yeah, she's standing right here, hold on." She sticks her arm out at me, the landline phone in her hand.

I stare at it. Goldie picks up the other phone/walkie-talkie. "Cards," she says into it. She listens. "Have you gone up on the epi?" She shakes the hand with the landline phone at me, frowning.

I take the phone. "Hello?"

"Mari, how are you doing?" Doc is whispering. He's probably whispering because his wife is sleeping.

"Fine," I whisper back. Goldie power walks off, still barking questions into the walkie-talkie.

"I'm sorry I didn't get to stop by today. I couldn't get away."

I don't say nothing. I shouldn't be pissed. It's his day off. I know how doctors' schedules work. They can't always be in the hospital. But I am kind of pissed. I thought he was more than just my baby's doctor. He told me he would be here today. He shouldn't have said nothing if he couldn't keep his promise.

"Mari, are you there?" He's talking regular. Must've stepped into another room. His voice does something to me. I feel small and scared. The anger and attitude all stripped away.

"Yeah," I say, hating that my lip is trembling.

"Dr. Moses called me after the surgery and Dr. Goldstein has been updating me regularly. I've also been checking in with Maggie and Gloria, to make sure the others were giving me the real scoop." He gives a chuckle, but I don't feel like laughing. He clears his throat.

"So do you understand what's been happening?"

I stay quiet, so he starts telling me.

"Angelo's had a rough time. But he's doing as well as can be expected. I don't want to give you false hope, but I'm very pleased with how this day has ended for him. The arrest was horrible, but it pushed our hand and made us give him the surgery earlier than we would have, which is really what he needed."

He pauses, giving me time to say something. I still don't.

"Maggie told me you were there when it happened. I can't imagine what that must have been like for you."

I turn away from Angelo's bed, curling in on myself. I don't want Bertie or Dave or anyone to see me like this.

"I wish I could've been there, Mari. But I heard José came by. Is it good that he's there? Is he supporting you?"

I let the pause draw out, knowing I've got to say something. "I guess." The words sound thick and shaky.

Doc sighs. "Look, I am really sorry I wasn't there for you today. As soon as I can get away, I'll come by for a visit. Okay?"

"Sure," I say, trying real hard to sound bored.

I hang up.

Bertie's awake, watching me. "Who was that?" he asks.

"The doc," I say, looking at the ground, hoping Bertie can't see my face too well.

He doesn't say anything else. Even though I'm pretty sure he already saw my face.

# DAY THREE

We take turns sleeping and watching over Angelo. Bertie makes me go back to my room since he just woke from a nap. We're kind of lucky. I thought the night nurse was nasty, but she pretends she don't see when one of us dozes off in the rocker.

I come back at five thirty. Right after the OB doc's visit. She said I'd be good to go home today. They let me stay an extra day as it is. I don't think she noticed how scared that made me. I don't want to leave Angelo. My place is with him. Plus, I don't even know where I'm gonna go.

Bertie looks like a mess when I shake him awake—clothes rumpled, hair sticking up all over, face all pasty and confused. I send him to my room, tell him no one should bother him for a few hours.

Angelo looks more swollen. I didn't think it was possible. Now even his face is all pooched out. The night nurse is wearing a blue paper gown and getting out a tray with bandages on it. Someone else is sitting in Dave's spot. He says his name is Francisco and he goes back to arranging the heck-no heart-lung machine. Amelia's asleep. The chairs around her are empty. Helen and Howard must be home. I bet they have a nice big bed and they sleep holding on to each other all night long.

I settle into the chair, the high one so I can see Angelo. Since night nurse is here, I don't try to touch him. Though I really want to. The monitors are all quiet without any beeping, so Angelo must be all right. Though he looks less like a baby and more like a weird blow-up doll than ever.

I'm about to ask the nurse about the bandages when a team of docs in blue pants and white coats come over. Someone flicks on the overhead lights, making me blind for a moment.

"Are you the mother?" one of them asks.

"Uh-huh," I say, giving him the evil eye. Why do I have the feeling he's gonna tell me something I don't want to hear?

"I'm Dr. Mitchell. I work with Dr. Moses. We're going to change the dressing on your son's chest. Gloria will give him some extra pain medication so he won't feel a thing. Would you mind waiting outside for a few minutes?"

"But I just got here."

They're swarming around Angelo like bugs. Picking at him, touching him. I don't know what they're doing, but I don't like the way they're doing it. Like Angelo is just a toy and not a real baby. My baby.

"Miss Pujols, this won't be good for you to see. We have to

expose his chest. Now, please." He pauses and points to the door. "I'll come find you when we're done."

I stomp away, trying to make as much noise as possible. I don't like being dismissed like I'm a little kid or a dog or something. *Coño.* I stop at the oven with the blankets, grab a few, slam the door closed. But no one's looking at me. They're putting on blue gowns and masks and circling around Angelo so tight I can't even see him anymore.

The waiting room is empty. I've just settled onto one of the plasticky couches when the elevator dings. Helen walks out, a big bag from the bakery in one arm and a smaller bag from Starbucks in the other.

"Mari? Don't tell me you slept out here."

I sit up. I can't help but smile seeing as she's so concerned about me.

"Nah, I still got a room. Was visiting, but they kicked me out. They're doing some dressing change thing."

"Oh, really?" She looks down at the bag. She slides her bottom lip back and forth against her upper one. "Do you want some coffee?"

I nod, though I don't drink coffee. Not really. I mean, I was pregnant, and you're not supposed to have caffeine when you're pregnant. Not that I ever really started before that. But something hot to drink would be real good right now.

Helen reaches in the bag and hands me a cup. I've never had one of these fancy coffee drinks before, the ones with whipped cream and sprinkles of spice on top. I take a sip. Warm gingerbread with milk. It tastes exactly the way Starbucks smells. I lick the cream off my upper lip. I want to thank Helen, to tell her how much the drink rocks, but she's still chewing on her mouth.

"Why do you look like that?" I ask, nervous all of a sudden. "Is the dressing change dangerous?"

"Oh no." Helen gives a quick smile. She puts down the other bag and runs her hand along the sleeve of her blouse, smoothing out a wrinkle I hadn't noticed. "It's just, I know when they do procedures like that, they won't let other parents back either. Guess that's what I get for coming so early." She gives a little laugh as she sits next to me. Her hair is done pretty and her face has makeup. The dark smudges that were under her eyes when I first met her are gone. I wonder how she had time to do all that—sleep, do herself up, and get breakfast for everyone— seeing as she was here so late. Maybe she didn't sleep. Maybe it's just all makeup.

"Sorry," I say, feeling guilty that Angelo's keeping her from Amelia.

"Don't be silly." She taps my thigh, like she's brushing off a flying bug. "It's not your fault. Or Angelo's."

She's doing that mind-reading trick again.

"Here, take one." She hands me the pastry bag. Muffins. I grab a carrot one and dig in.

"Thanks," I say, crumbs falling out of my mouth.

Helen takes a book from her backpack, *Child-Rearing for the Special Needs Child*. She rests it on the sofa while she adds sugar to her coffee and stirs.

"Want something to read?" she asks.

I kind of do. But I don't want her to think I haven't done any reading.

"This one's really good." She hands me one with a picture of a papi lifting a baby in the air on the cover. Both baby and papi are laughing. I feel a little jealous of that baby. Of how much her papi loves her. I open to a random page and pretend to read. But really I just look at the pictures. I still don't want to jinx myself.

It seems like forever before Dr. Mitchell comes out. Helen stands and touches my arm before excusing herself. The doctor doesn't say anything useful. Just that they did what they said they was gonna do and it went fine.

The night nurse, Gloria, is still cleaning up, her gloved hands fisted with blue towels stained with blood. I didn't need to see that. Maggie is back. She's talking with Gloria, taking notes in a notebook. Angelo, my little puffed-up baby, has clean, white bandages on his chest. He's been moved a few inches lower in the bed. I go and wait for my turn at the sink behind other parents. They rush down the hall in the other direction, smiling and holding hands. Folks are lining up behind me to wash, too.

"Excuse me," I say, pushing past a woman as I try to get to my baby.

"Mari?"

I turn around. My breathing stops. Abuela is next to one of those sonogram machines, holding on to it like it's keeping her from falling. Her other hand clutches a yellow notecard with Angelo's bed space written on it.

I don't know what to say. I don't know what to do. They must have let her in while I was talking to the doctor. You can't see all the elevators from the waiting area.

Abuela's standing there, her face wrinkled, purple-brown hair dye almost all washed out. She looks scared and lost, like a mangy mutt out in a thunderstorm.

She's Angelo's *bisabuela*. Parents and grandparents are allowed 24/7. Guess that goes for great-grandparents, too. She don't need my permission to be here. But when I look at her, I see the person who told me to get rid of Angelo. To give up on him. I see the person who gave up on me.

"We was going to come yesterday, right after we heard—"

I hold up my hand. Don't want her excuses. Don't even want

her here. If I open my mouth, something bad's gonna come out. I keep it closed. For Angelo's sake. I turn to my son.

"How'd he do?" I ask the nurse. "With the changing thing?"

"Fine," Gloria says, not looking at me.

"Is that your mother?" Maggie asks, motioning to Abuela.

"No," I say. Helen's holding Amelia in the rocker. She's humming to her. The look on her face is pure happiness.

That's how it's supposed to be. Mamas are supposed to love their daughters. They're not supposed to dump them and cut them out of their lives when they become inconvenient. Same goes for abuelas.

"I don't have a mama." I put my hand on Angelo's bed, looking at Maggie to make sure this is allowed. I don't have a papi neither. Everything about him was lies. All lies. Especially those letters. And I most definitely don't have an abuela.

Maggie's watching me, her forehead all creased. She gives me a nod when she sees what I want to do.

I put my finger against Angelo's palm. When he grabs on, it's like he's squeezing the tears out of me.

I don't have anything before me. No family. No love. But I have something after me.

I have a son. *I have you, Angelo.*


"So are you going to tell me who that lady was or do I have

to call Veronica at the front desk and ask?" Maggie's holding a plastic see-through box connected to one of Angelo's tubes. She opens something on the bottom and dumps the liquid in another container.

I look behind me. Abuela's gone. Maybe the sight of Angelo scared her off. Good. It's not like I was gonna welcome her with *abrazos y besos*.

"That's my papi's mama."

"Your grandma?"

"Yeah." I'm staring at Angelo's feet. They look like miniature versions of Bertie's. Except for the puff.

"She didn't want to stay and visit?"

I shrug. "Don't know. Don't care."

Maggie goes for another bag. "Was she the one you were living with before?"

I nod. There's some truth there.

"So who are you and Angelo going to live with after he gets out?"

I'm surprised how she brings it up like it's a done deal. Like he's definitely going to get better and go home. But the way she talks makes it seem like he's in jail. Like he's serving some sentence. How could babies go to jail? They're innocent. Unless they serving time for the sins of their families. I don't want to think about that. I don't want to think about how what's happening with Angelo may be God's way of getting back at me.

"They're gonna stay with me." Bertie's back. His hands are in his pockets. His shoulders are humped over like he's preparing for a blow. "I mean," he looks at me, eyes all nervous, "if they want to, they can." His clothes are even more wrinkled, but he's awake. His pants are hanging off his hips. His hands are probably what's holding them up. I should've saved him some of the muffin. I feel bad I didn't even think about it.

"How's he doing?" Bertie chin-nods at Angelo, shuffling closer. He's not looking at me. Maggie waits to see if I'm gonna talk. When I don't, she tells him about the bandage change.

Bertie's staring at my hand holding Angelo's. "Can I do that, too?" he asks, eyes still nervous as they lift to Maggie.

"Sure can! You washed your hands, right?"

"Yes, ma'am."

Angelo's other hand is on the board, wrapped in bandages. The only holdable hand is the one I've got.

Bertie licks his lips and looks at me. "You don't got to," he says. I know he's talking about living with him and his mama. Not about letting go of our baby's hand. I nod my head, telling him I know, but not giving him an answer.

I take my hand away. Bertie reaches out, real slow. Like he's afraid to touch him.

Maggie chuckles. "He won't break."

Bertie smiles. Real brief. "Yeah, but he was born broken."

"I know," she says. "But we fixed him for you."

'Cause it looks like this is going to take a while, I grab Bertie's hand. I press it on top of Angelo's.

Bertie sucks in air, real quick. He opens his hand, lets it cover Angelo's. His hand is bigger than mine. His fingers reach all the way up to Angelo's elbow.

"He's warm," he says. He smiles. And it's not slow. It's not fake. It's not lazy. It's a real smile. And it lasts for a long time.

D id you mean it?" I say. We're out by the vending machine. The heart doctor came by, the same one from that first night—Dr. Gupta. She's taking a sonogram of Angelo's heart, and there's not a lot of room by his bed with the two big machines there.

Bertie buys himself a Pepsi. He asks if I want one, too, but I'm still full from the coffee and muffin.

"Mean what?" he says.

"That Angelo and I could live with you."

"'Course I meant it. Wouldn't have said it if I didn't." He cracks open the can, chugs down the soda.

"And your mama?"

He takes another gulp. "Oh, she still *bien quillao* at you. What you did, with her *peluca* . . ." He shakes his head and grins his half smile. It's the first time since Angelo was born that I see the Bertie from before. The relaxed, not nervous, not tired Bertie. Ever since he got to hold Angelo's hand. "But she be cool. She has to be. He's her *nieto*. That's real blood. It's more import-ant than any bad blood between you. Besides"—Bertie takes the brim of his Yankees cap, pulls it up so I can see the green in his

eyes—"she love babies. 'Specially cute babies that look like me."
There's that grin again. The one that hooks you in, makes you
want to stay awhile.

Living with Bertie would be good. Not great. I'd have to
see his mama's ugly face and deal with her ugly talk and living
each day. But it'd be better than sneaking a baby in and out of
Heavenly's. I was going to ask Yaz. Her abuela's always loved
me. More than my abuela ever did. And there's no way I'm
asking Carmen to take us in. Like I said before, I don't do
begging.

A kid shrieks. Some abuelos chase a toddler. The parents
must be inside visiting a new baby. Makes me think of my abuela
and how I'm glad she's not here.

"Hey, did you call Carmen? Tell her about Angelo?"

Bertie crinkles the empty can. He throws it to the garbage
bin. He looks tired again. "Blood is blood, Mari." He goes to
walk back inside.

"But . . . but . . ." A thousand words run through my head. *I
didn't want that. You didn't ask. How could you?*

Bertie doesn't stop. He keeps going like he's already decided
not to listen. So I decide I might as well not say anything. Don't
think I've ever done that before.

"Ah, Mr. and Mrs. Pujols." Dr. Gupta is pushing the sonogram machine down the hallway. Bertie gives me a look like,

*We've got to change Angelo's name already.* I ignore him. I kind of like the sound of Angelo Pujols.

"Your baby's heart function looks very, very good. Today, we are going to start to wean off the ECMO."

"You mean take away the heart-lung machine?" Bertie asks. His eyes glint like the Yankees just made it through the play-offs.

"Exactly," she says.

"What about his puffiness?" I say. Amelia doesn't look puffy, not like Angelo.

Dr. Gupta gives a little laugh. "Ah yes, it is common to be volume-overloaded after heart surgery. But we will work on that, too. Do not worry, we will bring all the fluid back to normal. Hopefully by the end of the week."

She pushes the machine past us, promising to come back in a few hours to check on Angelo. She almost runs over a guy in the hallway. She can barely see what's in front of her when she's bent over shoving at the machine like that.

"That thing should have a warning beep on it." Bertie cups his hand to his mouth. "*Cuidado, cuidado*, small Indian lady doctor driving oversize machinery. *Chicas y nenas, refugianse.*" He imitates Dr. Gupta's accent so perfectly, I laugh. I'd forgotten how Bertie can do that. Make me laugh.

&

"Maggie!?" Alarms go off. "MAGGIE!!" Helen, it's Helen. She's shouting.

*Angelo.*

Bertie and I take one look at each other and bust down the hallway. Other people are running, too. Nurses and doctors. Dr. Gupta. They shove me out of the way. They're running toward Angelo.

*No. Not again.*

Bertie's faster than me. He gets there first. He grabs me as I come around the corner. He pulls me close, presses my head against his shoulder. He doesn't want me to see.

"No!" I shout. "NO! Let me GO!" I twist. I buck.

"Shhhh, shhhh." His mouth is hot against my ear. His fingers dig into my back. His arms trap my arms.

He drags me away. It don't matter that I'm fighting him as hard as I can.

And then I hear it. A wailing so loud it breaks me in two.

Bertie's still talking to me. I haven't been listening. All I'm doing is trying to get back to my baby.

"*No es Angelo, no es Angelo.*" He says it over and over. It's not Angelo. He's shaking his head. He puts his forehead to mine. His eyes are right there. Green with gray and brown and gold. Like he's trying to show me what he saw.

The howling gets louder. Helen. Some nurse I don't know is leading her toward us. Toward the waiting room.

The door bursts open. Dr. Mitchell and two other white coats fly by.

Helen and the nurse pass us. Her bawling gets quieter when the door shuts. And now it's like Bertie is holding me up. Because I'm falling apart.

Eight minutes. That's how long it takes for Dr. Moses to get here.

Thirteen minutes. That's how long it takes for them to realize there's a clot in Amelia's heart.

Twenty minutes. That's how long it takes for Howard to come.

Forty-eight minutes. That's how long it takes for a baby to die.

I'm wrecked. Beaten. Hysterical.

But Helen is worse. She won't get off the floor.

Bertie leaves me long enough to help Howard get Helen on the couch. Dr. Moses comes out. He's stooping-through-doorways tall. White hair. Clear blue eyes. He sits next to Helen. He takes her shaking hand in his big, steady one. How can hands that large fix hearts that are so tiny? Doc told me your heart is about the size of your fist. Do you know how small a baby's fist is?

Dr. Moses's voice is deep and solid like a priest's. He tells

Helen that Amelia has passed. He tells her that sometimes this happens. He tells her that they did everything they could to save her. He tells her that he's very sorry. Howard holds Helen. She's sobbing, and he is, too. Dr. Gupta and Dr. Mitchell stand behind Dr. Moses, heads bowed way down, like in church at a funeral.

All I can think of is how it isn't right. How Helen did everything perfect. How Howard did, too. How hard it was for them to make Amelia. How much they wanted her. How much they loved her. How none of it mattered.

Snot is dripping out of my nose into my hair. My gown is wet. From tears or milk, maybe both. What are they going to do with the milk? All that milk Helen had been saving for her baby? What happens to a baby's milk after she dies?

Bertie's beside me, shoulders keeping me up. He doesn't cry. He just shakes his head back and forth.

"Oh my God, oh my God." He says it over and over.

Howard's hand is on Helen's back, her arm, her neck. It's the one part of him not shuddering. Helen's sobs have turned to murmurs of "No, no, no . . ." interrupted by Amelia's name. Dr. Moses is still holding her hand. He doesn't say anything. He just sits, a quiet witness to their grief.

I'm still whimpering. I want to go to Helen. To put my hand on her shoulder. To let her know I'm here. I'm a witness, too. But if I move, I'm gonna retch.

I smell Heavenly's perfume. And then she's pulling my hair out of my face. Teri's on her knees in front of us, the gold of her dangling cross winking. I reach for her, but Bertie's already there. He's on the floor. He's in her arms, sobbing.

There's another baby in Amelia's spot. A black baby. Baby Boy Lark. His name is Jordan. They've been calling him Jordy. His mama, Edith, is a nurse over at St. Barnabas in the Bronx. She's real chatty. They didn't know about the heart disease 'til after he was born. She keeps telling me how, when they found out the baby had a heart problem, she made them transfer him here. This is the place to be! Where miracles happen! I don't tell her about Helen and Howard and the miracle of their baby, Amelia, dying. I think about it though. Maybe that would shut Edith up. I don't want to be friends with her. I don't want to be friends with someone else whose baby might die.

Bertie's waiting for me when I come out of the breast-pump room. I didn't go there to pump milk. I went there to be alone. To lock myself in and curl up on the sleeper chair where no one could see me or touch me or cry with me. Bertie had gone home to shower. Teri wanted to go with him, but he said no. Yeah. Bertie and Teri. Guess that's what happens when you cut people off and treat them like *ratreria*. I keep thinking I should be pissed. That I should yell, and scream, and stomp. At both of them. But all I feel is sad. And scared. For Helen. For Amelia. For Angelo.

Bertie's standing against the wall a little way down. Not stalker close, but close enough that I'll see him. Toto's with him. I guess he and Abuela came back. They're talking. Too low for me to hear. Toto sees me first. He nods at me then puts a hand on Bertie's shoulder. He holds his fist up. Bertie touches it with his. Toto nods again. Then he walks away. Bertie had no papi growing up either. Sometimes, I forget that.

Bertie's hair is slicked back. It's flat and smooth when it's wet like that. He walks toward me, hands open. His eyes are red. Not the whites of them. The skin around them. Like he's been rubbing them with sandpaper tissues or scratching them with his nails. He licks his lips. They're cracked. Like he's been using sandpaper tissues there, too.

"Mari." His mouth says my name, but I don't hear it. Did he speak it out loud? Or did he only mean to say it, but then couldn't? He comes closer. His hands are still out. He's reaching for me.

I step away.

Bertie stops. His hands don't go in his pockets. They don't cross in front of his chest. They just hang there.

"Listen." His voice breaks. Even his sigh is beaten down. "*Lo siento. Por todo.* But you have to know. Nothing's happened. *Te lo juro.* I swear it. I wouldn't do that to you. I wouldn't do that to us. Teri and I, we've just grown close is all." His hands rise up a little. Like he's pushing the air. "There was no one else. I had no one else to talk to." He's shaking his head. So slow I don't notice at first. As if he knows what I'm gonna ask him next.

"You want to be with her?" I don't ask it like I'm angry. 'Cause I'm not. I feel empty. And tired.

He doesn't answer 'til I look at him. "I want *you.* I've always wanted you." He runs the back of his hand across his chapped lips. "Since that first dance."

It was by the river. Prince Royce was singing "Corazón sin cara" and I leaned in, like I was gonna kiss Bertie's ear. I bit it instead. Not hard. But enough it got his attention. He squeezed me around the waist. He pulled back and gave me that lazy, teasing smile. The bite worked. Because Bertie saw me. He really saw me.

"Love has no face, Mari." Bertie remembers the song, too. "I love you. I love that you're such a *galla.* I love that you fight. I love that you fought for our son. But, *por favor,* don't fight me. Come. Live with me and Mami. Let me take care of you. I'll take care of you both. I won't leave you. I promise."

I want to say yes. I want to say yes so badly. Bertie said what I wanted to hear. But it's not enough. Not anymore.

I saw the way Teri looked at Bertie. She's never been with a guy. Not like the rest of us have. She's too good for most all of them anyway. But Bertie, he's good, too. He'd be good for her. Maybe this is the trade? Maybe this is God waiting to see if I can let something go before He lets me keep something else. I already decided Angelo comes first.

Besides, words can lie. Like I said, Bertie's good. He wants to do the right thing. But he's gonna have to show me. What he really wants, what he needs. I don't wanna make Bertie do something he don't want to. That doesn't lead anywhere good. I should know.

Bertie moves in. Like he's gonna take my hands. I lean against the wall, fold my arms in front of myself. My lip prickles, wanting me to scratch at it. But I wait, and it passes.

"I know you'll take care of us. But we can't stay with you."

Bertie frowns. The stubble on his chin and along his jaw is all shaved off. "Who you gonna stay with?" he asks.

I don't want to look into those Dominican green eyes anymore. So I look at the artwork beside me. Some is for doctors and nurses—medical stuff. Some is for kids—nursery rhymes and quotes from books. *If that diamond ring turns brass, Papa's gonna buy you a looking glass. . . .*

"Don't know yet where we'll be." I almost say, *We've got options,* but I tear up thinking about how Amelia and Helen and Howard got no options anymore. "We'll just wait and see." I close my eyes and pray that Angelo will get better and that he and I will have options to face. Together.

"I understand." Bertie's looking at his shoe, scuffing out a mark on the linoleum with his toe. "You're punishing me. You're still punishing me."

I take his hand. I squeeze it 'til he looks at me. Bertie can't hold my gaze more than a second before he's glancing away, blinking real fast. "I'm not." I wipe at my face with my other hand. "I need you. Angelo and I, we both gonna need you." If we're lucky, if Angelo makes it out of here, Angelo and I are gonna need everyone who's willing to have us. I'm not writing anybody out of my life. Out of our life, Angelo's and mine. Not this time.

Bertie takes back his hand. He half turns away, covers his face with his long fingers.

I swallow, and breathe, 'til I can talk and not cry. "I'm counting on you, Bertie," I say, trying hard not to think of my papi and of how much Bertie looks like that boy in the photo in Abuela's living room. "You promised you wouldn't leave. Angelo and I, we're gonna hold you to that."

I leave Bertie alone beside a poster of the inside of a breast showing where the milk comes from.

Yaz is waiting by the elevators. She opens her arms, and I walk into them. We rock from one foot to the other. Her elbows hold my head against hers. We're sniffling but not full-on crying. She heard what happened to Amelia. She whispers to me that she and Iris—that's her abuela—have room for us. They want Angelo and me to move in. I mumble *Gracias*, and hug her some more.

"Let me think on it." I pull away. I need to see my little man.

Yaz touches my cheek, drags a finger down a tear trail. Her nails are painted again. Tiny purple half hearts next to big, full red ones. I look away real quick. I don't want to cry no more.

In the NICU, someone's sitting next to Angelo. Keeping watch. The maroon-colored hair gives her away.

"Eh, *¿cómo te sientes?*" Toto comes to stand next to me. He gives the heck-no machine guy, Francisco, a nod. Francisco lifts a hand and nods back. Toto's staring at me, hands in pockets, waiting for me to answer. I'm trying to figure out how I feel about him and Francisco chatting. I decide it's a good thing. I decide they're all on Angelo's side.

I shrug and murmur, "Okay."

Abuela turns when she hears me. One of the machines makes a noise and she turns right back around. She's holding Angelo's hand.

"*Mira.*" Toto has his phone out. He's showing me a picture of something. It's a bassinet. For a baby to sleep in. It looks like it's in my room.

I take the phone so I can see the photo better. I bring it real close, then think of Heavenly and her eyes and bring it down again.

"This for real?" I hold it out toward Abuela.

She stretches her lips, like she's got food stuck on her teeth. "*Sí*," she says. She traces the tip of one of Angelo's pudgy fingers. "You both belong with us."

Toto pushes the rocker closer to Angelo and motions for me to sit. "*Por favor. Di que vas a regresar.* Please. Come home. We'll help. We'll both help."

Abuela's nodding. "*Sí. No te dejo solito.*" She's whispering to Angelo. I won't leave you alone. Her baby voice isn't as good at Helen's. But maybe she just needs more practice.

Abuela looks over at me. "I been here, holding his hand, since Bertie left. I no leave him. *Te lo prometo*, Mari. *Pero, por favor. No te vayas.* Please. Don't you leave, either."

I drop my chin to my chest. I'm blinking real hard. I'm not gonna leave. I'm gonna stay with my Angelo.

"He looks like he's doing pretty well for post-op day number one."

I swing around. Doc is at the computers behind me. I leap out of the rocker. My heart leaps, too. But I just stand there. Like a *ñame*.

When did he come in? Why wasn't he here before? Maybe if

he was here, he could've saved Amelia. Because he's Doc. He's safe. And I trust him.

Doc's got his white coat on. He's wearing those classy glasses. He's staring at the screen, scrolling with the mouse, blond excuses for eyebrows bunched together, serious.

"Weaning the ECMO, fluid coming off nicely." He looks up, finds me, and smiles. He takes four quick steps toward me. I think he's going to take my arm. Or my shoulder. But he takes two more steps to Angelo's bed without stopping.

"Good evening, Ms. Dominguez." He nods at Abuela as he puts the stethoscope in his ears. How he remembers her name is different from mine should surprise me. But it doesn't. That's just Doc. "So nice to see you. I'm sure Mari appreciates your being here." He closes his eyes to listen to Angelo's chest. He touches Angelo's toes and fingers and speaks with Dave, who's back on ECMO watch. Maggie comes out from the supply room with new bedding. Gloria trails her, her pen scribbling over a piece of folded paper.

"Ah, Dr. Love!" Maggie says. "I hear congratulations are in order!"

"Thank you, yes, we are very lucky." He takes off his gloves and pushes his glasses back on his nose. Is he blushing?

"Uh, Mari? Would you come with me, please? I'd like to talk to you in private." He's standing beside me, waiting. I'm staring at the white sleeve of his coat thinking about what Maggie just said. I'm trying to wrap my head around the fact that Amelia's dead, but something happened to Doc that's worth congratulating.

I follow him into the room. The same room Bertie and I waited in while Angelo had his surgery. Doc motions for me to sit. I sit. But he stays standing. He paces back and forth. I'm starting to breathe hard. He said everything with Angelo looked good. So why does he look nervous?

"There's something I've been wanting to tell you. To share with you," he says. Pace, pace, pace to the door. "I've wanted to tell you for a while. But I didn't think it was appropriate." Pace, pace, pace to the chair. "But now that Angelo's out and doing well, I think I can." He takes the seat across from me. I try to swallow, but I can't. My throat's too dry. My hands hold on to each other. My palms are sticky. I don't know what Doc's going to say. I don't know what I want him to say.

"Sandra and I had a baby. A baby girl. Last night."

That's not what I thought he was going to say.

I blink. My eyes are scratchy dry.

"That's why I wasn't there the night Angelo came. We were in the hospital." He looks at his hands. They're clasped together the same way mine are. "Sandra was in the hospital. Her blood pressure was making everyone nervous. They almost induced her, but then she went into labor all on her own."

He had a baby? His wife was pregnant and he didn't say nothing?

And then . . .

He came to see me and Angelo when his wife was in the hospital. When she was having their baby.

"Is she okay?" I squeak it out. "The baby?"

Doc exhales, like he'd been holding his breath. "Yeah, she's great. Eight pounds, four ounces. Healthy as can be." He's smiling like he can't hold it in. He sees me staring. He reaches out and takes my hand. "We're lucky, Mari. Sandra and I. We know how lucky we are."

I believe him. Because if anyone knows, it's him and all the other doctors and nurses who see all the unluckiness the world makes.

"I heard about your friend. About Baby Trope." His hand tightens around mine. He bounces our fists up and down a little. "I'm sorry."

"Amelia," I say. "Her name was Amelia."

He bends his neck, runs his free hand through his mane of blond hair.

"Amelia," he says it back.

We sit there, holding hands, not saying anything for a while. He doesn't tell me that he knows Amelia had the same heart problem as Angelo. He doesn't tell me what happened to Amelia won't happen to Angelo. Because he knows I would hear the lie.

He shifts forward and tugs our hands again. Our knees are almost touching. "We're lucky, Mari. In this moment, both you and I, we're lucky."

And for some reason, I'm remembering the way Abuela's lips lifted when she smiled, showing me the purple-pink of her gums and a bright red slash of lipstick on her front tooth. "*¡Un bebé es como agua de mayo!*" She was looking at the ceiling, her hands raised as if she were speaking to God. As if me being pregnant was an answer to her prayers. And it made me angry. That she was turning it into something for her. That Angelo was for her. I thought he was for me. Now I see Angelo was for all of us. Don't matter that his heart was born broken and that he can't pump red and blue blood like he's supposed to. Our hearts might be pumping blood the right way so we can work at Starbucks, merengue by the river, run away, and fight *pendejos* who talk smack about us or threaten our tribe. But our hearts aren't whole either. Mine, Abuela's, Papi's—even my dumbass mama. Maybe Angelo's here to show us that. Doctors got to fix Angelo's heart for him. But us? We got to fix our own hearts. Or learn to love in spite of them. Maybe Angelo *is* what we all needed. Like water in May. Maybe he's gonna be the one to show us what makes half a heart whole.

Doc takes me to see her. I don't want to go. Don't want to intrude. But he won't let up. Abuela promises to hold Angelo's hand 'til I get back.

Doc's wife, Sandra, is on a different floor than me. A floor where they let the babies room with the mamas. It works out perfect, 'cause when we go in, Sandra is taking a shower. So I don't even have to see her. I don't want to see that Doc's wife is as beautiful and perfect as he is. Turns out, I don't need to see her to know that. Their baby is so beautiful and perfect there's no way the mama isn't. Teeny, tiny nose, lips pink like spring flowers, itty-bitty fist curled against her cheek. No tubes, no wires, no machines. Just baby.

She's sleeping, but he asks if I want to hold her. I say no, but he's got her up already. Her eyes open, big and blue like mountain water. As I take her, her hat falls off. Her hair! It's not blond—it's black. A great forest of it. Just like Angelo's.

I put her to my shoulder, hold her head real good with my fingers, careful not to squeeze her. My other hand cups her tiny baby butt. She's warm. She nickers against me. Her little face burrows, looking for something. My boobs are tingling, swelling. I turn and my cheek touches the smooth newness of her forehead. My nose is in the soft down of her hair. She smells like baby shampoo and talcum powder.

"She wants milk," I say, choking out a laugh.

Doc laughs back. "I know. She's always hungry."

Her head is bobbing, mini mouth gumming my shoulder. We both laugh. Doc takes her back, explains to her that her mama's still in the shower. He rocks her 'til she's sleeping.

Rosemary. That's what they've named her. Doc says Sandra wanted Rose, but he wanted his daughter to grow up strong. Says he told her he knows someone with "Mary" in her name who grew up strong. Someone who makes her own decisions and doesn't let anybody pressure her into anything. I turn away. I don't want Rosemary to see me crying.

As he puts her back in the bassinet, he says he's going to miss her.

"What do you mean you're going to miss her? Where you going?" I put my hands on my hips, pulling my gown to cover me more. Holding that baby made me feel naked.

"Don't worry, I'm not going anywhere. I'll still be around to take care of Angelo." He's smiling his lion smile down at Rosemary, tugging her hat back on real slow so as not to wake her. "Sandra's been living in Texas. She's got another year and a half of fellowship to complete. She's training to be a cancer surgeon."

A surgeon. For people with cancer. Makes perfect sense.

"Wait, you've been here and she's been there?" I say.

"Since September. They gave her December and January off as we wanted the baby born here. In the Children's Hospital. But then it will be back to racking up frequent flyer miles."

"But how's she going to take care of a baby alone and be a doctor?"

"She won't be alone. Her mother's moving down there to live with them. She'll take care of the baby while Sandra's working."

"But what about you? Won't you miss her? Miss them? Sandra and the baby?"

He takes off his glasses, gives his eyes a good dig with his fists. The glasses go back on. "Yeah. I'm going to miss them. Heck, I already miss them, and they haven't even gone yet." He scoops up the baby and hugs her to his chest. She makes a baby grunt but doesn't wake.

"But you know, Mari. Better than me. You do what you have to do." He's looking at me, his eyes bright and slippery. "That's life."

Abuela's in the same spot. She's talking to Angelo in Spanish. Telling him how he looks just like his *abuelito*.

"I saw him," I say. I hand two plastic cups to Maggie. My milk's come in real good now. Thank you, Rosemary.

Abuela looks up. Her face is still smiling for Angelo.

"Who you see?"

"Papi. I went to Sing Sing. A week ago. Seeing as I'm an emancipated minor with the pregnancy and all, I got in."

Her eyebrows do a dance. Well, the eyeliner that is her eyebrows do a dance seeing as she don't have real eyebrows no more. Her lips are doing something funny, too, like she's either gonna sneeze or cry.

"Those letters. He never wrote them, did he?" I don't say there's no way the skeevy excuse for a man I met—the man she raised—would ever have written about kindness and love. I could. I could hurt Abuela. Part of me wants to. Part of me thinks she deserves it. For lying. And for all the other crap she's done over the years. But part of me still sees Doc's face, him clutching his new baby girl to him, knowing he's going to have to say good-bye. I see Helen, cuddling Amelia, all smiles and candy, not knowing that she wasn't even going to get to say good-bye.

*You do what you have to do.*

And I see Angelo lying in that bed, fighting as best he can. I see him loving everyone back, even if they didn't always want him. Forgiving them. Even with only half a heart.

Abuela's still holding Angelo's hand. She's not looking at me anymore. Her mouth is moving, but no sound's coming out.

I could tell her I know she wrote those letters. I could tell her I understand why. That she wanted something she couldn't have. That she had to make do with what she got.

"He no want you." That's what she's saying. But it's not to Angelo. It's to me. "From the beginning, he no want you. He try to get your mami to *stop* the pregnancy."

My mama told me it was Abuela who wanted her to get an abortion. Maybe it was my papi, too. I believe it, considering what he said to me.

Abuela's still talking. "They only fifteen. But she no do it. She proud to be pregnant." Abuela glances at me. "Like you. So Luis, he drop out of school. Make the money with the drugs. Got your mami hooked on them, even. After you born."

I almost tell her what my papi said. What he told me himself. But I don't.

Abuela grabs for a tissue. She dabs her eyes. "You know how you lived with me sometime? From when you was a baby until you had four years old? *El gobierno.* They kept taking you away from her."

I remember going to Abuela's apartment with my pillow. Sleeping over when my mama went on a trip. Always waiting for her to come back. Praying to God at night and in the morning, promising to be a better kid, to listen better, to not scream or talk back, if He'd just send my mama home to me.

"Then your papi, he in jail. Your mami, she stay sober for a few years. But raising a child, ¿*es duro, sabes?* Especially when you alone." Abuela's shaking her head. "I know I not perfect, but I offer your mami to take you. Make it easier for her. But then she disappear. Maybe is better. *El daño limitao.* They can't hurt you. Since they no here."

Her makeup is running. She's mopping at her face so hard her earring falls off. I bend and pick it up. She's staring at me. Like she's real angry. Not at me angry. Angry at the world angry.

"You was always yelling. Always fighting. You never did what I told you. Like you knew you deserved *más*—more than what you got. Toto says is because I held the blame on you. If you hadn't been born, maybe Luis he no turn out that way, ¿*sabes?* Maybe he don't go to the drugs? Maybe he don't go to the jail? So I try to do something to make it up to you. Give you something you deserved. Something you no think come from me."

Abuela's hand is holding mine. The damp tissue is squashed between our skin, one side light and one dark.

"*Lo siento por las cartas.* Those letters? I wanted you to know the Luis that I loved. The Luis that should have been your papi. Your papi, he gone. *Por las drogas. Ese hombre* at Sing Sing? He no your papi anymore. I no want you to meet that man."

*I never wanted you.* The words ring in my head even though I never heard his voice say them. But I'm glad I met my papi. It's better to know the truth. Even if the truth breaks away another chunk of your heart.

"Then you was having a baby," Abuela says. "And I think, *eso es mi oportunidad*, my chance to be better. Better than I was to you. Better than I was to Luis. Babies, they so easy. They love you no matter what you say, what you do. It's when they grow up it gets hard. But a baby with a heart problem? A baby that could die?" She shakes her head again. Tears flood her cheeks.

"I no want what happened to Luis *y tu* mami to happen to you. I no want what happened to me to happen to you. I no want you to suffer."

I don't tell her that having Angelo was my decision and that she shouldn't have butted in. I don't tell her how much I suffered because she didn't want me, how I roamed the streets like a homeless person, the baby inside me the only thing keeping me warm.

I don't tell her how she's right and how much I'll suffer if something happens to Angelo. How ever since Amelia died, I've been wondering if I made the right choice.

Maggie circles around us, back from storing Angelo's milk. She pretends not to see Abuela's tear-wrecked face. Or that now she's missing an earring. And an eyebrow.

Maggie drops a bag onto the rocker. "These are for you," she says. "Helen was sorry she couldn't give them to you herself." One of the canvas straps falls over. A book slips out.

I pat Abuela's hand and let go. I walk to the rocker. I slide the bag of books to the floor so I can sit.

I think of all the things parents do for their babies. Some of it good. Some of it bad. But maybe everyone's just trying to get along? Doing what they think they got to do.

I pick up the book that fell out. *You and Your Baby. Your Baby and You.*

Me and Angelo. That's what it's about. Me and my son. I got to take care of him. I got to be here for him. I'm the one who's got to not leave. But I'm scared. Scared that he'll be taken away and I'll be alone. I know that if Angelo leaves, now or in a few weeks because God takes him, he don't have control of that. Even if he leaves when he's all grown up, because he gets a girl pregs or falls in with drugs, maybe he don't have control of that neither. Maybe none of us do. Maybe even if I promise not to leave, even if I promise to be better than all the other mamas and papis in my family, better for Angelo, better for me, maybe I won't be able to. But I can fight for that promise. I'm strong. I'm a good fighter. I don't need no one to tell me so.

I open the book. I start reading.

# EPILOGUE
## EIGHT MONTHS

Angelo's gonna be eight months tomorrow. Bertie's mama wants to throw a party for him. She still calls me *canillas*. But she crazy loves that baby. Abuela, too. Totally *enchulao*. Toto keeps trying to get him to play with this stuffed soccer ball he bought him. No matter Angelo can't even sit up by himself yet. Doc told me to expect that, the delay in his development. But it don't make it any easier. 'Specially when all the other babies in our mommy-'n'-me program started sitting two months ago.

But Angelo's doing good, considering all the months he spent in the hospital. I got to take him home for the first time on Valentine's Day. There's something about holidays and important events with this kid. Bertie spent that first week on my bedroom floor. Felt like I was the one with only half a heart I was so scared. Didn't help that Angelo came home with tubes and monitors—for feeding and checking his oxygen levels. Doc said over half of HLHS babies go home with them. *Coño*, nothing can wake you faster than your baby's oxygen monitor screaming at you in the middle of the night. Even when pretty much every time it's because the sticker fell off his foot.

At first, we was at the hospital every week for appointments. And there was therapy, too—PT, OT, and speech. Who knew a two-month-old needs help with speech? But turns out speech therapy also covers sucking and swallowing. Angelo needed big-time help with that. Bertie came to a couple of appointments. But he had to work. So my girls took turns taking me and Angelo. Toto even came once. Need two of us just to get in and out of the subway with that stroller, it's so big. You should see the looks we get boarding the 1 train. But I just show them my don't-mess-with-me smile and nobody says nothing.

When Angelo turned five months, we was back in the hospital for surgery number two. Compared to surgery one, it was *manso*. We was home in two weeks! Dr. Moses said he never seen a HLHS baby with obstructed pulmonary veins do so well. That's what they call that hole that was closing too early when he was inside me. Don't think I've ever been more proud.

My life is real busy. I ain't lonely no more. Angelo's always with me. I don't let him out of my sight for no one. Except Dr. Moses. Bertie keeps trying to get me to do that GED program with him. Teri says it'll be easy for me. Teri's helping Bertie study, and Yefri, her boyfriend—her first boyfriend—don't even mind. The merengue dancer from the park with the cool gray-blue eyes? He's one of Bertie's friends, another ex-associate of Skinner's. Turns out he likes smart girls. Bertie reintroduced them.

Maybe after Angelo's a year, I'll do that GED. There's no way I'm gonna leave him with someone else 'til then. But it would be nice not to have to sit and watch Cacata Mama make drooly faces at Angelo during their playdates. She is such a *furufa*. But Bertie and I, we agreed to let her have that party. Bertie's mama wants to invite Doc. I said sure, because I know he'll be down visiting Rosemary and won't be able to come. Don't really want him seeing the inside of that woman's apartment. And I'm sure they'd make Doc dance. Merengue, salsa, bachata. You know what they say about white men. And I know Bertie'd feel weird about it. Even though he said it was okay with him, Bertie's still jealous about Doc. Not that he has reason to be. I don't mind it though. The two of us are still just chillin', taking it one day at a time. But Bertie's being all possessive about me and Angelo? That makes me feel good.

Yaz and Heavenly are coming over to help me pick out Angelo's outfit for the fiesta. Don't know which of her five pairs of designer eyeglasses Hev'll be wearing, but I know which outfit she's going to want for Angelo. Hev is partial to the teddy-bear look.

Abuela's home already, banging away in the kitchen. She left work early. She does that sometimes now that Angelo's around. Abuela's making flan and *torta de guayaba*. Who knew she could bake? And my Angelo? He's sleeping. Right here next to me on the bed, tucked up inside my arm under the coconut tree, his face pressed up against my boob doing his baby elephant snore. You'd never know from looking at him that this kid has half a heart. If you saw him with his family, everyone laughing and smiling and loving him, you wouldn't know Angelo was ever not wanted. If you had to guess, you'd say the opposite.

# ACKNOWLEDGMENTS

This book would not have been possible without the assistance of multiple individuals.

To the amazing, thoughtful, and ever helpful Jim McCarthy, thank you for believing in Mari as much as I do. To Anne Heltzel, editor supreme, thank you for your passion and for the expert guidance that enabled me to enrich Mari's world.

Thank you to the folks at SCBWI for creating and sustaining such a warm community of aspiring and accomplished children's book writers and illustrators. My writing education came from you. Thanks especially to Lin Oliver, with whom I had the fortune to spend a breakout session at one of my first Winter Conferences, and who showed me, on a ripped-out scrap of notebook paper, how to plot a novel. I never knew one could do such a thing!

Innumerable thanks go to the inestimable Carolyn Mackler, who is not only one of my first mommy friends but also my first writer friend. I could not have done this without your counsel (both the babies and the books!). You are my role model on so many of life's fronts. Thank you to the incredible and talented Maria E. Andreu, Lisa Hansen, Mary Ann McGuigan, Betsy Voreacos, Tisha Hamilton, and Gigi Collins for your honesty, insight, and laughs. Thank you to the very early supporters of my writing career, who include not just those listed above but also: Laura Ruby, Christine Heppermann, Barbara Seuling, Michelle Wolfson, Rachel Lewis, Trudi Leone Lord, and Sara Truog. Thank you to Pilu Torrejon and Adriana Orozco Kothari for your feedback on dialogue and slang. Thank you to John Rudolph for your expert guidance, wisdom, and long-term friendship (Go, Jeffs!—oops—er—or whatever mascot we are when you are reading this).

Thank you to the physician/scientist colleagues, mentors, and friends who helped shape me as both doctor and writer: Charles Kleinman, William Fifer, Welton Gersony, Jane Newburger, Julie Glickstein, Daphne Hsu, Stéphanie Levasseur, Amee Shah, Lynn Simpson, and Rosalind Korsin, among many, many others. Thank you to Jonathan Rhodes, who, when I was a medical student, provided my first stunning example of how to deliver bad news to a patient's family with compassion and humility. Thank you also to all of the students, residents, and fellows I have had the pleasure of knowing. Every one of you is a warrior when it comes to these lives we touch.

Thank you to my patients, and their parents, for what you teach me. You inspire me. I am forever grateful and humbled to know you.

Thank you to my family: my parents for their undying love

and support and for forever telling me anything is possible; my brother for not raising eyebrows when I told him I was writing a book; my sister-in-law for our long (never uninterrupted!) conversations on work, life, and family; and my in-laws for their ferocious pride. Thank you to my abuela, who was nothing like Mari's—except for pushing *pan y mantequilla* like a dealer. You were always there for me, and not a day goes by when I don't think of you. Thank you to my beautiful girls for showing me how powerful and all-consuming the love of a parent for a child can be. And last and most important, thank you to Marc. To quote the late, great Barry White, you are my first, my last, my everything.

*A portion of the profits from* Water in May *will be donated to* support research benefiting children with heart disease.